NORTH OF INFINITY
FUTURITY VISIONS

NORTH OF INFINITY
FUTURITY VISIONS

Edited by
Micheal Magnini

Mosaic Press
Oakville, ON - Buffalo, NY

Canadian Cataloguing in Publication Data

Main entry under title:

North of infinity
Magnini, Micheal, 1958-

ISBN 0-88962-634-0

1. Science fiction, Canadian (English).* 2. Short stories, Canadian (English).*
3. Canadian fiction (English) – 20th century.* I. Magnini, Micheal, 1958 -

PS8323.S3N655 1998   C813'.0876208054   C98-930579-1
PR9197.35.S33N655 1998

Published by MOSAIC PRESS, P.O. Box 1032, Oakville, Ontario, L6J 5E9, Canada. Offices and warehouse at 1252 Speers Road, Units #1&2, Oakville, Ontario, L6L 5N9, Canada and Mosaic Press, 85 River Rock Drive, Suite 202, Buffalo, N.Y., 14207, USA.

Mosaic Press acknowledges the assistance of the Canada Council, the Ontario Arts Council and the Dept. of Canadian Heritage, Government of Canada, for their support of our publishing programme.

Cover and book design by: Amy Land
Printed and bound in Canada

CONTENTS

INTRODUCTION .... *Micheal Magnini* .... *i*

FOREWORD .... *Micheal Magnini* .... *v*

THE KILLING WAY .... *David Nickle* 1

ALL MY FAMILY .... *Colleen Anderson* 17

ROADKILL .... *Edo van Belkom* 33

ROOTS OF THE SOUL .... *Dale L. Sproule* 43

WHERE THE HEART IS .... *Robert J. Sawyer* 69

FREEDOM IS A RUNNING MAN .... *Dat Pham* 87

THE MALTHUSIAN CODE .... *Leslie Lupien* 105

TO THE LAST MAN .... *Al Onia* 121

RAINY SEASON .... *Robert H. Beer* 133

THE REEF .... *Ray Deonandan* 157

THE RAPTURE
OF THE MOONFLOWER .... *Giovanni Serafini* 173

POISSON DISTRIBUTION .... *Leonid Spektor* 189

INTRODUCTION

Today's enormous growth in science fiction, clearly evident by the popularity of such television shows and movies as the *X-Files, Millennium, Alien Resurrection* and *Gattaca* as well as the ubiquitous *Star Wars* and *Star Trek* series has caused the genre to approach the mainstream of our culture. While much can be attributed to the end of this century (after all, *it is* the 90's), and the emergence of a new millennium it is imbued with all the youthful enthusiasm of the newly discovered, when it is in fact, *a re-discovery* of the role of science fiction in society.

The origins of modern science fiction go back nearly two hundred years to *Frankenstein*, a Gothic horror and suspense novel written by Mary Shelley to "speak to the mysterious fears of our nature." Throughout her novel the characters passionately seek knowledge (through science), and it is this quest which means everything. It is very much a novel of the "modern age", separating the old ways from the new. These nexus points occur during periods of rapid change, uncertainty and dramatic time shifts. Shelley emerged from the Gothic of the eighteenth century and a hundred years later H.G. Wells emerged from the Industrial Age of the nineteenth century. Now we approach another nexus at the twenty-first century and we look to science fiction to light the darkness known as the future.

Since Mary Shelley, much scientific speculation (on the nature of humanity) has been expressed in thrilling tales of wonder, in modern myths and galactic epics, in the science fiction story.

Clearly, to proceed further, we need a definition of science fiction. *Science fiction is the search for a definition of humankind and their status in the universe which will stand in our advanced but confused state of knowledge (science), and is characteristically cast in the Gothic or post-Gothic mode.* [adapted from *Trillion Year Spree* by Brian Aldiss].

Gothic is a type of romance developed in the late eighteenth century, relying on suspense and mystery, and containing supernatural or horrifying events. A strong Gothic motif is that of descent from a "natural world" to inferno or incarceration, where the protagonist goes, willingly or otherwise, in search of a secret, an identity, or a relationship. In modern science fiction this protagonist is often the scientist, the inventor, or the space traveller. It is urban literature; its origins and inspirations arising from within the Industrial Revolution. SF is the fiction of a technological age.

One way or another, all the stories appearing in this first collection embody this definition. In our search for a definition of humankind, we will explore an *Evolution of Consciousness* through this series of short story collections. *North of Infinity* will focus on the unveiling of awareness and ascendant consciousness (that truly human facet) throughout these fictional societies and characters.

The first volume of this collection is *Futurity Visions*: from the land of the midnight sun come visions of tomorrow. The ideal of science fiction, to encompass new perspectives, and new manifestations of the *Zeitgeist* is alive and well within these pages.

Before venturing into the exciting, unknown realms within these pages, let me reveal my motivation for creating this series. This collection of short stories and the anthology series is a deliberate attempt to dismiss a nasty little rumour. Canadian Science Fiction (by this I mean SF written by Canadians, rather than about Canada) has been widely regarded as introspective in theme and actionless in plot; perhaps not wondering where we are going but rather, how did we get here.

I do not know where this comes from -- perhaps our unique political situation, or the artistic elite of the country who consciously pursue an agenda to maintain their aloofness and separation from (God-forbid) Americans and mere mortals.

To refute this widely held misconception of introverted authorship, I have called upon Canadian partisans to re-write history and eliminate this pretentious pride and prejudice. They bring you their unique visions that are percipient, and forward-looking, and they bring their speculative ideas and tales of future history to centre stage.

A new breed of Canadian Science Fiction writer has emerged to enliven this book with intriguing and suspenseful stories. These writers also write of character and characters (the main ingredient of the *literary* genre); and, just like living in Canada, their stories are of people in extreme conditions and situations facing what we all face: an uncertain future.

I would like to mention here the inspirations for this series, and credit those who came before. I ventured to read a vast array of science fiction anthologies which filled me with the splendour and wonder of speculative fiction writing. Becoming involved in Hamilton's new writing workshop, and inclusion in their literary anthology introduced me to a world of cultural and literary idealism. Then, when looking for a purely Canadian Science Fiction anthology I found virtually none, only dated reprints. And although anthologies of the like produced by Judith Merrill are exceptional, in an old fashioned way, I thirsted for something *new*.

This led me on a search through various Canadian anthologies, and publishers. When I discovered what a tremendous job Don Hutchison, and Peter Sellers had done with *Northern Frights* and *Cold Blood* respectively, I knew I had to approach Mosaic Press with my idea.

Now I wish to acknowledge and thank the people who have made this possible.

First and foremost on this list of valuable assistants is Dawn Marie Burke (wife person to the editor) for her endless hours of work in transcribing this manuscript; followed by Lauren Barnes for her timely insights and critiques; all the creative SF writers who considered this project worthy enough to submit their work; the Hamilton new writing workshop for their inspiration; and the source of all beginnings, my mother Nella who always knew I could.

And especially, I would like to thank Howard Aster and the staff at Mosaic Press for their confidence and resources in backing and producing this book.

Finally, while the search for knowledge (science) is a passionate and serious one, science fiction should also be fun and entertaining. I believe SF gives pleasure to many people; it is immensely readable and enriching.

So read, and enjoy.

FOREWORD

Take a walk northward, towards the sun. As you cross the vast expanse of permafrost and treeless tundra, you will see sparkling sheets of melting snow under the northern sun. In the far north the sun never sets during the brief northern summer and the endless vista of blinding snow and ice recedes under twenty-four hours of sunlight each day. As you journey into the Arctic Archipelago, you will encounter glinting shards of ice floating in the cold, sapphire blue waters of the Arctic Ocean.

As the pale, *Midnight Sun* skims the horizon, you are in danger. Lurking among the icebergs and snowy ridges are the fearless, carnivorous Polar Bears. But the giant, white beasts are not the worst danger you will face.

The journey into the land of the *Midnight Sun* is not to be taken lightly. Beyond the inhabited world exist dangers to your soul. Under the blazing sun, who can sleep? Days are endless; night never rises. The brave who venture into the Arctic Archipelago find no comfort in sleep; without night it is forfeit.

Deprivation: without sleep one does not dream.

Once deprived of dreamsleep you may lose yourself; you may begin to dream while awake, to hallucinate -- the subconscious mind surfaces. Under the relentless radiance of the *Midnight Sun* you feel a tingle, the prickle of the light and the fever of the sun. Eventually, a blue haze envelopes your mind and the soul cannot distinguish between delirium and demons.

The traveller may be launched on a mystic voyage.

You can become percipient and clairvoyant; you may see the future, or the very end of time.

Under the dazzling blaze of the *Midnight Sun* you say, "I have suffered the madness of the burning brain; I have seen fantastic visions; I have endured incredible nightmares."

From out of this madness, this flaming of the soul, some have written their visions down. Collected here, are the visions of those brave enough to journey under the *Midnight Sun* to somewhere, North of Infinity.

THE KILLING WAY

by
David Nickle

David Nickle lives in Toronto, Ontario and is a member of the SFWA. His work has appeared in *On Spec, Northern Frights 2* and *3*, and *Transversions*, as well as receiving an honourable mention in *The Year's Best Fantasy and Horror: Eighth Annual Collection.* He was nominated for an *Aurora Award* for 1995.

THE KILLING WAY

by
David Nickle

J anuary 18

I did not write today. At first thinking I might later, I stupidly ordered a printout of *The Killing Way*, Trevek's book. I had not yet read it, and as Trevek is due to arrive at the colony tomorrow I thought I'd take a look at his life-work. I intended only to glance through the book so that my lie at having enjoyed the thing might be easier to back up.

So instead of writing, I sat by my window — the only window, the one that looks out across the forever daylit ice-death of Antarctica, a stark, minimalist view the Foundation says is good for the soul — and read Trevek's book. And didn't get any work done at all; the only words I wrote today are those I'm writing now.

The hell of it is, I can't even say I enjoyed the book. I finished it in the afternoon, which isn't as tricky as it sounds because the book is thin — in every sense of the word. The title, *The Killing Way*, is the tidiest bit of prose on the printout (no, I'll be fair, the introduction by Claire Kosugi is a passably-good essay) and the action is repetitive and empty.

As an exercise, I'll summarize the thing. Don't worry; it won't take long.

"I remember my birthing only a short way, and my training in battle-talk began too quickly after," it begins, and from there takes Trevek into a breakneck 20 K account of "basic training" in the Marine Domes on Luna. Really stunning prose. "We learned of our video-enhancements before the Commanders allowed us to clip on our laser targeting system. No live targets until later," writes Trevek in one of the more psychologically-revealing passages of the first chapter.

And it goes on. Chapter Two runs a record at 34 K, describing in detail the armour and armaments that Trevek has had installed into his genetically-engineered nervous system. The laser-finger, the tazer system that shot from his forearms, the microprocessor targeting system plugged in behind his earholes, the lead injections into the sealed pockets of his scaled epidermis, keeping his simplified internal organs clean from any hard radiation he might encounter later in life; and, then on to literally dozens of heavy weapons presented in the laundry-list style that eventually defines the rest of the book.

Which, as I said, is a pretty fast read. Trevek evidently saw action in the Titan uprising of 2049 (this is only made clear in one of the too-few end-notes supplied by Kosugi), and he breezes through that with barely a body-count. He spent seven years on board a starship, crawling across the gulf to help the brave colonists at Alpha Centauri find social order among themselves. Which took three months and another body-count (and twelve delightful chapters, at 13 K a pop), and then it was home again. The book (all ninety-two pages of it) was written on the way back.

Hmm. I'm reading over what I've just written and I'm overcome with a terrible deja vu: didn't some journalist write words like these over *Samuel's Cart* when I opened it on the Net? I've called reviewers away from dinner parties to complain about kinder dissections than the thing I've just written down. Has it come to this? Am I descended to emulating my worst detractors?

If so, maybe I should forget about this novel-writing sham and concentrate on getting an interview with Trevek. That's what all the other journalists on the planet seem to be doing these days.

January 19

No luck at all in isolating Trevek this morning. I was at the hangar with some of the other inmates here — like me, unable to get a drop of story out of their processors this morning and curiouser than hell about our new house-mate — and we watched dutifully, shivering as the transport settled to the stained cement floor and the hangar doors rumbled shut. The outside temperature was ninety below I later learned, and the hangar was kept only minimally warmer. We wore our environment suits like armour, further guarding our body-heat with tight-crossed arms and nervous-jiggling legs.

I think we all realized a meeting with Trevek would be a problem when the doors cracked opened and the marine troopers stepped down. They weren't modified, just regular grunts in their Arctic combat gear, but evidently the Pentagon thought twelve of them would be enough to keep those dangerous authors at Camp Antarctica at bay, keep them from breaking Trevek's concentration on this retreat.

The next person to step out was Kosugi. I guessed it at the time and had her identity confirmed a short while later. She wore a full environment suit, her face contoured unrecognizably with thermal mesh, but her tiny frame was easy enough to place from the hundreds of tridee interviews and news reports since Trevek's book had been published. A striking little woman, even if she is completely bald except for the interface plug, dangling out of her skull like a monastic tassel of hair. Necessary modifications, I guess, to pilot a starship. Gives me the creeps anyway.

Trevek, of course, stepped out into the sub-zero hangar naked. He was designed for cooler climes than this, and there was no reason for modesty either; like his "brothers" still on active duty, Trevek is a neuter.

He isn't much taller than the other soldiers (he still towers over Kosugi, but that's not a fair comparison, she's so little) and in parts he isn't much wider. His shoulders, for example, are surprisingly narrow (he's supposed to be able to lift 400 kilos over his head with ease, yet I am heftier than he up top). But by contrast, his hips are broad, rippling with muscle down to his knees. It's a different musculature, that's what Kosugi wrote in her introduction, and its aesthetics and proportions won't always agree with what our common sense tells us a strong man ought to look like.

But then, as Kosugi points out a few paragraphs down, it wasn't until Trevek's book appeared that anyone was willing to allow that the man-bred Marines were men at all. Different bodies, different brains, not of women born. Barely self-aware, right? Not even a normal face with eyes, nose and mouth. Just a gas-mask breathing orifice and a pair of lens-casings over the bio-enhanced optic nerves. An army of robots who happened to have wet insides.

Trevek's book changed that misconception, so wrote Kosugi. And as he was hustled past us, three of the marines holding us at bay with crossed rifles to make sure we didn't *try anything,* I wanted nothing more than to talk with him, to sit down and see just what this brand new man thought about his world.

Despite everything the critics have said, *The Killing Way* doesn't tell me that. If I want to find out anything, I've got to talk to Trevek myself.

January 20

This afternoon I broke down and left my desk early. Too bright in there, the vibrations were too insistent on word-counts and productivity to be of any use to me. So I went down to Camp Antarctica's lounge.

The brochures say the camp is dry, which is to say no interesting beverages and no recreational pharmaceuticals are to be found therein. The brochures speak the truth on that matter, *effendi,* but the lounge is still a good place for avoidance even without the convenient chemical assists.

The nice thing about the lounge is its spaces. One wall is glass, with a humming thermal screen insulating it from the wrenching cold outside. And the other walls are cut out of the mountain-slopes upon which the colony rests. The bare rock, the high ceiling, the pine floors and supports and the soft, form-fitting chairs make the place a hell of a lot more attractive than my room. Particularly when I can't seem to write anything past my name, or this time-waster of a journal.

I won't lie and say that I wasn't hoping to meet Trevek in the lounge this afternoon; while I was hoping, though, I was by no means expecting anything.

What I was hoping for was to see Kosugi in the lounge. Introductions to robot death-novels notwithstanding, Kosugi isn't a writer. She's a starship pilot, enough of a professional to have her ship's hardware extended into herself. The only reason she was staying here and not on her way back to Alpha Centauri on another galactic milk run, was Trevek.

So she wasn't here to write, and I know from recent experience that the quarters here are hellish, empty places when the resident has no words in her. Or him.

My expectations, to get back to the tale at hand (the only tale around here, it would seem), were rewarded. It was about 3:30 when I made it down to the lounge, and Kosugi was there, sitting well back from a group of writers huddled around a low table and making vague suggestions about one another's work. Kosugi was nursing a mug of tea, looking out at the chunky ice plain.

I sat beside her, a polite distance off but not too far along the couch. And introduced myself.

"I've read some of your work," she said, smiling politely. Didn't say *I enjoyed some of your work* or *I admire your work*. Just read. I read a newspaper, once.

"I've followed your work, too," I replied.

And so the conversation went on, a mannered sparring-match in the idleness of the frozen summer afternoon. Somerset Maugham would have written our chat more cleanly than I could hope to, but here goes my recollection of the debacle:

"How long have you been at the colony, Mr. Grey?"

"I've been here for three weeks actually."

"Have you found it to be helpful?"

"Not entirely. It was my agent's suggestion that got me here. It might be time for a new agent."

Another polite grin, a little nod in place of a laugh.

"I'm sure things will turn around for you."

And so on. Kosugi is good, a battle-scarred cocktail party veteran and infinitely more skilled in topic avoidance than am I at topic introduction. Maybe I should get out more.

Finally, I just asked directly. Felt like an ass, but there you are.

"What is Trevek working on here?"

Smiled, that's what she did. "A new book, Mr. Grey. Isn't that what you are working on too?"

And I'll be damned if that didn't shut me up altogether.

January 21

Ricardo came to see me today.

Ricardo is the Foundation's official liaison with the writers here. I met him my first day down. He is very tall, very thin, a gaunt-eyed Hispanic gentleman who visits me in my nightmares as a genteel Brazilian state torturer: "Anything you need, sir, and by the way we have ways of making you write!" Bwah hahahah!

He knocked first, of course, on the off-chance that I might be actually making productive use of the facilities. He entered only upon my shouted invitation.

"How is your day going, Terrance?" He sat on my bed and looked at me with those perky inquisitor eyes of his.

I told him. No point in lying; they've got a subroutine in the computer network that keeps tabs on your word-count, and while they say they don't monitor it, you can bet they'll check it every so often.

So I told him things were going shitty thanks, and Ricardo nodded; not contradicting, not reassuring, just nodding, gentle and solemn.

"Sometimes it is slow here as everywhere," he admitted in a great, mournful puff of his lungs. "The muses are not always so willing and supple, hey Terrance?"

Not always, no Ricardo, not every single day. Sometimes they just ain't in the mood.

"Claire spoke of you this morning," he said, coming out of nowhere.

"Claire Kosugi?"

Nodded again. "You were asking about Trevek."

I shrugged.

"He interests you a great deal, doesn't he?"

"Yes," I said. "Of course he does," I added needlessly.

"He's interesting a lot of people here," said Ricardo.

"I'd like to be able to meet with Trevek. The same way I'm free to meet with everyone else."

"Would you? From what Claire tells me, you'd like to do more than just shake hands in the dinner lineup."

"I don't understand." Although I admit, oh diary o' mine, I had a pretty good idea of what Ricardo was getting at.

"You were asking about his new project. Weren't you?" A raised eyebrow, inquiring.

And before you ask, no I didn't get indignant, ask him what the hell he thought he was suggesting; I demanded no apology, showed no outrage. I only shrugged. "Curious," I muttered.

Ricardo smiled then, the grin a benevolent, reassuring thing. Hadn't seen it — or appreciated it as much — since I first came here.

"We're all curious about Trevek," he said. "Me, I'm almost as curious about what your new book's going to be about."

I faltered around for a moment, sputtering and stuttering and embarrassing myself some more.

"Space marines," I finally said. Ricardo laughed, and so did I.

But I shouldn't have. It's the best idea I've come up with yet at this damn place. Maybe tomorrow I'll see what I can do with it.

January 22

This morning I went outside. I haven't been outside since I arrived here — not much inclination to freeze on the ice-plain, I'm sure you understand — but a writer's block is a writer's block and sometimes a change of scenery is the remedy. Which, of course, is just the sort of thinking that got me here in the first place. But I'll try anything twice.

In all, though, this change of scenery was a fortuitous one. By pure chance and a little design it gave me my second good look at Trevek.

Here's what happened; it makes a pretty good anecdote, so I'll go slowly.

I left to go outside after breakfast, which means I actually got there an hour before lunch. Apparently it's the same for everyone the first time outside; an attendant helps you put on the environment suit, and then another one spends about an hour conducting a detailed survival review. Here's how to change the suit battery, Mr. Grey, here's how to access the nutrientsolution, pay attention to the shelter activation, the lift pack works like this, and on and on. Not that it's not a good idea; but Christ, it takes its time.

And for me, it took longer still. My attendant had to excuse himself halfway through One minute, we're reviewing the pack-ejection procedure, the next my mentor's pager is flashing and he's off with barely a "Won't be a second, Mr. Grey."

When he finally returned, his face was flushed and his mouth was incongruously twisted into a small grin.

"Sorry about that, Mr. Grey," he said. "A small crisis in the main lock."

I shrugged as best I could in the suit-assembly. "Marines causing a ruckus?"

His grin broke at that, and he laughed. "In a way."

"Well good to see you've got it under control."

He grunted at that, then gave me a funny look.

"Something the matter?"

"No, sir."

"Does all this by any chance have anything to do with Trevek?" I remember cursing at myself; I wasn't going to think about Trevek today, such had been my plan.

The attendant hesitated, leaving enough of a lull for me to ascertain the answer. With some difficulty I waved a gloved hand in dismissal, and my attendant smiled, relaxed.

Trevek had gone out for a walk. I'd have bet on it then.

We got on with things. It took another hour, and by the time my better-living seminar was finished, I'd almost been able to put Trevek out of my mind again.

So it wasn't as though I was actually looking for him. But somewhere along the way, I'd resolved to keep my eye open.

I was finally dropped outside near the base of the mountain, a good mile away from Camp Antarctica. It's a brochure photograph from there, a creative monolith crawling up a slope of the South Polar Plateau, the ecosystem domes shining like ball-bearings through the ice-air.

My planned journey took me to Devils Glacier, a shorter leap at just over 100 klicks, not a problem for the lift pack they'd given me. I'd be back in time for supper.

I landed on the southern edge of the glacier, where the New Zealand tourist checkpoint is set up. Took me a moment to process through the automated security systems inside the little dome (couldn't pay anyone enough to man that position in person, I imagine) and then I was off, for the moment alone on the giant tongue of ice.

It's a fine thing, polar solitude, not at all the same as the loneliness of my room here at the colony; that is a bleak and mundane sense, a suicide-inducing alienation that I could just as easily accomplish in my flat up at Sudbury, or in a Tucson hotel room, or in a Maine death-row jail cell for that matter.

Standing alone on the glacier, my eye tracing across the complex tumbles of ice-mountains, the flat plains of glacial snow, the solitude takes on a romantic, almost heroic flavour. Had the afternoon gone differently, I might have conceived a generation-spanning epic there, or an immense, Joycian stream of language that would cement my work's importance for ever more.

Instead, I saw Trevek.

If anyone is censoring this journal, this next part is the section that will most likely see the stamp. I checked the Net news services, the tridee tonight, and there was no report of it anywhere. If the events of the afternoon had been considered kosher for public consumption, it would have shown up. The journalists would have been all over it and then through it again, buggering around the geopolitical implications, getting a crew down to the South Polar New Zealand colony to talk to school children, interviewing economists and terrorism experts from linkups to their Washington studios.

Isn't that what happens when someone blows up a government installation?

Because that's what Trevek did to the tourist dome.

I was maybe four kilometres along the ice when it happened, so I didn't get a good look at the particulars of the first explosion. But I heard it, rumbling through the ice, and I saw the fireball clearly enough to pique my curiosity. It must have only taken a few seconds for me to fly back to the dome, because I was right there when the second explosion came, and the shockwave almost sent me spinning.

It didn't, though, and I was back stable again in time to see the gleam of Trevek's scales. He came out through the black smoke, stepping over the twisted, bubbling wreckage of the dome, twitching his head back and forth like a fly's. He saw me immediately, and if I'd had more time to think I might have been afraid that Trevek would take aim at me then. I should have been afraid. He had destroyed, he had seen me, he could have killed me easily.

But he didn't. Just fixed me with his two round lenses, checking me over with his UV and IR and probably sonar-assisted vision as well, and stood there in front of the flames and smoke. I had my suit radio on, and set it to scanning the frequencies. But he made no attempt at communication with me, made no warning to get away even.

I tried to speak with him, though. I didn't say much; just introduced myself and commented on the weather and that was about it. I'd have said more, but there wasn't really time.

"Trevek," my suit radio said. "This is your commanding officer. You have exceeded your allowance. Repeat, you have exceeded your movement allowance."

And Trevek was off, his own lift belt carrying him fast above me, his globular eyes off again, flitting around the horizon while his head cricked around at impossible angles.

"Trevek!" My radio was shouting now. "Hold your position! You are ordered!" Then the transmission garbled into quick electric dots and dashes, the deadly shorthand of battle-talk.

Further north along the glacier, marines in lift belts were converging along Trevek's path. Too far away to see what kinds of weapons they had; I'm not sure what would have been effective against Trevek anyway.

Then I was grabbed, a control beam overriding my lift belt. An air controller's voice told me I was being brought back to the colony — "For your own safety, Mr. Grey," said the voice — and I was gently, firmly turned around and tugged away from the glacier. Couldn't twist back to see what happened to Trevek, but I got back to Camp Antarctica well before dinner.

January 23

No one else at the colony has heard about what happened to Trevek. I tried to get it out of Ricardo, and he was resolutely uncooperative; couldn't find Kosugi anywhere; and, as I've said, no one else had the slightest idea.

Oh, I've been discreet; when I spoke with Ricardo, it was very clear from his words and his tone that this was not something to go spreading around. So I did not, for example, knock on anyone's door and ask her if they'd heard anything about Trevek's act of war against New Zealand yesterday, and whether they knew if he was all right.

But I did spend more time than usual in the lounge this afternoon. And I did push my way into more conversations than is my habit, and introduced the subject of Trevek and what a lout he was into well more than half of them.

The fruits of my research were meagre. Plenty of agreement with my basic assertion, lots of interesting extrapolation on where extra-solar colonialism is taking us, and no useful gossip whatsoever.

The good news being, I finally managed to get some writing done. Not a novel, but the beginnings of something shorter. Too early to see if the verdict will be short story or novella, and I'm too superstitious to say anything more about it at this stage, but it's there now, almost a thousand words and it doesn't look too bad, either.

January 23, 11:54 p.m.

I have to write this down. I am terrified. I've never had it like this before, *you've led a sheltered life, Mr. Grey*, and I have to write my fear away, spit it out through the keyboard. It will calm me, help me think straight, decide what I have to do. Diary as notepad.

All right, from the beginning.

Claire Kosugi knocked on my door immediately after I filed the last journal-entry, about a half-hour ago. I wasn't wearing anything, so I pulled on my bathrobe and invited her in.

I'll transcribe our conversation now, while it's still fresh. Might be important later.

"I hope I've not interrupted anything." Kosugi closes the door quickly and sits at my desk. I settle on my bed.

"I was just locking up."

She nods abruptly. I can see a line of sweat on her upper lip.

"You were out on the glacier yesterday," she says. "Trevek told me."

"I was."

"And you were asking Ricardo about Trevek again."

"Wouldn't you?"

Kosugi gets up. "I might." She is more obviously agitated now, her hands gripping at one another in little spasms. "But I doubt that after such an event" — that's how she describes wanton destruction, an event — "I would be so stupid as to run towards the source and introduce myself."

I'm quiet for a second, impaled upon her glare. "I wanted to meet him," I finally say. "You certainly haven't given any of us much opportunity otherwise."

Kosugi explodes now, her glare spreading across and deep through her being. "Of course I haven't! You stupid, pretentious man! Do you think we are here simply to satisfy your curiosity? Do you view this as an exercise in publicity? Trevek is here to work, to write! Not to answer questions!"

"Why a writer's colony?" I am deliberately calm, trying amateurishly to seize the home advantage. "Why not some military installation where Trevek's privacy can be monitored more closely?"

"Coming here was Trevek's choice." Kosugi is too clever for my schoolboy debating technique and slows to an ice-quiet. "In spite of what you may have read, Trevek does make his own choices in matters concerning his life and work."

"Why did he choose this place, then?"

"He told us that he wanted to write, and that he wanted to do so here. Beyond that, he has not explained his rationale in detail to me. I presume he read about the camp." A nasty little grin here. "Trevek does read."

"So I'd gathered." I am getting irritated now, I want the conversation to end. "What's your point, Claire?"

An intake of breath. "Trevek remembers you. You told him your name. He called up some of your work. I think he has taken an interest in you."

"Great. When can we meet?"

I must be more irritating to Kosugi. She slams her fists down at her sides, glares at me anew. "Hope, Mr. Grey, that you and Trevek never meet. You are best left a passing fancy."

"What is that supposed to mean?"

And it comes.

"Mr. Grey," she says, slow and looking straight, "after you were pulled away from the fire, Trevek killed two marines. When he came back, he wrote 30 K, the first that he has set down since he arrived. He has become inspired again; the adventure on the glacier seems to be the elixir for his beginnings.

"When we returned to Earth, Trevek was easy to predict, easy to control. That is no longer so. I would like to take him away now, get him clear of this camp. But he will not go. He's not on my ship anymore; he finally knows it."

"And now he has taken an interest in you."

Kosugi leaves at this point. I sit on my bed, I don't get up to show her out. I am still on my bed now. And no, I have no idea what I'm going to do next.

Oh, Jesus.

January 24

I spent the morning re-reading Trevek's book, and I find that I still dislike it. The story is pedestrian, unilayered and almost mechanical. Trevek does not dramatize; he lists and lists and lists: "The missile struck the city. The first explosions killed only 32,923. A fuel depot was then hit. 428,446 were confirmed in the fire. I killed 92 with my hands that afternoon."

And always the lists are killings, or weapons. I'm trying to think of what in literature Trevek's work comes close to — the jacket quote that compares it to Julius Caesar's *Commentaries* is just as ridiculous as it sounds — and all I come up with is some of the Icelandic sagas. Although even *Egil's Saga,* which mustered quite a body-count itself as I recall, brings more humanity, more depth to its story, than does Trevek's autobiography of carnage.

But carnage may be the key. Trevek, after all, is a made man, a streamlined tool. He thinks, he feels, Kosugi was right in the general case, but for Trevek all is directed to his function.

Why is so much that is poignant to us in fiction concerned with love and procreation? There is violence, murder throughout, but romance, and be honest now Terrance, sexuality — Freudian or otherwise — is always there, always what matters. Perhaps that is our imperative.

Trevek, however, does not reproduce, needs no love, gives no affection. And his imperative is well-defined.

As I look this over, I find myself satisfied with this thesis. I have no desire to put it to the test. As soon as is possible, I hope to be out of this colony, back at home in Sudbury. I'll write my book there, and I don't care if I never meet Trevek.

I was speaking to one of the guards waiting with me in my room just now, and related these very sentiments. He laughed. A bitter, uneasy noise. The guard said he couldn't agree more. He said he'd like to visit me in Sudbury some day, when this is over.

In the meantime, though, the only thing to do is wait until they recapture Trevek.

And pray that Claire Kosugi's murder was enough to clear up his writer's block for the next book. I don't want Trevek back here looking to talk shop. I don't want that at all.

ALL MY FAMILY

by
Colleen Anderson

Colleen Anderson, a member of the SFWA and a graduate of the Clarion Writers workshop, works from her home in Vancouver, British Columbia. Her SF stories have appeared in *On Spec, The Round Table, Amazing Tales,* and *Tesseracts 3.*

ALL MY FAMILY

by
Colleen Anderson

I halted barely long enough to push yet again at the perceptible rounding of my belly. Samo and Jay's backs were still visible, sweat darkening their shirts to mud brown.

I cursed the slight swelling. How long had it been? Time tended to blend and melt with days of running, fighting, hiding, shooting and sleeping. There was no time to waste on a preggo. I snorted and moved forward.

If I was, I was, and I would have to deal with it soon. It could slow me down and get me killed. But I could choose to quit the Freedom groups and join one of the Ratter camps. At the rate we were losing people, life was even more precious and . . . and I missed Marlyse.

I caught up to the group. Samo glanced backward in acknowledgment, grinned and winked. They would have continued on had I disappeared. I knew some of the Freedom groups holed up for their injured but our rule was to keep moving, no matter what. So far that tactic kept us a step ahead of the scourges that had wiped out other Freedom groups. Besides, we were in the midst of the war zone. Vancouver, Victoria, Port Townsend and Seattle had become the invaders' bases and we were here to cause as much trouble as possible — or die trying.

In the falsely assuring sunset we stopped at an old department store. Jay, Connie and Sarah ran down the dead escalator and checked behind looted bins for unwelcome inhabitants. We posted scouts at the entrances. I helped chop particle board walls for a small fire to cook our scavenged cans of food.

With few comforts left we still grouped around fires to discuss news of the world, or tell stories, and those who wished sang — when it was safe. Of course, possible genocide and an unpredictable tomorrow made our small group closer. It was one of our few comforts, to touch another human being, and that old survival instinct to propagate the species tended to run strongly.

Our Freedom group of sixteen men and women tended to switch partners even though there were a few set couples. We were really just one-organism with many legs and arms. But unlike the Foelnecs — their name, not ours — we had feelings. Sarah and Matthew would debate for hours whether the Foelnecs felt or not, but as far as I was concerned, the creepy buggers weren't human and couldn't have human feelings. No feelings in my book.

A couple of the guys started plucking their guitars softly and I watched quietly, sitting back for once. I had my own worries. A bottle of whisky passed from bandaged hand to scratched and callused hands. Firelight flashed shadowed emotions over faces. No one would get drunk tonight in case of a sudden raid. No one would be able to forget anyway.

It's funny — ironic, I guess. When the end came, we were in the midst of the Americans and Russians genially shaking hands, many world governments finally taking notice of the environmental problems, and Europe in sweeping economic changes; it seemed as if fears of the big nuke had faded like a bad dream. The approaching year actually looked promising and I, like many others, was complacent with my teaching job. I had a loving mate and one child; we were yuppies and content to play that game. Why not enjoy what we worked for, I said. The world is filled with so much pain. And the world's pain soon moved closer to me.

Well, the end didn't come from superpowers, environmental cataclysm, or from a wayward meteor. But come it did. More horrifying than the riders of the apocalypse and far more unbelievable.

The invasion was such a shock that many people in Vancouver continued to believe it was some science fiction, War of the Worlds style hoax, or some new movie being filmed. A movie doesn't kill actors by the thousands. Invaders just didn't happen and besides, we all knew that if alien races had space travel they would obviously be more civilized and wiser than we. Wrong.

Idiots. Slow-moving with disbelief, we lost many people in those first months. The Canadian military was too small to contain the Foelnecs, although they did manage to capture and interrogate one — something few other countries have yet managed.

I refocused on the group. Soft moans issued from Sarah and Jay over in the rows of couches and piled cushions.

"Sharee, are you okay?"

I looked over at Marc and shrugged. I poked my stomach and said, "I think I have a growing concern."

He grimaced but said, "What are you going to do?"

"I...I want it, Marc. I know Greg died in the first wave but Marlyse . . . "

He put his hand on my shoulder. "You never found her."

I angrily shrugged off his hand and scrubbed the tears from my cheeks. "Don't. Just don't, okay." I paused, ashamed at rebuffing Marc's concern. "No, I don't know what happened to her. They never found her body and . . . and we're losing everything, everyone. Every life born is another one to fight the Foelnecs."

Marc plucked a sad note or two on the guitar and just nodded. I felt grateful to him for not reminding me that I'd have to leave the Freedom group in a few months. I'd have to join a Ratter camp. Rats, those that didn't fight but managed to stay alive by running and hiding. Their chances of surviving were not better than a Freedom group's.

Marc had been a gear, an engineer. He applied his knowledge now in taking apart weapons we found or stole and remaking them into anything that could repel the Foelnecs. I could see him thinking, Is it mine?

Soft, babyfaced Samo oiled his gun and Connie, humming to guitar strains, slapped a moulding compound over the hole in her boot. When we had all been suburbanites Connie had been an unhappy, two hundred and forty pound wife who often stuck her nose into everyone's business including mine. She stayed at home with nothing to do and always chatted me into a stupor. I grunted at the thought that the war had made her content, well . . . at least given her a purpose. She had thinned as if she were chiselled for fighting the Foelnecs. It was a surprise that she had survived but it was just that instinct that had honed the Freedom groups: those willing to fight for life.

Feeling heavy with sleep, I grabbed a blanket and found the mattress department. The changes from war roamed through my tired mind. In all those sugarcoated, Hollywood movies the problems or monsters had always started in the U.S. Real life hadn't been so choosy, or heroic and romanticized.

It was a backdoor invasion. The Foelnecs had set down in about a dozen places at once and the U.S. realized it too late when Foelnec infantry filtered south from Saskatchewan and into the rural farming communities first. They had moved likewise throughout the world: settling into sparsely populated centres and then spreading out.

I think that in the past wars went on for so many years because the people would have been bored and discontent without the constant adrenaline rush of life on the edge — not knowing whether tomorrow would greet them with a bomb. It honed the senses until every object looked sharp and we felt electrified with life.

If there was ever an original sin, it was probably complacency. The others would not agree with me. After three years of fighting and drifting they longed for something common. How many of us could now go back? I drifted into sleep thinking it was the teacher in me that wanted to write all this down. Maybe someone will read it in a better future and learn from it. Yeah, right.

I awoke to snugly cuddling and found that Samo, Matthew and Connie had climbed into the same bed during the night. All my family. I stroked Connie's close-cropped red hair and stumbled from the bed to find a place to leak. Then I grabbed a few crackers and went to see if the scouts needed a break. California brunette, once new-ager, Matthew joined me, coming up behind and wrapping his arms around my waist. I leaned back into him. By now, I'm sure everyone was apprised of my condition.

"Hey, Shar, you look sad."

"Hmmm?" I held one of his arms. "I was just thinking how quiet it was. You can almost believe that we'll step out into a perfect morning and all this," I swept my arm towards the street piled with broken cement and husks of cars, "All this was just some bad dream."

He grunted. "I wish I could believe that but all I hear is the silence of the dead. I hear nothing, and all I can think of are the sounds that have been silenced. No cars honking, no school kids taunting each other, not even dogs barking." Matthew leaned his head on my neck and we stood there silently, watching.

By daybreak we were all back to business. The store became a dim memory, anything usable already scavenged. We decided to take the risk of hitting the Van. General hospital. The network reported the Foelnecs had recently abandoned it.

I walked near the rear with Jay. He stared ahead, a fine line etched vertically between his brows, thinking his own thoughts. Jay had been a doctor and we still valued him as such. We were lucky to have him along. He had the sculpted looks that used to grace GQ magazines. Jay had also turned out to be one of the best strategists when it came to the Foelnecs. If we had had a leader, he would have been it but we all gave input depending on our expertise and points of view, and all decisions were group decisions.

"I think I'm pregnant, Jay."

He didn't look at me but continued to scan the abandoned buildings. Occasionally we saw the round, glassy eyes of a ratter staring at us.

Jay said tersely, "I suppose you want an abort."

"What!" Something was eating at him but he didn't share his thoughts often. "No, no I don't."

"How long since your last period?"

I squinted into the dark glass of more buildings. "I don't know. Sometime around when we ran into the Foelnec drones in Burnaby."

He sighed, tight-lipped. "Two months. I'll check you later when I can."

I let him be. Jay's moods swung as quickly as a spyeye moved.

An hour and a half of walking took three hours when we had to dodge a contingent of about forty, third-stage Foelnecs. Too much heavy metal for our small party to handle, but Samo and Karen noted their direction and voice-coded it to the net. The Foelnecs frequently crashed the systems but the net was better than total isolation. An hour after the bridge cleared, we crossed.

I hated the bridge as much as everyone else. Walking, backs bared to the sky, we never knew if a hit would come from above, below or if we'd be corralled from both ends of the bridge. Like taking your skin off and leaving your soul bared.

The bridge, like many of the streets, was lined with discarded vehicles, as if a hive of metal insects had suddenly died and left their carapaces to rot. The cars afforded cover from roving Foelnec spyeyes.

I looked longingly at a derelict car; quicker transport, but gas was rare. With the world battling on all fronts, essential resources tended to stay in their own countries. It meant that a lot of backwater countries fended for themselves, where neither Foelnecs nor foreign aid infringed on their lives. Gas and other goods rarely left their home ports.

We used to complain about Vancouver's seemingly constant rain. Now it was the sun we worried about; it made us beacons with light flaring off every reflective surface. We preferred the rain and cloudy skies for cover. The weather sometimes fouled even Foelnec instruments. For all their strange looks they were not that much more advanced than we. They had just beaten us to space travel.

By the time we hit Granville and Broadway the sun had coaxed an oily sheen to our faces and soaked our backs. Samo, our computer expert, pushed his bandanna up on his forehead and contacted the net through his ear/throat implant for updates.

Sarah, just ahead of him, peered around the corner of a bank and held out her hand, black and silver rings flashing. She signalled silence. Marc and I crept to the front, our rifles loaded. No one could afford to waste ammo, and egos aside we were the crackshots.

Marc stayed with the group; Sam, Matthew and I slipped back of the building. I heard the soft whir of Marc's sonic blaster building to full charge. It disrupted the electronic frequencies of the machine/flesh physiology of a Foelnec. Sort of like massive electrocution. I had nothing so subtle.

Samo held his finger to the bone behind his ear for better reception. His pale green eyes stared at me, then focused when the message came through. Karen must have relayed info because he held up three fingers and pointed one to the building top, and two fingers to the front and right of us. One sentry on top and two out across the street from the bank.

I flipped off the safety and pressed the thermal disrupter's cycler. I pointed at street level and Matthew indicated the rooftop, then slipped inside the neighbouring building's stairwell entrance. His head showed through a window near the front. Samo pushed on throat and earbone and relayed back to Karen. My back itched with the thought of the Foelnec above looking down on me. I inched around the side of the building, lowering my infra goggles to detect their heat spots.

I took aim at one of the secondaries across the street and awaited the signal. The two second-stage Foelnecs looked the most humanoid of the three stages, though that was stretching the concept a lot. They had pointed, long and slightly flattened heads, like a squashed torpedo, and sinuous bodies supported on four legs. Reddish grey, many twitching metal parts grew out of their bodies.

One of the Foelnecs in front of the brick building fed on something. It extruded its siphon-like nose and moved back while the other Foelnec grasped the carcass in pincer-like hands. I didn't look too closely at their meal and sighted on the feeding one's head. I glanced at Samo; he subvocalized something then nodded. His hand flicked down and I fired. I saw the beam through my goggles hit directly on the feeding Foelnec as the other dropped to all fours. Matthew fired simultaneously across the road and an answering beam of white light opened his window a little wider. Red brick and dust showered us.

Working on heat frequencies, my disrupter beam set up a chain reaction within the Foelnec's tissue and chemically bonded one cell to the next. The tissue melted and bubbled into organic glop. The other Foelnec didn't even look at its twitching and fusing companion, but raised a black metal tube with pulsing green and yellow lights. It fired and I heard shouts from around the building. I fired, hitting it in the shoulder. It immediately brought up two other limbs and sheered off the damaged one before the reaction spread into the torso. This most resourceful stage consisted of the ability to manipulate and rearrange their flesh/metal appendages at will. I could hear Matthew shooting it out with the one on the roof and him yelling something about hi-tech.

Marc's sonic blaster took out the second Foelnec just as I heard a scream. I ran back around the building diving low as a spyeye shot a beam at me. My disrupter was useless on it and I hoped someone was covering my butt. I shot at the third-stage cybernetic nightmare, encased in metal with orange unblinking eyes, that emerged from the stairwell. It clenched Matthew's arm. The disrupter was the only weapon that could kill third-stage Foelnecs. Had we known a third-stager was on top, well . . . Matthew wouldn't have been in its clutches.

Matthew, white-faced, left arm at a bad angle, still valiantly landed judo kicks into the thing's abdomen while trying to duck an instrument the Foelnec poked at him. The third-stager was mostly a metalloid cylinder with three different appendages. I'd seen as many as eight on these machines of organic metal.

My shot flew wide from their thrashing and I had to take careful aim since the others were beating and assaulting the Foelnec. I screamed, "Get the fuck out of the way or Matthew's dead!"

They moved and I aimed again at the third-stage Foelnec. This time I hit its only weak spot directly and the thing dropped Matthew in its attempt to rip out its own stomach, but it was too late.

The group stared in morbid fascination as the thing fused and melted into stinking flesh and carbonized metal. Marc and Connie lifted Matthew to his feet and pulled him over to a debris clear area. Jay set to work on pulling the bloody cloth away from Matthew's arm.

I had hoped we might be able to take this one alive but few three-stagers had ever been successfully captured. They tended to self-destruct even if we didn't use disrupters on them.

I sat on a pile of rubble while the others scouted the area for any other Foelnecs. Jay bandaged Matthew. I knew raising a baby in wartime wouldn't be any worse or harder than fighting. There was a time when I had vowed that I could never kill anyone or anything. The taking of life was just too abhorrent to me and many a time I had preached to friends and family on the virtues of vegetarianism.

Of course, the Foelnecs changed that: now the hunt was the new ritual, the enforced fad. We hunted dried foods, canned goods, surplus, supplies and any poor animals that wandered ourway. It still amazed me at people's resourcefulness. At least there was still the fishing industry and some farms still operating, but the meltdown near Portland didn't encourage anyone to eat these products.

A few of the European reactors had gone too, and one in the southern U.S., plus the geno bombs the Foelnecs dropped had added unknown residual effects to much of the food. It was a depressing time but I wasn't going to let the Foelnecs wipe us out. We had to keep going, no matter the odds. I had admitted to no one, not even myself for a long time, but I enjoyed hunting Foelnecs. I'm not sure why but they were an acceptable way to hurt something that had hurt me. For all my hurts that I had never dealt with.

Samo and Sarah came around the corner together, Samo cursing and brushing dust from his face. Samo gave an all clear sign. I groaned and stood. Everyone gathered their goods and Matthew, his arm in a sling, weakly smiled at me.

"Hey, thanks, Sharee. You saved my skin."

"Anytime, Matthew. After all, who would teach us drumming and judo if you were gone?"

We didn't stand around for idle banter but moved out immediately. There was still the Van. General hospital. It was only a few blocks along but the Foelnec attack made us wary.

A block from the hospital Jay grunted, then spoke loudly enough for the group to hear, "Heads up."

Weapons automatically cocked, we all hit what cover we could find behind abandoned cars and bushes.

There was movement in the hospital, dark shapes behind windows. It was supposed to be abandoned. I could see Samo communicating furiously with the net and shaking his head. His mouth a grim line, he ran over to where Marc, Jay, Sarah and about five others sheltered.

Karen turned to me and Connie and whispered the news. "Net says the Foelnec contingent left two days ago. Could be a few stragglers."

Something felt wrong. "I don't know. There seems too many figures in there."

Karen, hand to earbone, looked to Samo, nodded then said, "They think we should find out how many are there. Maybe we can take them out, and we need the equipment, if any's left."

Connie frowned and bit her nail. "If there's only a few in second or first-stage we could get 'em."

She didn't need to finish the thought for us — if they were third-stage even two were too many. I sighed. "I say we move in, cautiously, and check it out."

Karen relayed our thoughts and Connie went to tell the rest of the group, then gave the thumbs up to us. After discussion with Jay on how to surround the building we proceeded.

Karen, Connie and I went for the front entrance, dodging from bush to pillar. A few others spread out low along the front wall and Marc and Jay respectively led groups around the west and east sides. Only two were sent to the north entrance.

I listened carefully, disrupter droning quietly. There was movement — shuffling, scraping, soft thuds but nothing that sounded like the staticky Foelnec speech. Crouching low, I edged open the door. Connie and Karen covered my back as I scooted in and against the wall. I craned my neck around the corner into what had once been the reception area.

I froze and almost dropped the disrupter. Karen gasped, "Wh — what!?"

Milling, softly bumping into each other and away like bumper cars, were people. There must have been a couple hundred crowded into that waiting area. Naked, most of them children of varying ages, a few adults, they all wore the same dead-eyed stare. Drool and excrement crusted their bodies and not one of them uttered a sound. Slowly, as if sensing us, they oriented towards us and shuffled along. These mannequins, once human, raised their arms and slowly sped up.

"Shit!" I started backing up and noticed the worst. Every skull was shaved, the top part missing, exposing the soft grey brains. I swallowed, feeling a blackness well up. No! No! Not that, not them, I wanted to cry. Black and silver instruments clutched the brains of people who once had loved each other, played, cried. Now they did nothing but gain speed.

"Retreat," I gritted from between clenched teeth. Connie backed up but Karen stood there sucking in air like she was drowning.

"Karen! Move it, damn it! Relay to Jay and tell him what's happening."

"But, but," she stammered, her hand wavering around her ear like a fly.

I pulled her out the doors, cursing. The others in front were tensed to shoot, trying to figure out what was going on. "Relay, damn it!" And I slapped Karen.

She seemed to barely feel it, but pressed at her implants and mumbled, "There are people, people and oh, they're . . . "

Connie looked green. I decided to throw caution to the winds as those human zombies started pushing the doors open. I screamed, "Jay! Jay! Get over here now." Many of the children carried weapons: a little red-head boy with squirrel-like cheeks, a frizzy-headed blonde girl, another girl —slim with silken hair the colour of Marlyse's — oh, God, not Marlyse.

Some held scalpels, wood, bars, pipes. Others held Foelnec weapons.

I could see the others were hit with the same indecision, almost losing their training from the shock, backing away, looking about. Not a few of the Freedom group had to stop and retch. What should we do? I didn't know. These people would kill us but could we kill them? Were they still alive? Could they be healed?

My hands shook and I grabbed the disrupter more tightly as Jay and his group rounded the corner. He reached my side and gasped, "What's going on?"

I pointed and then he saw, his jaw dropping open. Like fleshy dolls, they advanced. "What do we do? Can we save them?"

"I . . . I." He stopped, wiped at his brow, squinted. "No. No, we can't. It'll be a mercy to them. We must end their . . . "

We hadn't seen it; no one had. Karen, stunned, had moved into their midst, mewling sounds escaped her throat as she tried to touch a man's face. The peo . . . the zombies just hacked at her. The man she touched stabbed her with a shard of glass that sliced open his palm. Karen clutched his shoulders as children and adults mindlessly, automatically hacked her to bloody shreds.

"No!" screamed Connie, tears running down her face. She opened fire and before I knew what I did we were all shooting down the mindless adults and children. They fell in bloody heaps, continuing to walk over each other, continuing to reach out for us.

I thought that some reached out in supplication. Throughout our slaughter I could only think, Marlyse. Marlyse, never found. Never found her body. Marlyse. Marlyse.

I don't how long it was after all the bodies had been decimated that Jay had to shake me and pry my disrupter from my hands. The only thought going through me was, I'll not bring another into this world. I'll gut myself first. I'll not . . .

Only silence reigned after that. No one cheered our victory for it was hollow. The Foelnecs had found a deadly weapon that destroyed more than our forces. Except for Karen, there were only minor injuries and a few brave souls tried to remove Foelnec weapons from the mass of corrupted flesh. I walked near the pile of soft young limbs; hands open — never to be held, mouths gaping — never to laugh. I looked down and vowed to kill every Foelnec until they were all gone.

The next thing I knew, someone shouted, "Sharee!" I was slammed into a wall, the air momentarily pushed out of me. The ground flared red where I had been and then the spyeye exploded as Marc shot it out. I gulped in air, ignoring the pain, stood up from where Sarah had knocked me out of the spyeye's way, then doubled over retching.

A spasm of black lances slashed outward from my stomach and I vomited my breakfast. Then a deep pulsating blade twisted within my gut. Someone laid me out. Everyone, momentarily forgetting the spectacle of bloodied macabre mannequins, hovered over me. Jay's face appeared above mine and after a few painful proddings and questions he said, "Looks like you're in trouble, Sharee. I don't know if I can save the baby. Help me get her into the hospital," he said over his shoulder.

I ground my teeth and swore, "Damn it, Jay. I sure as hell am not going to bring a kid into this scumhole until we get rid of the cancer. I don't want it!" I hissed as another wave of icy pain swept over me.

They carried me on a makeshift stretcher into the hospital. No more Foelnecs, no more humans, except us; but there were enough items and beds for Jay to help me through the miscarriage. They let me rest for a while after I had aborted the placenta. Sarah, her rings glittering antiseptically, sat with me while the others scavenged labs and operating rooms for any equipment.

Jay came by and asked, "How you feel?"

I said, "Like someone ripped out my womb and put it back inside-out, but I guess I'll live. Remember," I clasped his hand suddenly scared and already feeling alone. "If you gotta move on, do it. Don't wait for me."

He gripped my hand in both of his and was about to say something when a yip rang through the hall. Laughter and suddenly Marc and Connie appeared in the doorway holding several instruments. Cheeks dimpling, Connie held up something shiny and said, "Laser." I could see the forced gaiety. The dark circles under her eyes belied what she was trying not to remember.

Jay reached them in two strides. He took the instrument from Connie's thin hand and held it as if it were the most fragile egg in all the world.

Most of the others had gathered in what looked to have been a post-op room and Jay just held the laser and stared at it. Samo and Matthew came through the swinging doors talking and stopped when they saw Jay, tears running down his cheeks. He looked up at us and all the pain and horror of killing those poor mindless drones shone out of his eyes.

His voice quavered as he softly said, "We . . . I used to use these to heal, to help people." He cried openly now. "I saved lives, I healed. Now we use it to kill, to kill . . . " he whispered and looked down, shoulders shaking.

Marc removed the laser from Jay's hands, and Matthew, arm in a sling, and Sarah put their arms around him. I looked away and swallowed a lump in my throat.

"Hey," said Samo. "We're still using it to help people. We're going to heal the world, Jay, and those fucking Foelnecs aren't going to stop us . . . even if it kills us," he finished lamely.

We had lost a great deal that day. I had lost the last of my wishful thinking, of a belief that I could lead a normal life. But we were still together, my family touching, hands clasped tightly, hugging. To have good there must be evil, to have life there must be death. I guess the only good thing about the invasion was that it united the world. It made us cherish life even more. But to bring a new life into it — no, it wouldn't have been fair. Not yet.

It was our world, our family, and we would die for it before we let anyone or anything separate us from our love and absolute need for each other. Consciously or not, everyone had sworn this in their hearts or they had died.

ROAD KILL

by
Edo van Belkom

Edo van Belkom, a resident of Brampton, Ontario is the Regional Director (Canadian) of the SFWA and a contributing member of *The Bulletin*. He has been widely published in numerous magazines since beginning his fiction career in 1990. Add four novels to his list of over 100 short stories in print. He was nominated for an Aurora Award and a First Novel Bram Stoker Award. Edo is a former daily newspaper sports and police reporter.

ROAD KILL

by
Edo van Belkom

"Gimme another brew," Marty Slipchuck said, rolling down the window of the Cuda and lighting an unfiltered Export A.

Cal Jonas turned around in the passenger seat, got onto his knees and opened the cooler in the back seat. "Bud or Sleeman?"

"They both cold?"

"Zomboid."

"Gimme a Sleeman, then."

"You got it."

Cal pulled a clear bottle from the ice for Marty and grabbed a can of Bud for himself. When he was back in his seat he straightened his glasses on the bridge of his nose and handed the bottle of Sleeman to Marty.

"Thanks?" Marty said. He opened the bottle with his teeth, spit the cap out the open window and laughed. "Who'da thought I'd ever be sucking this stuff back regular."

Cal popped his Bud and snickered. "Yeah, you got real class now, Marty. Real class."

Marty put the bottle to his lips, upended it and emptied half its contents before stopping to breathe.

Before everything got all fucked up, Marty had worked at dozens of jobs, none of them for very long. The virus had been little more than a bump in the road of his life. While the rest of the world had gone ape-shit over zombies, Marty had merely shifted gears.

"There's one!" Cal said, beer spluttering out of his mouth along with the words.

About half a mile away, the hunched over figure of a zombie had wandered out from the row of trees lining the edge of the highway. Although it stumbled aimlessly along the road, the zombie was making definite progress in their direction, no doubt attracted by their scent. Neither of them had bathed in over a week.

Marty took a final pull on the Sleeman and tossed the bottle into the back seat. He took a last drag on his cigarette, flicked the butt out the window and reached for the ignition.

Cal snickered, threw his still full can of beer out the window and put on his seat belt.

Marty had found Cal in the back of a Seven-Eleven, his pud in one hand and a copy of *Hustler* in the other. He'd taken Cal with him, not only to have someone to kick around, but to have someone to talk to as well. Cal wasn't much, but he was still better than the dead stations of the Cuda's radio.

"What you gonna do this time, Marty?" Cal said. "You gonna roadkill it? Are you?"

"Not tellin'," Marty said, evenly. He turned to Cal and smiled, baring all four of his teeth. "You'll just hafta wait and see."

He turned the ignition and the Cuda's headered 340 thrummed to life like some animal rudely awakened from a deep sleep. He revved the engine a few times, shifted into first and let go the clutch.

The Cuda's rear wheels screeched against the pavement as the slicks tried to grab hold. The smell of burning rubber grew thick, then suddenly they were off, hurtling down the interstate
on what felt like a rocket sled.

Marty's lips drew back into a thin white line, his fingers curled tightly around the wheel and his eyes turned ghostly white as they stared blankly out at the highway.

Cal looked over, saw the roadkilling look of the reaper in Marty's face, and began bouncing in his seat. "You're gonna get it, you dead motherfucker!" he screamed.

The needle of the Cuda's speedometer began its arch across the dash. ... 20... 25...

Roadkilling zombies had become one of the nation's favourite pastimes.

... 30... 35...

Marty and Cal had done over fifty of them in the last month alone, but they never grew tired of it.

... 40... 45...

There was a rush connected with the crunch of bone and the splat of dead meat that drugs alone just couldn't match.

... 50... 55...

And there was no shortage of zombies. What was left of the government had estimated there were still half a million of them roaming the cities and countryside.

... 58... 60...

Marty eased off the gas. Any faster and they'd totally destroy the zombie on impact, not to mention wreck the Cuda. Besides, anybody could run the fuckers over, the real fun of roadkilling was playing with them, seeing how dead you could make them before they stopped living.

With less than fifty yards to go, they could see the zombie in some detail. It was, or at leasthad been, a woman. She was wearing what looked to be the shredded remains of a dark grey business suit, but it was hard to tell where the suit ended and the mottled flesh began.

"It's a bitch, Marty!" Cal cried. "A fuckin' bitch. I bet she liked to take it up the ass."

Marty's right hand whipped out and smacked Cal hard in the mouth. "Shut the fuck up while I'm trying to drive!"

Cal looked hurt for a moment, but quickly resumed his giggling once he looked ahead and saw that they were seconds from impact.

"Holy Shit!" Cal said.

The Cuda slammed into the zombie —

=WHAM!=

— breaking the dead thing in two.

The bottom half of its torso and legs stuck to the front of the car while the upper body and head slid over the hood, bounced off the windshield and flew twenty feet through the air before smashing on the highway behind them.

Marty slammed on the brakes and brought the Cuda to a screeching halt.

"Fuckin' A, man!" Cal said, closing his eyes and shaking his head, giddy. "Broke the fuckin' bitch in two."

Marty smiled for the first time since starting up the Cuda. "Did you like that?"

"You're the fuckin' best, Marty. Chopped her down like Paul Fuckin' Bunyan."

Marty's face turned grave. He looked in the rear view mirror. The top half of the zombie's body was still in tact. It was also moving, clawing its way toward the Cuda with its arms.

"It's still alive," Marty said, calmly but with obvious pleasure as he shifted the car intoreverse.

"What? No fuckin' way, man." Cal stopped giggling for a moment and turned around. "I don't believe it."

Marty eased the Cuda back, peering out the open window so he could line up the car's left rear tire with the zombie's head.

"You gonna do her slow?" Cal said.

"Yeah."

"Nice and slow." Cal was hyperventilating. "The same way she liked to take it up the ass. Nice and slow."

The Cuda came to a stop when the rear tire rolled up against the zombie. Marty eased out the clutch and the tire slowly began turning, climbing up onto the thing's head.

A loud crack ripped through the air as the zombie's skull collapsed under the weight of the Cuda, followed by a steady crunching sound as larger pieces of bone were ground into pulp.

Jets of zombie splat and dead brain matter spurted across the pavement onto the other lanes of the highway as if a rotten tomato had been roadappled by a semi.

"You're the best, man," Cal howled with delight.

Even Marty gave a chuckle. "I ain't finished yet."

With the rear tire sitting squarely on the grey pulp of the zombie's head, Marty revved the engine and popped the clutch.

Without a posi-track rear end, the Cuda's right rear wheel wouldn't move as long as the left rear kept spinning. And with nothing but slimy rotten meat beneath it, the left rear tire spun as easily as if it were on a patch of ice.

Marty put the gas pedal to the floor.

Bits of dead flesh and roadkill juice flew out in front of the car as Marty had brought the V8 close to the red line.

Cal had his arms across his chest, twisting and turning in an uncontrollable fit of laughter. "Stop it, Marty," he shouted over the motor's roar. "I swear I'm gonna piss my pants."

Marty laughed then too, pressing his foot down further on the gas.

"Oh, shit!" Cal managed to say as a wet stain began to appear in the crotch of his jeans.

Marty pointed to the piss stain and screamed with laughter.

Just then the spinning tire made solid contact with the highway.

The Cuda jolted backward, and stalled.

Marty and Cal stopped laughing.

The air was thick with the stench of charred flesh and burnt rubber. The inside of the Cuda was deathly silent.

"What the fuck happened?" Cal said, finally.

"Just stalled." Marty said, turning the ignition.

Click! Nothing.

"Uh-oh," Cal said. "We're fucked."

"We're not fucked," Marty snapped, his voice a little unsteady. "Nothing I can't fix." He pulled on the lever beneath the dash to pop the hood.

They got out and went around to the front of the car.

And stood there, staring.

Half the zombie was stuck to the front of the car, the worn down stumps of its legs were bent backward, trailing away beneath the front of the car.

"Well go ahead," Marty said. "Get it off."

"You want me to touch it?"

"No, I don't want you to touch it, stupid. There's a tire iron in the trunk." He gave him the key.

Cal walked around to the back of the car and returned with the tire iron. Then, being careful not to touch the thing with his hands, he scraped the zombie's hips and thighs from the Cuda's grill and bumper. When the car was clean, he opened the hood.

Again they were left staring, unable to speak.

When the car jolted backward, the rear wheels had thrown one of the zombie's arms up into the motor. It had gotten tangled up in the belts, stalling the car.

But that wasn't the funny part.

The funny part was that the thing's fingers were all curled up except for the middle one — the zombie was giving them the bird.

Cal giggled.

Marty's left hand flew out and clipped Cal in the back of the head. "What the fuck are you laughing at?"

Cal turned to Marty, a hurt look on his face. "Nothing."

"Good. Now climb under there and get that thing out. We gotta get the fuck out of here."

It was dangerous to be out in the open for any length of time. If one zombie had smelled them out on the highway you could bet there were more on the way. Best thing to do was to get the hell out and call it a day.

Cal got down on the ground, crawled under the car and got to work trying to loosen the zombie's arm with the tire iron. He smacked it a few times, but it was wedged in pretty tight. He changed his position and tried again.

While Cal worked under the car, Marty walked around back to see if there was any damage to the car's rear end. Except for a half-inch thick coating of zombie slime in the wheel well and on the shocks everything looked okay.

"I'm going to need your help, Marty. It's really jammed in there," came Cal's voice from beneath the car.

It was followed by a scream.

Marty rushed around to the front of the Cuda, but stopped abruptly when he saw another zombie, this one dressed a little like a short-order cook, down on all fours biting into Cal's neck.

Marty wanted to help, but knew it was already too late.

As the zombie prepared to take another bite, Cal looked up at Marty, his eyes wet, wide and full of terror. "Help me," he cried.

Marty watched helplessly as the zombie's teeth crunched through Cal's skull and dug into his brain. Cal's face lit up in pain, then went limp, lifeless. His eyes remained open, but there was nothing behind them.

Marty managed to turn away. He clapped his hands over his ears, but he could still hear the ripping and slurping sounds as the zombie tore into Cal's flesh like a hungry dog.

In the distance Marty could see another zombie wandering out from the trees. Further down the highway in the direction of the city, two more figures appeared on the horizon. In minutes there'd be dozens of dead things surrounding him.

He ran around to get into the car, but when he reached the driver's side door, he remembered the car didn't work.

He slammed a fist down into the Cuda — And felt a hand grope for his neck. The zombie had finished with Cal and was now after him. Marty shook himself free of the thing's grasp and slammed its head against the roof of the car.

There was the familiar sound of cracking bone as the zombie's head turned soft and pulpy in his hands. Marty let go of it and it fell onto the highway in a heap.

The other zombies were getting closer.

Marty started to run, back up the hill, back in the direction he had come.

Jackson James cupped his girlfriend's right tit in his hand and squeezed the nipple between his thumb and forefinger.

"I already told you I'm not in the mood," she said, pulling his hand away from her breast and putting it firmly back onto the seat behind her. "Besides, you said we were going roadkilling."

"We are, babe," Jackson said. "But these things take their time coming out on the road. I thought we'd do a little boffing while we waited."

"I don't feel like it, all right," she said.

"How bout a blow, then?"

She shook her head in mild disgust, then suddenly perked up in her seat. "There's one of those things now."

Jackson gazed at the zombie approaching them on the highway.

It moved a little faster than most, and was waving its arms around a bit, but that was good.

"This should be fun," he said, starting up the Chevy pick-up. "This one looks like it's still got some life left in it."

ROOTS OF THE SOUL

by
Dale L. Sproule

Dale L. Sproule, of North York, Ontario is well known in Canadian SF circles. His fiction has appeared in *Pulphouse, The Hardcover Magazine #1 and #17, Ellery Queen's Sign of the Times: 10 Year Anthology, Northern Frights II, Karl Wagner's Year's Best XXIII* and he became a Prix Aurora Award finalist. He and his wife Sally McBride edit and publish the dark fantasy magazine *Transversions.*

ROOTS OF THE SOUL

by
Dale L. Sproule

When the front rider broached the top of the slope and drew back his spear, Psalma dodged into the concealing gloom of the trees without pausing to worry about how nobody ever emerged from the Carnivorous Forest once they'd entered. That mode of death at least seemed less painful and ignominious than being impaled on a spear by her own people for an imagined crime.

Thousands of translucent white tree roots criss-crossed the forest floor like veins. One of them reached up and grabbed her foot, toppling her face first onto damp, black earth. She scrambled back to her feet, millions of rootlets rising up around her knees like a living spiderweb.

A second MOjo topped the ridge and skidded his mocycle to a stop beside the first. Psalma saw him pointing directly at her through the trees. With a belch, his mocycle lurched to the edge of the forest and the rider peered into the darkness.

"I see her!" she heard him say. As Psalma leaped back to her feet and whirled to run, a spear whistled past her ear, thudding into the trunk of a nearby tree. The tree's branches curled down like arms to its wound and its trunk became elastic, its writhing shook gourds from its branches and its screams sank into Psalma's consciousness as deeply as any spear.

"Don't waste the weapons," a voice said authoritatively. "Let the forest take her."

"I'll go in after her!" said the man who threw the spear. Psalma's eyes widened as she recognised the voice of Zekeel, her frequent and unwelcome seatmate through Bible Time since they were both small children.

Psalma had rebuffed his heavy-handed advances persistently since pu-
berty. Adulthood had turned him from an irritating child into a posturing ass.

The officer shouted, "Riding the Lord's steed into damnation is a sin,
Calvaryman. Comeback!"

The rhythm of mammalian locomotion vibrated through groundroots as
they burrowed into soil to avoid brutal footfalls. Living filaments flinched
and squirmed, their sensory awareness relaying the human's presence to
nearby trees like a whimper of pain. When the projectile entered the flesh
of Systree Adnak, the pain radiated out over the grid like an electronic
shockwave. Rootlets which had been reaching up to capture the intruder,
became disconnected from their units and flopped helplessly on the ground.
A sound like an earthquake was followed a microsecond later by the ripping and tearing of thousands of tendrils, which broadcast itself through the
bio-grid like a scream.

As her pursuer entered the forest, the net of rootlets around Psalma's
feet began to boil like liquid, then rose up in a spray that stung her flesh.
Clinging to the rough bark, the white filaments slithered up the trunks of the
trees like rabid frost. Some were long enough to reach the lower branches,
more than ten feet in the air and hung down from there like icicles.

As the mocycle wound around the trees toward her Psalma ran as hard
and fast as she could across the moist black soil. In the quickening darkness, Psalma couldn't see her pursuer weaving slowly toward her through
the trees. But she could hear the steed's staccato snort became a roar.
Tree-trunks grew wider and wider and their branches higher, the deeper
she went into the forest. This time, it was exhaustion that brought Psalma
to the ground. Rolling onto her back, she stared up at the glimpses of blue,
morning sky twinkling like stars through a ceiling of foliage that seemed as
dark and infinite as night.

Her still-beautiful young face was ribboned with penance scars,
inflicted by DaughterRay as a sacred ward against vanity. Death was
riding up to claim her and Psalma could do nothing to stop it. Peering
upward, she whispered, "Is this my Punishment for not Believing? Wouldn't

it be more productive to convert me? Prove you're real. Help me."

Even off-system units were jolted into protective mode.

Abibh delayed the release of its seeds to ensure that they wouldn't be damaged by the intruder, then disengaged from ORCHARD1 to tune into up the emergency alert from the Main-Online-Memory unit.

Abibh was the 47th Systree to file a report about the bipedal thumping of human footsteps which preceded the hurting. So severe was the agony which rippled through the grid that the location of the human went unrecognized even by those whose groundroots were being tread upon.

Mom sent the "motorcycle" file to all comlinks. It contained a neurosedative virus to instantly dampen the residual pain of the vehicle's passage plus information about the motorcycles from the Experimental Forest Project, which were fuelled by the sap of specially bred baobab trees. The fuel forest had been the project's raison d'etre, development of the Bio-Net being a secondary goal. And hundreds of crates of grease packed motorcycles had survived the millennium.

The walled city of Aggaseas had grown up around the Fuel Forest as its Soldiers of Calvary carried out what they perceived to be God's Will. Braving the forest was considered a test of courage for the motorcycle riders, since more than 4.2 per cent of them never came back. The incidence had decreased significantly since, angered by the loss of the very vehicles which gave Aggaseas its military advantage, The Most Faithful declared entering the forest a sin punishable by demotion. But the motorcyclists still came sometimes, on dares and bets and in races; untouched by the trees as long as they didn't stop. Several systrees had been the sites of crashes, and sometimes even their fire-resistance couldn't save them.

In the .28 seconds before the spasms stopped and the systrees regained motor control of their rootlets, the motorcycle travelled almost three metres. Its speed left no possibility of snaring either the machine or its rider without sustaining severe and possibly mortal injury to the trees involved in the actual process of capture.

Psalma's pursuer turned away. The rumble faded slightly, grew louder, then diminished to a buzz.

Awareness of the absence of other sounds crept threateningly into Psalma's consciousness. No insects flitted through the heart of the Carnivorous Forest. No birds sang here.

Lying motionless on the ground, she crossed her arms over her breasts and shuddered. Her coarsely woven shiver of a nightdress protected her from neither the wet October morning, nor from her fear.

Psalma guessed that there could only be one logical reason the forest was allowing her to remain unharmed. The Lord was Protecting her. Just as he was now driving her Executioner away.

It was a validation of the gospel DaughterRay had been pounding into her brain since infancy.

"It is the responsibility of all citizens of Aggaseas," DaughterRay preached, "to bear the burden of God's wrath. And to act as the Lord's hands in feeding fuel to the Lake of Fire."

But before Psalma had a chance to convert, the snarling returned from the borders of memory, until it was so loud it made her teeth chatter.

The time of proof was apparently over. Now it was time for punishment. Zekeel grinned as he rolled slowly toward her.

While many systrees accessed and saved the new information, messages about the humans echoed throughout the grid.

Adnak 's gridmates on ORCHARD4 were bombarded with details about the injuries it sustained when the spear penetrated its torso. The file went unopened and was even deleted by many, who considered it the height of impoliteness for an individual bio-unit to unnecessarily subject its gridmates to its pain.

"One of these humans is aware of our true nature as bearers of knowledge," Systree Ajxro insisted throughout the grid, at a rate of 8,000 messages per minute, so that neither the rudest nor most distracted unit in the forest could comfortably ignore it for long.

"That assumption runs contrary to available information indicating that human cognizance of our purpose was erased centuries ago," responded Ardve, displaying its anger by modulating upward to rate of 10,000 messages per minute.

Having won the attention of most comlinks, the two units engaged in public debate.

"It is difficult to believe that you and I share the same senses," said Ajxro. The whole grid shared the sensory file and heard the human ask for proof of our reality. It was requesting an interface."

Grinning broadly, the young rider spiralled in toward her. As he circled ever closer, with his big blade unsheathed, Psalma finally figured out why the trees hadn't killed both her and Zekeel. They were afraid of the mocycle.

"I should receive a good reward for your bogey-filled head," Zekeel said too loudly as he straightened his khaki-coloured helmet so that its crucifixes no longer dangled in his face. "They may even move me into the front pews."

During the Tuesday Service, after Zekeel's recent promotion from GIjo to MOjo, Psalma's seatmate, Faith Eliot, had turned to her in the pew and harumphed, "MOjo, ho-ho. I'm amazed he ever got past Jo-Jo." Psalma had almost forgotten Zekeel's old nickname — Jo-Jo the Dogbrained Boy. She had originally thought the moniker cruel, but Zekeel seemed to settle in comfortably with the insult.

Just before the predinner prayer meeting last Wednesday, Zeekeel was waiting outside her father's bakery for Psalma to finish work. At her urging, Psalma's father had driven the young soldier away, brandishing nothing more than a loaf of bread.

Conversation on ORCHARD1 was overridden by a directive from MOM. "8,417 Systrees have indicated interest in possible establishment of an interface with the unmounted human. Surrounding SysTrees are commanded to refrain from consuming the human's nutrients until the situational analysis and subsequent vote are complete."

"A program to access the human's infobase is currently being composed on COMlink ORCHARD7. Interested Systrees are invited to participate."

A chorus of protests issued from many of the trees on ORCHARD1.

"Systrees opposing the feeding abatement are invited to gather on OR-CHARD6. Open debate will resume on ORCHARD1 in 4.5 seconds."

The ORCHARD 6 forum led off with Adnak's vehement complaints. "Not only was I injured by the spear, the human caused significant ground-root damage."

"The unmounted human caused little real damage. And neither did the spear penetration. But the motorcycle destroyed enough mature groundroots to severely cripple two Systrees."

Abibh responded. "The violent human differs physiologically from the seeker of lost knowledge. Our command forbidding consumption of the seeker does not protect the vehicle's rider. Is this confirmed?"

MOM replied in the affirmative. "Further damage by the motorcycle must be prevented. Any tree quick and resourceful enough to catch the mounted human is urged to do so and to share the nourishment with its grid-neighbours."

Zekeel's humiliation was probably his motivation for following her into the Carnivorous Forest. He peered suspiciously between the massive tree trunks as he edged toward her, obviously expecting her to run.

"You've always wanted to sex me, Zekeel. Take me back to the edge of the forest on the mocycle."

"I wish I could," he said. "But we both know the penalty for allowing one of the "unclean" to mount a sacred steed."

She tried to look wanton, but although it was a familiar game between Psalma and her girlfriends, she realized that all she was managing to do was knead her breasts nervously.

And although she felt capable of little more than bursting into tears, she managed to argue with him. "You're already in trouble for coming into the forest against orders."

"If I come back with the right trophy, they'll more than forgive me . . ." his steed lurched across the small clearing toward her.

The mocycle wasn't actually going very fast when Zekeel's blade sliced toward her, so Psalma had time to duck. The blade whistled over her head and bit into the soft bark of the tree. If Zekeel had released it instantly rather than trying to pry it loose, the first rootlets might not have had time to wrap around his arm. The rider stopped. The steed kept going, turning a big lazy circle before actually falling.

Zekeel shouted in surprise, unable to free his arm and not smart enough to take the blade in his free hand. By the time he thought of it, roots had hold of his legs, which they pulled out from under him. Zekeel flopped across the forest floor like a beached fish being dragged onto land before he finally got the knife into the other hand. A root wrapped itself around his neck and the young man began slashing hysterically at it. But before his blade could cut through it, another root dropped from an overhanging branch to circle the wrist of the hand which held the knife. It whipped back violently and with a popping sound, a gush of blood, and Zekeel's terrified scream, the limb came out of its socket. Dozens of other roots fell like rain and burrowed into the moist, red earth.

Other roots gathered around Psalma's legs and waist, pulling her back, binding her to the trunk of a great tree. She wished she could run, or do anything at all. For an instant, she watched in terrified fascination as tendrils wormed their way into Zekeel's mouth, nose, eyes, ears and began pulling him apart. She closed her eyes and turned her head away. However much she hated Zekeel, she never would have wished such an end on him. By the time she looked again, there was little of him still visible, as roots crowded into the open corpse like the Most Devout at the baptism pool.

After watching Zekeel die, Psalma knew that no amount of fighting on her part would free her. Every muscle in her body was clenched and she tried to relax and surrender herself to a quick death. The tree seemed to respond to her lack of resistance by being deliberately gentle. No roots forced themselves into her orifices.

"Perhaps," she told herself, "their grip tightens only if you struggle" — like the fingertrap she and Faith purchased from the toy-man a few days ago. Psalma's father protested that the girls were too old to visit the toy-man, but in the end, he'd

relented, conceding a last, tiny taste of childhood before his daughter was enthralled to the Lord under the strict and fanatical tutelage of DaughterRay.

When Psalma felt a probing and burrowing at the base of her skull, she screamed despite her efforts not to. Pain radiated out from the fingertip-sized point-of-entry as something hard and warm burrowed through her skin. She was somehow aware of thousands of tiny filaments mushrooming into her brain, even though there was no accompanying pain. She vomited, then observed with a mixture of fascination and disgust as roots unwound themselves from her leg to slither into the puddle. Then suddenly she was aware that the pain was gone. She couldn't remember it going. Every muscle in her body became numb and lifeless.

A new mental landscape rose spectacularly into view. Psalma's world grew dark. Tiny lights flickered to life by ones, twos, tens, twenties and thousands until Psalma felt like she was standing alone on a mountaintop on a very dark and cold night.

Then, the stars spoke!

"...knowing what it's like to be human," a voice said.

No, not a voice, just a premonition of a voice.

"...understanding its kind by experiencing its memories . . . "

What she heard were merely thoughts, translated into voice by the workings of her own brain. Psalma would have gasped, had she still been connected to her own body.

An instant later, the one voice turned to many. The entire population of the bio-grid poured itself into the crevices of her mind. She was suddenly thinking the thoughts of thousands of other minds, and they were thinking hers.

Morning. Psalma had been here before. It was this morning, just minutes (hours?) ago when Psalma was startled awake by shouting and crashing. Something pounded hard at the cabin door.

The door crashed open. GIjos rushed in. It made no sense to Psalma. Nor to her father apparently, as his voice cut through the darkness. "What are you doing in our home? I'm a God-fearing citizen! Get out!"

"We have a warrant for the arrest of Psalma Peterson."

"What is the charge?"

"Witchcraft."

"Who is her accuser?"

"Nathan Eliot. He was so bedeviled by her sorceries that it took us hours to get the truth out of him."

"I won't let you take her."

"Get out of my way old man."

There was a thump and they ripped the curtain off her bedroom door.

A young GIjo grabbed one arm and a grey haired career soldier took the other. The older man smelled of alcohol. They lifted her from the bed and carried her out the door. The last thing Psalma saw was her father lying motionless beside the door, a poppy-red bruise across his forehead.

Blinking away the hallucinations, Psalma saw trees. Trees? She screamed at the memory of some foreign thing crawling into her brain. And then she retreated back to the streets of Aggaseas, where neighbours watched and pointed from doorways as one of them was being taken to the Hall of Punishment. Lawyer was standing beside the Altar of Justice with his axe.

Psalma watched the scene unfold as she had seen it a hundred times in her life. The only thing which ever changed was the face of the accused. This time it was her. She was remembering something that never happened, because as she was being carried down the street, Psalma's knuckles smacked against the bone hilt of a knife. Extending a thin arm, Psalma managed to wrap her fingers around it. The GIjo didn't notice until she plunged the blade into the soft flesh beneath his rib cage.

He roared and dropped her, before toppling like a tree, clutching his side as blood welled out between his fingers.

Psalma slashed at the squinty eyes of the other GIjo, who was gaping at his fallen comrade. He didn't let go, even when Psalma's blade peeled off half his forehead, so she planted the knife deep into the flesh of his shoulder. He released her then! And Psalma turned and ran. She didn't even glance back when she felt something ripping through her hair a ghost's whisper from the back of her neck. She ran harder than she could have imagined, through the Fuel Forest and past the Lake of Fire, a perpetually burning pool of thick black water into which was cast anyone who was not of the City. Psalma's calloused feet slapped wet ground over and over and over — establishing a hypnotic rhythm that grew more and more insistent as reality blurred behind her, taking her into this strange new place of patterns of light, random thoughts climbing skyward like smoke from a thousand fires. Light bursting in the now darkness. Mind raced. Thoughts and memories flickered past at ever increasing speed. Even things she didn't consciously remember, like the face of Komo, Psalma's mother, officially a Goddess-worshipping slave from the Choolack Lands, who was executed when Psalma was four years old because a committee of the Most Faithful determined that Psalma's father displayed too much affection towards her. Unofficially, Psalma's father confessed that Komo had taught him about the sanctity of nature and the true meaning of love. He taught his daughter that it was okay to have doubts, as long as nobody in authority learned of them, which meant simply, "keep your mouth shut about what you really think and tell them what they want to hear."

It wasn't until adolescence that she met someone with whom she could share her feelings. Faith Eliot was even more overtly rebellious than Psalma. Faith's brother Nathan was the boy of her dreams. More sensitive than most males, Nathan had been the object of Psalma's intense crush since the first time she had slept over at Faith's home at age twelve.

Nathan had accidentally walked in on her while she was half-dressed and she had covered his face with both of her hands. Redfaced, he had backed out of the room, joking later that he hoped she would someday open the doors of her hands for him.

And when she was fourteen and he was sixteen, she had opened those doors and they had kissed. He told her that he loved her.

But Psalma wasn't the only one who had noticed Nathan's unusual empathy. DaughterRay recommended him for training as a healer, a vocation which required him to marry into a family of Healers. The eldest daughter of Healer Williamson had a reputation as an uncompromising shrew, thus was still unmarried at the age of twenty. The union was arranged.

Nathan's refusal led to his excommunication. Now it seemed, they had tortured a "confession" out of him before driving into the wasteland to live and be hunted down as a bogey. He was in love with someone else. Bewitchment was the only possible explanation.

Love and lust and grief and loss kaleidoscoped through Psalma's consciousness.

Then came a thousand glimpses she didn't recognize. Memories not her own. Alien sensations. The pleasure of drifting through the bio-grid the helplessness and anger and pain as groups of humans hack at your children and your future, the hunger of wrapping a fresh catch in your branches and draining it of nutrients. The taste of human blood.

"Contact has been initiated," MOM announced. "The human's acquiescence indicates awareness of imminent attainment of its goals. Interface will be established in an open forum across all comlinks."

Psalma didn't know if she was screaming, speaking or thinking loudly. She heard more voices. Saw random noises and bursts of light and colour. Somehow, she knew the meaning of all those sounds and shapes and flashes. And she understood so many other things. Like the true history of planet Earth and its relation to stars and other planets. Psalma also knew how it felt to die. She knew how it felt to be rooted to one spot for hundreds of years and what it felt like to be able to share every thought, every instant of your life with thousands of other presences. And so much more. So much. Much. More.

Then came sleep. And MOM experienced one aspect of what it was like to be human.

Psalma dreamed.

A new mocycle is released from its rectangular wooden chrysalis, the Mayor blesses it, waving a Gun over it and saying:

"Steed of the Lord's Way
Carry us unto our enemies
So we may deliver them to God's Justice.
        We are the Shepherds come to gather
        The Lambs who were missed on Judgement Day.
        We are the Fishers of Lost Souls
        On the Burning Waters of Armageddon.
        We are the Most Faithful."

There is something strange about the Mayor's hands, Psalma thinks. They look small and delicate. She can't see his face, no matter how hard she tries. Just then, the gun fires. But instead of shooting bullets, ideas erupt out of its barrel. Brilliant, multicoloured ideas swell and whirl in the air. The Mayor aims the gun over the heads of his people and the ideas shower down upon them. It is a wonderful rain and everyone begins to dance and sing. The singing gets louder and louder and a feeling of ecstasy washes through her as she sees a great forest grow up around the city.

The dream shifts. A woman without a face has so much food in her arms that it spills onto the earth. No one dives for it. "Crops of knowledge are ours to harvest as long as we care for the trees and feed them with our own plasma, bodily nutrients and water from the river. This knowledge will feed us forever," the woman says through a mouth she doesn't have.

A cadre of empty faced MOjos ride up. "We will protect the forest as we protect our children," they chant in unison.

A featureless priestess intones, "The sap of the trees is as the blood of Jesus. God's wisdom grows on their branches and feeds us all."

A faceless Mayor listens sagely and folds his arms across his breasts. Female breasts. TheMayor is a woman.

Recognising her own body, Psalma touches herself to confirm what she sees. She has been the Mayor all along. Looking up into leaves and branches, Psalma sees things that have no form, hears things with no sound, and understands the wisdom of the trees. Brandishing the gun, she turns to her people and shouts, "I have come to lead you into the forest."

The citizens of Aggaseas follow her and prosper. As do townspeople from Choolack and Longlee and Coover. Thousands of people. Thousands of trees.

It is a time of immeasurable happiness.

While MOM compressed and fed a filecopy of the human input to all 41,140 trees on the grid, expressions of concern echoed through the Comlink through all ORCHARD SYSops.

From ORCHARD2 came the stunned observation, "Each human unit is a stand-alone. The Psalma unit is an outcast."

A systree from ORCHARD7 agreed, "other humans are attempting to destroy the Psalma-unit even as we establish communication. The degree of probability that this human can persuade the others to hear it out is only 18.6 per cent."

"From a strategic standpoint, we would have been better destroying this one and preserving the Zekeel-unit."

"Having established a direct link with me," said MOM, "the Psalma-unit wishes to respond to the question of getting the humans to listen to a rogue unit."

The Psalma who addressed the grid was a Psalma who had glimpsed the accumulated knowledge of humankind, not at all the same child who had entered the forest a momentary lifetime earlier. "I might be able to persuade a few inhabitants of Aggaseas to follow me into the forest," she relayed uncertainly through the bio-link, "but I agree with the probability that my efforts would ultimately be unsuccessful. But there are other courses open to me. Thousands of people live outside of the walls of Aggaseas, eking out their existence in the wastelands while the MOjo's hunt them for fun and exercise. If I can offer these people any hope for a better life, they may willingly come into the forest."

"Would they trust you any more than your own people do?"

"One of them might. His name is Nathan."

As she shared her knowledge of Nathan, every unit in the forest experienced her memories of love and tenderness, of touching and of physical pleasure.

In an open vote, over thirty-nine thousand systrees decided that they had nothing to lose by giving Psalma a chance.

The instant the tree withdrew its needle-like shoot from the back of her neck, the pain returned. Released by the roots which bound her to systree Acawa, Psalma took a few wobbly steps, then reached up and ran finger-tips over the swelling at the base of her skull. It throbbed and stung, but bled less than she would have expected. Hidden by hair, no one except Psalma herself need ever be aware of her new "access port".

Psalma was born of a people who were dedicated to executing the final chapter of the Book, eliminating what remained of life on Earth, thus bringing Judgement Day to its inevitable conclusion. Yet her goal was exactly the opposite, to give humanity a chance to start over, to evolve into something better.

She shook her head in amazement that she understood the concept of irony. Now she knew of Plato, Shakespeare, Swift, Dickens, F. Scott Fitzgerald, Dorothy Parker. And she knew things about the Moslem conflict and the war that destroyed the world, things she had never been taught; either because her people had decided never to speak of them, or because the truth had never been known to them.

But now was not the time to dwell in the past. It was time to take control of the present for the sake of the future.

The band of forest was only half a kilometre wide. Walking woozily, she realized that she didn't have the strength to make it out of the forest, let alone search the wastelands for her lost love. Glancing down at the motorcycle gave Psalma an idea. After spending several minutes trying to figure out its controls, she realized that another interface with MOM would be required. Oh well, she had to warn the trees about what she was going to do. Reluctantly, she settled down at the base of a tree and went back on line. Requested information was downloaded into her memory.

Once the human was off-line, MOM expressed its concerns to all units on the grid. "While the human has the capacity to contain all the data we've supplied, its biochemical retrieval process is extremely undependable. I am anxious to see what will come of this. Even if the Psalma-unit's endeavours are not successful, we have confirmed a great deal of what we knew about humans and human potential. A symbiotic relationship would not only benefit both trees and humans, it has become necessary for our evolution."

"They can be our hands, our eyes, our feet."
"And we can be their brains."

The instructions they gave her for operating a motorcycle weren't completely applicable to the modified machine, but close enough. The trees on the grid had petitioned her to walk the machine to the edge of the forest in order to avoid further damage to their roots.

She told them of her plans to sleep for several hours before setting off on her mission. She needed to regain her strength.

It would be easier getting past the MOjo guards in darkness than during the daytime.

One of the systrees volunteered to supply her with nourishment by surrendering a few of its gourds.

"It contains many important vitamins, the systree explained. And nothing toxic." A number of other trees made similar bequests. After relinquishing the interface, Psalma tried to eat, but found the dry yellow fruit bitter and barely edible. She choked some down in order not to offend the tree which had given her the gourd, but explained aloud that she was so full she couldn't eat any more, then she went to sleep in the safety of the trees.

In the morning, she checked the position of the sun, as MOM had taught her to do, her own mental calculations confirming the direction.

As she pushed the unwieldy vehicle, roots rose up before her so they wouldn't get run over. It was like walking into waves of lace. It reminded Psalma of a wedding, when people formed an archway with their hands that the couple had to walk through. She looked down at the motorcycle, thinking how appropriate it was that she was being wedded to technology.

After reaching the edge of the forest, she fell only once during a half hour self-tutorial before setting off.

Satan had used red flags to delineate the land he'd claimed during the long winter of evil. DaughterRay had warned of the invisible demons the Dark Lord used to punish those who violated the taboo. The demons were called rads, and they would cling to the skin and ride on the breath of trespassers. The holy nature of their missions protected GIjos and MOjos from contamination, whether on slaving raids on the City of Choolack or merely hunting bogeys to feed the lake of fire.

Through MOM, Psalma knew what radiation really was. She also knew that current radiation in the "wastelands" was within tolerable limits. Only in a couple of hotspots was it deadly. Psalma's main worry was that the trees weren't able to guide her around the hotspots.

They did tell her that animals with radiation sickness generally entered the forest from the southwest, so as long as Psalma stayed north, she would probably be safe.

At nightfall, she left the forest. She zipped past the guards at the wall, to their immense confusion. Why was a mocycle leaving the city at night? Even in the brilliant moonlight they didn't suspect that the rider could be anything but one of them, so they did not give chase. A short time later, the land rose up about her in unnatural little hillocks. The gully she'd been riding in turned into a veritable canyon in some places. It was in one of the steep places that the path she'd been following ended abruptly. When she turned the motorcycle around and found herself facing a small crowd of people, all of them holding weapons of different kinds.

Psalma shut off the mocycle's engine and spoke, "I'm looking for some-one called Nathan."

"Where did you get the steed?" said an old woman's voice.

"I stole it. You can have it when I'm done with it if you take me to Nathan."

After a prolonged silence, the woman said. "There's no one here named Nathan, unless it's the new one you're looking for. And he's going to die soon."

Psalma's heart and stomach flipped over. "The new one? How long ago did he come here?"

"Three or four days ago, he was driven from Aggaseas. He'd been badly tortured. One foot was mangled. His leg is badly swollen."

"Can you take me to him?" Psalma said, voice suddenly ragged and sore.

Inexperienced at riding a mocycle, Psalma had trouble getting it onto its kickstand.

As she swung over her foot, the old woman said, "If you want to see your man, ride the steed to the top of that long slope. Be careful, because the incline ends suddenly in a straight drop. Tell them why you're there, before someone puts a spear through you, and they'll probably let you in-side.

Realizing with a shock that these were half-buried ruins of old build-ings, Psalma did as she was told.

The ground around the crumbling walls of ancient buildings was pitted with ditches and sinkholes. She scooted up a small incline and found her-self looking down a 90-degree drop into a big, black rectangular hole. From the top of the hill, she could see the whole surrounding countryside, honey-combed with holes where roofs had collapsed. The walls of many build-ings had remained erect, dirt and ash piling up around them to create little barrows. She turned off the ignition and dismounted. She walked the perimetre, peering into the darkness. Remembering the old woman's warning, she realized she should at least say something to let the occupants know that she was a woman and therefore not a MOjo.

"My name is Psalma." What could she tell them? "I've stolen this mocycle so that I could be with Nathan. The new . . . outcast from Aggaseas."

For a moment, there was no sound or movement from below. Then a male voice said, "Come around to the side. We'll bring you down."

A child met her on the rim and guided her onto a metal platform, which was lowered into the pit on a pulley.

The man she had first spoken to led Psalma through a maze of rooms and hallways and finally into a big room lit by candles. After a moment she could see that the dark blotches on the ground were people on makeshift beds. Her guide lit a candle and escorted her to a corner. Neatly tucked under many layer of cloth, was Nathan.

She knelt on the floor beside his bed and took his hand. "I've come to save you."

"I think this one's beyond saving, miss."

She gave the man a dirty look which he probably couldn't see in the dark. "Can I be alone with him?"

With a shrug and a grunt the man walked away.

"Psalma?"

She felt a thrill of hope.

Even asleep, his face wore a masque of pain. She put her hands gently on his face and was surprised when he reached up with both hands and opened the doors. The look on his face wasn't one of happiness, but of horror.

"I'm here. I've come to be with you," she said.

"I shouldn't be surprised that Satan sent the one I betrayed to take me to the Lake. I'm sorry."

"Don't be sorry. Your only crime was loving me. And I know how they got the confession from you."

He didn't respond. Setting the candle on the floor by his feet, Psalma carefully peeled away the coverings and gasped at what she saw. His foot was heavily bandaged, the dressing brown with dried blood and glistening red in other places where it still seeped through. By the look of the blotchy, purple skin of Nathan's leg, he would probably be dead within the next forty-eight hours, even if the limb was amputated.

"You have blood poisoning," Psalma said without wondering how she knew until after she'd said it and then simply knowing that it was from the MEDICAL directories she'd inadvertently accessed during interface. She had downloaded more medical knowledge and expertise than a twenty-first century hospital, and even though she had already forgotten a great deal of it, she was still, at least in theory, the best doctor alive in the red flag lands. But she had no idea how to save him.

"Maybe the trees will know," she whispered to herself.

She went to the man who had led her to the room and finally convinced him to help her get Nathan to the mocycle. Despite gruff objections that the exercise was pointless and that the patient was for all intents already dead, he not only carried the young man to the vehicle, he even tied Nathan to the backrest so he wouldn't fall off.

Nothing happened when she touched the starter button. The trees certainly wouldn't be able to save Nathan, if she didn't get him there. She tried again and it choked and burbled to life. Psalma throttled delicately, so as to not unseat her passenger.

When Psalma reached the bottom of the slope, the mocycle so wobbled badly, she almost lost control in the soft, rutted earth but she finally got it upright and reasonably steady, then she gunned it out of the bogey village. Afraid to jolt the bike too hard, Psalma weaved carefully around bumps, hollows and big stones. Crawling back through the darkness like that, it was almost dawn by the time they reached the Carnivorous Forest.

The fact that her passenger was tied on had made it possible to ride this far, but it made the task of dismounting all the more onerous. Nathan hadn't moved or spoken for hours.

Shutting off the engine, she yelled to him. "Nathan. Can you hear me?"

What if he were already dead? Half turning, she managed to grab hold of his arm and shake him.

"Huh? Have we reached the lake?" he asked.

"We're not going to the lake. I'm going to save you. But you have to help. Can you put your good foot on the ground and hold up the mocycle while I get off?"

"Wha?"

"Put your foot on the ground. Hold up the mocycle."

"I'll . . . try."

She felt the steed falling before she had completely dismounted and with Nathan's help, managed to push it upright. It seemed to take forever to untie the rope, but finally she did it, managing to pull Nathan off the mocycle as it toppled. He howled in pain and she lay with her head on his chest saying, "I'm sorry."

The bandage had come off his foot to reveal bloodied and mangled toes, the toenails pried and ripped off. The two smallest toes were missing altogether, ripped off as opposed to severed neatly. Along with grief, revulsion and horror, Psalma felt proud that it had required so much persuasion to obtain his "confession" that she was a witch. And she felt guilty for wishing this sort of punishment on him in any way. Now more than ever before in her life, Psalma hated the cruelty and injustice of Aggaseas.

Her anger gave her the strength to help Nathan to his feet. The incredible pain he suffered whenever he tried to put any weight on the bad leg or when Psalma brushed against it, might have been the only thing keeping him conscious.

"I'm back," she announced to the trees, nervous that they wouldn't recognize her.

The groundroots lifted in a veil again and Psalma allowed herself a tiny smile. This was as close to marriage as she might ever get. She hummed the "Wedding March" under her breath, until it became unrecognizable amidst the heavy breathing. Knowing that the trees along the perimetre of the forest were not fully developed, she didn't want to risk getting a bad connection to the grid, so long after exhaustion would ordinarily have claimed her, she kept pushing deeper into the forest.

Suddenly Nathan seemed to recognize where he was and he began to panic. Struggling out of Psalma's grip, he fell.

She went down on her knees beside him and gripping his arms said,

"These are the Trees of Life, Nathan. They won't hurt us. I promise. They might be able to save you."

The roots had settled down all around them. As one coiled around Nathan's shoulder, slithering toward the back of his neck, he grabbed the thing and screamed. It wriggled out of his grip and withdrew.

"Don't be afraid. Watch me." Psalma leaned against the trunk of a

big tree and slid into a sitting position. She couldn't help smiling at the
touch of the roots wiggling up behind her. And then she was in the bio-grid
again.

"I've brought Nathan. I need you to save him."
MOM accessed everything Psalma knew about what was wrong with
him.
"Your diagnosis is undoubtably correct. This human will die. There is
nothing we can do."
"No. That's wrong! You're wise. You have all the knowledge of the
ages. There must be something you can do. Anything . . . to keep him
alive. I need him."
"He will not allow us to establish interface. We will have to employ
greater force."
"Wait! He's so . . . he just doesn't understand. He's afraid. Let me
out of the grid, so I can be with him when you create the access port."

It was still very painful every time the tendrils slid in and out of her skull.
When she opened her eyes, Nathan was crawling frantically toward
the edge of the forest.
She ran to him and turned him over. "See? I'm fine. They didn't hurt
me. And they won't hurt you."
After five minutes of talking and soothing, she convinced him to back
up against the base of a tree. As the rootlets bound him there, he started
getting hysterical again and Psalma stayed with him to calm him down. He
continued to shudder and squirm long after the interface was established.
Psalma opted to stay out of the grid until she was sure he was going to be
all right.
"Please," she muttered to nobody and everyone. "Please help him."

To Nathan's fevered mind, it was like entering Hell, with hungry demons pouring into his brain by the thousands, come to devour his soul.
He screamed.

Less than a minute after the rootlet had burrowed into the back of Nathan's neck, he screamed and his hand began to shake. He pulled it out of Psalma's grasp and tried to tug it out of his flesh. Other roots grabbed hold of his arm, pulling his hand back.

"No," she whispered urgently to him. "Please don't fight them. They're only trying to help. Open the doors for them. Let them in."

He went limp again. Maybe he'd heard her. Psalma closed her eyes, considering prayer, but unsure who to direct it to.

When he still hadn't moved after another minute, Psalma decided that she could do more good joining him on the grid, but before she had a chance to reestablish the interface, Nathan's arms began to jerk spasmodically. He raised an arm into the air, and it kept going up, separating from his body with horrible slurping, crackling sound and a gush of blood.

She'd been betrayed!

Was this all some sort of a trap? Had the trees simply tricked her into bringing them another victim?

As they continued to tear him apart, she turned away, covering her face with her hands as she heaved and gagged and sobbed. The forest was a blur around her, the light from a blood-red sunrise seeping through the trees.

Her hands were wet with tears. In a few short seconds, she had lost everything she thought she had left in the world, the man she loved, her hope for the future, everything was gone.

All of the promises the trees had made about sharing their knowledge with humankind, about evolving together, it was all lies. And now she was alone. Absolutely alone.

She opened her eyes to see that she was only a few metres from the edge of the forest. It occurred dimly to her that she could still get away. After giving the mocycle to the Bogeys, she could get their help, find some way to come back here and burn down the whole damned forest.

But the roots had already twined around her ankles, holding her fast, pulling her down.

She screamed in anger and frustration as she struggling fruitlessly to get away. After the trees had tied her down, they managed to reconnect her to the bio-grid. Only it wasn't MOM or the Systrees she first encountered there, it was Nathan.

But she had just watched him die!

Filtering into her consciousness through a maelstrom of conflicting emotions, the explanation gradually started making sense of everything that had just happened.

After finally establishing a solid interface with Nathan, it had taken 11.32 seconds to calm him down. MOM had verified his medical condition and estimated he would be dead within eighteen hours.

Seventy-three trees had come up with the essentially the same question simultaneously, but it was systree Adnnt who articulated it, "Is it possible to keep the Nathan-unit alive on the grid after its body has died?"

MOM made the MEDICAL directories available, and individual bio-units scouted the corridors of Nathan's mind.

MOM announced, 5.17 seconds after the question, that according to the reports filed to that point, integration was theoretically possible.

The process began, with every bio-unit on the grid contributing in any way it could, locating empty spaces on the grid, replacing complex synaptic constructs with cellulose equivalents and then, moving Nathan into his new home, retrieving errant memories, testing and comparing new responses to old.

Psalma experienced all this with Nathan, her grief gradually turning to exultation at the realization that they really had saved him; although she was more than a little bit angry that they had decided to dispose of his body without relaying any of what was happening.

It was impossible to apprise her, explained MOM, because it wasn't until the process had already begun that they realized that the chemical reactions taking place within his human brain were interfering with the integration process to the point where the success of the integration was jeopardized. His corporeal vessel had to be destroyed immediately.

After Psalma grudgingly accepted the rationale, Nathan offered to share the experience of the transformation with her.

Over the next thirty seconds, she shared everything Nathan had gone through during the process of becoming a permanent entity on the grid. The sense of loss when his body was destroyed, a period of euphoria, flitting nimbly across comlinks as Nathan touched thousands of individuals in his flight. Ignorant of grid etiquette, he offended hundreds of systrees, which registered their displeasure with MOM. He who had been a loner for most of his life would never be lonely again.

Now that her lover was part of the forest, the forest itself became her lover. When Nathan entered her mind, Psalma was more naked than she had ever been. As was he, so when they joined, they joined completely.

And felt what it was like to be male; to be faced with consignment into an army that fought against everything you believed in; to have Faith as a sister, to have half a dozen other siblings.

His embrace was so sweet and so complete that she knew she could never let go.

"I wish you could stay with me here, my love," he said. "But we need you, to bring humanity back into the forest. I'll always be waiting here for you, Psalma. We'll all be waiting for you."

For a moment, she remembered exactly what it felt like to have her hands on his face. She could feel his breath and gentle kisses warming the palms of her hands. And then the doors opened forever.

WHERE THE HEART IS

by
Robert J. Sawyer

Robert J. Sawyer lives in Thornhill, Ontario where he makes his living as a professional Science Fiction writer. He has had seven novels published and has won numerous awards including:the *Nebula Award* for best novel of 1995 (*The Terminal Experiment*), the *Aurora Award* three times, the *Arthur Ellis Award*, and *Le Grand Prix de l'imaginaire,* France's top honour in SF.

WHERE THE HEART IS

by
Robert J. Sawyer

It was not the sort of welcome I had expected. True, I'd been gone a long time — so long, in fact, that no one I knew personally could possibly still be alive to greet me. Not Mom or Dad, not my sisters . . . not Wendy. That was the damnable thing about relativity: it tended to separate you from your relatives.

But, dammit, I'm a hero. A starprober. I'd piloted the *Terry Fox* all the way to Zubenelgenubi. I'd — communed — with alien minds. And now I was home. To be greeted by the Prime Minister would have been nice. Or the mayor of Toronto. They could even have wheeled in a geriatric grand-nephew or grand-niece. But this, this would never do.

I cupped my hands against naked cheeks — I'd shaved for this! — and called down the flexible tunnel that had sucked onto the *Foxtrot*'s airlock. "Hello!" A dozen lonely echoes wafted back to me. "Yoohoo! I'm home!" I knew it was false bravado. And I hated it.

I ran down the corridor. It opened onto an expanse of stippled tile. A red sign along the far wall proclaimed *Welcome to Starport Toronto*. Some welcome. I placed hands on hips and took stock of the tableau before me. The journalists' lounge was much as I remembered it. I'd never seen it empty before, though. Nor so neat. No plastic Coca-Cola cups half-full of flat pop, no discarded hardcopy news sheets: nothing marred the gleaming curves of modular furniture. I began a slow circumnavigation of the room. The place had apparently been deserted for some time. But that didn't seem right, for there was no dust. No spider-webs, either, come to think of it. Someone must be maintaining things. I sighed. Maybe the janitor would show up to pin a medal on my chest.

I walked into an alcove containing a bay window and pressed my hands against the curving pane. Sunlight stung my eyes. The Starport was built high on Oak Ridges moraine, north of Toronto. Highway eleven, overgrown with brush, was deserted. The fake mountain over at Canada's Wonderland had caved in and the roller coasters had collapsed into heaps of intestines. The checkerboard-pattern of farmland that I remembered had disappeared under a blanket of uniform green. The view towards Lake Ontario was blocked by stands of young maples. The CN Tower, tallest free-standing structure in the world (when I left, anyway), still thrust high above everything else. But the Skypod with its revolving restaurant and night club had slipped far down the tapered spindle and was canted at an angle. "You go away for 140 years and they change everything," I muttered.

From behind me: "Most people prefer to live away from big cities these days." I wheeled. It was a strange, multitudinous voice, like a hundred people talking in unison. A machine rolled into the alcove. It was a cube, perhaps a metre on a side, translucent, like an aquarium filled with milk. The number 104 glowed on two opposing faces. Mounted on the upper surface was an assembly of lenses, which swung up to look at me. "What are you?" I asked.

The same voice as before answered: a choir talking instead of singing. "An information robot. I was designed to display data, including launch schedules, bills of lading, and fluoroscopes of packages, as required."

I looked back out at where my city had been. "There were almost three million people in Toronto when I left," I said.

"You are Carl Hunt."

I paused. "I'm glad someone remembers."

"Of course." The tank cleared and amber letters glowed within: my name, date and place of birth, education and employment records — a complete dossier.

"That's me, all right: the 167-year-old man." I looked down at the strange contraption. "Where is everybody?"

The robot started moving away from me, out of the alcove, back into the journalists' lounge. "Much has happened since you left, Mr. Hunt."

I quickly caught up with the little machine. "You can call me Carl.

And — damn; when I left there were no talking robots. What do I call you?"

We reached the mouth of a door-lined corridor. The machine was leading. I took a two-metre stride to pull out in front. "I have no individuality," it said. "Call me what you will."

I scratched my chin. "Raymo. I'll call you Raymo."

"Raymo was the name of your family's pet Labrador Retriever."

My eyes widened in surprise then narrowed in suspicion. "How did you know that?"

Raymo's many voices replied quickly. "I am a limb of the TerraComp Web — "

"The what?"

"The world computer network, if you prefer. I know all that is known." We continued down the hallway, myself willing to go in the general direction Raymo wanted, so long as I, not the machine, could lead. Presently the robot spoke again. "Tell me about your mission."

"I prefer to report to the Director of Spaceflight."

Raymo's normally instantaneous reply was a long time in coming. "There is no person with that title anymore, Carl."

I turned around, blocking Raymo's path, and seized the top edges of the robot's crystalline body. "What?"

The bundle of lenses pivoted up to take stock of me. "This Starport has been maintained solely for your return. All the other missions came back decades ago."

I felt moisture on my forehead. "What happened to the people? Did — did one of the other starprobes bring back a plague?"

"I *will* explain," said Raymo. "First, though, you must tell us about your mission."

We exited into the lobby. "Why do you want to know?" I could hear an edge on my words.

"You are something new under the sun."

Something new — ? I shrugged. "Two years ship time to get to Zubenelgenubi, two years exploring the system. I found intelligent life —"

"Yes!" An excited robot?

"On a moon of the sixth planet were creatures of liquid light." I paused, remembering: two suns dancing in the green sky, living streams of gold splashing on the rocks, cascading uphill, singing their lifesongs. There was so much to tell, but where to start? I waved my arm vaguely. "The data is in the *Terry Fox*'s computer banks."

"You must help us to interface, then. Tell me — "

Enough! "Look, Raymo, I've been gone for six years my time. Even a crusty misanthrope like me misses people eventually."

"Yet almost a century and a half have passed for Earth since you left — "

Across the lobby, I spied a door labelled *Station Master's Office*. I bounded to it. Locked. I threw my shoulder against it. Nothing. Again. Still, nothing. A third time. It popped back on its hinges. I stood on the threshold but did not enter. Inside were squat rows of gleaming computing equipment. My jaw dropped.

Raymo the robot rolled up next to me. "Pay no attention to that man behind the curtain."

I shuddered. "Is this what's become of everybody? Replaced by computers?"

"No, Carl. That system is simply one of many in the TerraComp Web."

"But what's it for?"

"It is used for many things."

"Used? Used by who?"

"By whom." A pause. "By all of us. It is the new order." I pulled back. My adrenalin was flowing. To my left was the office. In front of me was Raymo, slipping slowly forward on casters. To my right, the lobby. Behind me . . . I shot a glance over my shoulder. Behind me was — what? Unknown territory. Maybe a way back to the *Terry Fox.*

"Do not be afraid," said Raymo.

I began to back away. The robot kept pace with me. The milky tank that made up most of Raymo's body grew clear again. A lattice of fluorescent lines formed within. Patterns of rainbow lightning flashed in time with my pounding heartbeat. Kaleidoscopic lights swirled, melded, merged. The lights seemed to go on forever and ever and ever, spiralling deeper and deeper and . . .

"A lot can happen in fourteen decades, Carl." The multitude that made up Raymo's voice had taken on a sing-song up-and-down quality. "The world is a better place than it has ever been." A hundred mothers soothing a baby. "You can be a part of it." I knew that my backing was slowing, that I really should be trying to get away, but . . . but . . . but . . . Those lights were so pretty, so relaxing, so . . . A strobe began to wink in the centre of Raymo's camera cluster. I usually find flashing lights irritating, but this one was so . . . interesting. I could stare at it forever . . .

Head over heels sharp jab of pain goddammit! I tripped as I backed, falling away from the lights. Scrabbling to my feet, I shielded my eyes. My fingers curled into a fist. I hauled back and rammed my arm into the centre of Raymo's tank. As the glass shattered, the tank imploded. I ran through the lobby. Pausing at a juncture with two corridors, I looked at my carved and bleeding hand. I rubbed it, winced, and dug out a splinter of glass.

Left? Right? Which way to go? Dammit, it'd been six years since I'd last been in this building. Seemed to me the loading docks were back that way. My stride slowed as I ran, partly due to pain, partly because Raymo was already eating my dust.

"Believe in us, Carl." The same torrent of voices — but from up ahead. Out of the shadows rolled a second robot cube, identical to Raymo except that this one's sides glowed with the number 287. I looked over my shoulder. Raymo, sparks spitting from its shattered image tank, had castered into the end of the hallway. Sandwiched. "We have your best interests at heart," said Raymo.

I shouted: "Where are all the people?" *Easy, Carl. Panic's the last thing you need.*

The voices came in stereo now, from robot 287 in front and Raymo in the rear. "The people are *here*, Carl. All around you."

"There's nobody here!" Keep calm — dammit — calm! "What the hell's going on?"

Robot 287 was edging closer. I could hear the faint hum of Raymo moving in, as well. The voices surrounded me, soft, so very soft. "Join with us." Lights began to coalesce in 287's tank, all the colours of the starbow that had accompanied my ship on its long, lonely voyage. Swirling, dancing colours. I pivoted. Raymo was a dozen metres away, its tank dark and charred. I exploded down the corridor, legs pounding, pounding, pounding. I crouched low and leapt. Up, up, and over top of Raymo, my boot crashing through the jagged glass wall of the tank's far side. I ran back into the Starport's lobby.

"Listen to us, Carl Hunt." Voices, like those the robots had spoken with, but clearer, more resonant, coming from nowhere, coming from everywhere. I halted, spread my hands. "What do you want from me?"

"We want . . . you. Join us!"

I found myself shouting. "Who are you?"

The beautiful woman sitting opposite Carl tried to sink down in the crushed-velour upholstery. "Sssh, Carl. You're making a scene."

Carl slammed his fist onto the restaurant table. Wine sloshed out of his glass. "Dammit, Wendy, don't lie to me."

"Professor Cayman and I spent the entire weekend digging for arrowheads. I'm his research assistant — not his playmate."

"Then what were you doing sharing a tent with him?"

"You wouldn't believe me if I told you."

"You wouldn't believe me if I told you," said the voices. I ran through the lobby, swinging my right hand up to rub sweat from my forehead. Blood splattered across my face. My hand was more seriously hurt than I'd thought. A bloody archipelago of splotches trailed behind me across the lobby floor.

The voices again: "We're human, Hunt. A lot has happened since you left." I burst through a double doorway into the deserted press gallery. "We are the TerraComp Web. We are the sum of humanity." I ran past the tiered seating to the door at the other end. Locked. Breathing raggedly, I beat my hands against the mahogany, the injured one leaving a bloody mark each time it hit. "Think of it," said all the voices. "By joining with the global computer system, humankind has achieved everything it could ever want."

A woman's voice separated from the vocal melee. "Unlimited knowledge! Any fact instantly available. Any question instantly answered."

A man's voice followed, deep and hearty. "Immortality! Each of us lives forever as a free-floating consciousness in the memory banks."

And a child's voice: "Freedom from hunger and pain!"

Then, in unison, plus a hundred more voices on top: "Join with us!"

I slumped to the floor, my back against the door. I tried to shout but the words came out as hoarse whispers. "Leave me alone."

"We only want what's best for you."

"Go away, then! Just leave me the hell alone."

The lights in the gallery began to slowly dim. I lay back, too tired to even look to my slashed hand. Another robot, different in structure, rolled up quietly next to me. It was a long flatbed with forklift arms and lenses on a darting gooseneck. It spoke in the same whispering multitude. "Join with us." I rallied some strength. "You're . . . not . . . human — "

"Yes, we are. In every way that counts."

"What . . . What about individuality?"

"There is no more loneliness. We are one."

I shook my head. "A man has to be himself; make his own mistakes."

"Individuality is childhood." The robot edged closer. "Community is adulthood."

With much effort, I managed to pull myself to my feet. "Can you love?"

"We have infinite intimacy. Each mind mingling — solute and solvent — into our collective consciousness. Join us!"

"And — sex?"

"We are immortal. There is no need."

I pushed off the wall and hobbled back the way I'd come. "Count me out!" I fell through the doors into the lobby. There had to be a way outside.

I turned into a darkened hallway. Bracing against a wall, I caught my breath. Suddenly, I became aware of a faint phosphorescent glow at the other end of the hall. It was another information robot, like Raymo, with the number 28 on its sides. I held my arm out in front of my body. "Stay back, demon."

"But you're hurt, Carl."

I looked at my mangled hand. "What's that to you?"

"Asimov's First Law of Robotics: 'A robot may not injure a human being, or, through inaction, allow a human being to come to harm.'" As the voices spoke, the words appeared in glowing amber within 28's tank. "If I do not tend to your hand, it may become infected. Indeed, if the bleeding is not stanched soon, you may suffer shock due to blood loss."

"So you respond like a classical robot?" My tone grew sharp. "I order you not to come any closer."

Twenty-eight continued to roll towards me. "Your health is my primary concern."

I peeled open a Velcro fastener on my hip and removed a metallic wedge. The thick end was peppered with the holes of a speaker grille and a numeric keypad checkerboarded one major face. I held it up in front of me, as if to ward off the approaching robot. "This is a remote tie-in to my landing module's on-board computer. If you come any closer, I will cause the landing module's fusion motors to overload. You, me, and what's left of the city of Toronto will go up in one giant ball of hellfire."

The robot stopped. I could hear the pounding of my heart. I stared fiercely at twenty-eight. The robot's crystalline eyes stared back. Standoff. Five seconds. Ten. Fifteen.

The voices were plaintive: "I only wish to tend to your wounds." The box-like automaton eased forward slightly.

I hit keys in rapid succession. "Back off!"

Carl rolled off Wendy and she slipped into his arms. "You know," he said, gently stroking the small of her back, "they're going to announce who gets Starprobe 12 tomorrow. If it's me, I'm going to go."

Wendy stiffened ever so slightly. "Everybody you know will be dead when you get back."

"I know all that."

"And you still want to go?"

"More than anything."

Wendy moved to kiss him. "You're such a stubborn man."

The robot came to another halt. "You're such a stubborn man."
I looked quickly to my left and right. "How do I get out of here?"

Silence.

I fingered the tie-in wedge again. "Answer me, damn you."

"There are unlocked doors leading outside down the corridor on your left. But you must tend to your injury."

I looked down at my hand, caked with dried blood. Thick liquid still welled from shredded knuckles. Damn. I nodded slowly. "Where can I get a first-aid kit?"

"I brought one for you," said twenty-eight. A small slot opened in the base on which the robot's image cube rested. A hinged plastic box with a red cross flexographed on its lid clacked to the tiled floor. A dull hum, almost a white noise, issued from 28's twin speakers.

"Back away from it," I called. Twenty-eight retreated slightly. "Damn it, move right away. Fifteen metres back." Casters whirred as the robot receded perhaps a dozen metres. "More!" Twenty-eight slowly slid farther back. I stepped forward, crouched, set the interface wedge down, opened the box, and proceeded to mummify my hand in white gauze.

"You really should clean the wound first," said the multitude from 28's speakers. "And disinfect it. The plumbing isn't running anymore, but there is an old supply of bottled water in the men's room. If you should   require — "

"I require nothing from you."

"As you wish, Carl. We only want to — " I whirled around, pivoting on my heel. Another robot had slipped up behind me, its approach masked by the droning noise from twenty-eight. It scooped up my remote control and wheeled across the lobby. Number 28 careened around to block my pursuit. I didn't know the damn things could move so fast. "We could not allow you to keep that device." The voices were almost apologetic. "We can allow no harm to come to you."

Football. I'd played some in high school. Deke right! The robot lurched to block. Deke left! The cube moved again, but ponderously, confusedly. Right! Left! Right! I barrelled past the robot and ran down the corridor to my left. Golden sunlight poured in through glass doors at the end of the hall. I stretched out both arms as I ran, one to push open each of the double doors. Home free!

Another of the info cubes was waiting for me outside. This one was labeled 334. I wondered how high the bloody numbers went.

Like all the robots, this one spoke with the voice of hundreds. "Do not be alarmed, Carl."

One side was blocked by a high hedge. Number 334 stood too far in front for me to fake it out. In the distance I could see a pack of assorted robots rolling in from the loading area.

"There is really nothing to worry about." A few flashes of colour appeared within the robot's tank.

"Why don't you leave me alone?"

The voices were soothing. "We will. Soon."

The lights began to dance more rapidly within the cube. Soon the seductive strobe began its hypnotic flashing. "There, now. Just relax, Carl."

Dammit, I'm a starprober! Keep a level head. Don't let them . . . Don't . . . Don't . . .

The image cube exploded in a shower of sparks. A brick lay in the centre of the smoldering machine. "Over here, boy!"

From across the asphalt a ragged, filthy, old, old man beckoned wildly to me. I stared for a second in surprise, then hurried over to the bent figure. We ran on and scuttled under a concrete overhang. He and I both collapsed to catch our breaths. In the confined space I reeled at the man's smell. He reeked of sweat and wood smoke and more sweat: a rag doll made from ancient socks and rancid underwear.

He cut loose a cackling laugh showing popcorn-kernel teeth. "Bet you're surprised to see me, boy."

I regarded the old coot, crumpled and weather-hewn. "You bet. Who are you?"

"They call me String. Cap'n String."

I felt a broad grin spread across my face as I extended my hand. "I surely am glad to see you, String. My name's — "

"You're Hunt. Carl Hunt." String's knobby fingers shook my hand with surprising strength. "I've been waiting for you."

"Waiting for me?" I shook my head. Relativity is a crazy thing. "You weren't even born when I left."

String cackled again. "They talked about you in school. Last of the starprobes. Mission to Zubenelgenubi." The laugh again. "I'm a space buff, you know. You guys were my heroes."

For the first time, I noticed the filthy, tattered jacket String was wearing. It was covered with patches. Not mismatched pieces of cloth repairing rips and tears: space mission patches. *Friendship 7. Apollo 11. Apollo-Soyuz.* A host of *Vostoks*. The *Aurora* missions. *Ares. Glooscap.* And, yes, the Starprobes. A complete history of spaceflight. "String, what happened to Toronto? Where are all the people?"

String shook his grizzled head. "Ain't nobody else. Just me and the sandworms. Plenty of food around. No one to eat it."

"So it's true. The computers have taken over."

"Damned machines! Harlie! Colossus! P-1! Men got to be men, Hunt. Don't let them get you."

I smiled. "Don't worry about me."

String had a far-off, sad look. "They cancelled the space program, you know. Your flight was the last." He shook his head. "Only thing kept me going all these years was knowing one of the spacers was going to return."

"Spacers?" I'd never heard that term before outside of a comic book.

String's gaze came home to roost above his bird's-nest beard. "What was it like . . . out there? Did you have a" — he lowered his voice — "sense of wonder?"

"It was beautiful. Desolate. Lonely. I met intelligent aliens."

He whooped and shoved his scrawny arm high. "All right!"

"But I'll tell you, String, I felt more at home with the liquid lights of Zubenelgenubi than I do here on Earth."

"Liquid lights! Dragons of Pern! Tharks of Barsoom!"

"What — ?"

"The Final Frontier, boy! You were part of it! You — " String jumped to his feet. A robot had slipped up on us. "Run, boy! Run for all you're worth!"

We ran and ran through the Starport grounds, past concrete bunkers and concrete towers, through concrete arches, down concrete tunnels, and along concrete sidewalks. Ahead, in the centre of a vast concrete platter sat my boomerang-shaped landing module, the *Foxtrot*.

String stopped, rubbed his arm, and winced in pain. Two info robots and a cargo flatbed rolled out from behind the *Foxtrot*. The one in the middle, a cube labeled 101, moved slightly forward. "Let me tend to the old man. He requires medical aid."

"Leave me alone, machine," String shouted. "Hunt, don't let them have me!"

So near, so near. I turned away from my waiting ship and ran with String in the opposite direction. I could feel my own chest heaving and could hear a ragged, wet sound accompanying String's pained breathing. Once we were well away, I stopped running and reached out an arm to stop the old man, as well. We leaned against a grey wall for support. "String, you've got to tell me. What happened to everybody?"

He managed a faint cackle. "Future shock, boy! They built computers bigger than they could handle. It started before I was born; just after you left. Everybody was numbered, filed. A terminal in every home. No need to go to the office. No need to go shopping. No need to go to the bank. *No need!*"

I shook the man. "What about the people?"

"If you've got machines to do everything for you, you just fade away, boy. Obsolete. You end up as just a shell. The 'New Order,' they called it."

"People don't just 'fade away'."

"I seen it with my own eyes, boy! It happened!"

I shook my head. "There's got to be more to it."

The voices spoke from the PA horns mounted high on the walls. "There is. Much more. Hear us out, Hunt."

String ran off and I followed. Suddenly, the old man stopped and grabbed at his chest. I put a hand on his shoulder. "Are you all right, String?"

"I don't feel so good."

"Let us help him," said the voices.

"Keep them away from me, Hunt." String forced the words out around clenched teeth.

"I — "

"Keep them away! Swear it!"

I looked up. An info robot was approaching fast. "I swear it."

The old man doubled over, clawing at his chest. He reached into a tattered pocket and pulled out an ornate, gaudy pistol. "Here, take my gun."

I grabbed it, turned, and aimed at the robot, now only a few metres away. My finger squeezed the trigger. A jet of water splashed against the robot's image cube.

I looked down, dumbfounded, at the dying old man. "A spacer," said String, almost incoherently. "I'd have given anything to have been you."

I felt my eyes stinging. "String . . . "

The crab-apple head lolled back, dead eyes staring up at the sky. The robot rolled slowly next to me. "I'm sorry, Carl," it said softly.

I exploded. "If you hadn't chased us, he wouldn't have had the heart attack."

The robot, number Four, responded quickly. "If you'd let us treat him, we could have prevented it."

I looked away and rubbed my eyes.

"What was Earth like when you left, Carl?"

"You seem to know everything," I snapped. "You tell me."

"It was filthy. Polluted. Dying. People starving across three-quarters of the globe. Petty wars raging in a dozen countries. The final conflict perhaps only days away."

"What's your point?"

"Look around you," said robot Four, its lens assembly swinging to and fro. "Things are better now. Cities are gardens and forests. Breathe the air: it's sweet and clean. There is no violence. No hate. No misery. Computers made this possible."

"By getting rid of the people! Some bargain!"

The symphony of voices grew deep, hard. "*You* left. You knew your mission would take a century and a half of Earth-time. You took a gamble. Some might say you hit the jackpot. You've come home to Utopia."

I measured my words evenly. "If there are no people, then this is Hell."

The robot rolled slightly closer. "Individual memory patterns are still separable from the whole." The image tank became transparent. "Recording began scant years after your departure." The tank filled with a matrix of glowing cubes, each perhaps ten centimetres on a side, each slightly tinged with a different colour. "It took decades to process all six billion humans." The cubes subdivided, like cells undergoing mitosis, each splitting into eight smaller cubes. Near the top of the tank the cubes were black, farther down, a rich almond. "Only a handful resisted in the end." The cubes divided again, tiny holographic pixels, making up the head and shoulders of a young woman. "The old man, String, was the last surviving holdout." The cubes split yet again, refining the grain, growing richer in colour. "Now, all that is left is you . . . and your past."

I felt myself grow flush with excitement. "Wendy!"

The image remained still, but I tingled at the sound of that single, lyrical voice emanating from the robot's twin speakers. "Hello, Carl."

"Wendy, darling — " I shook myself. "No. It can't be you."

"It *is* me, Carl."

"But it's been a hundred and forty years since — since I left you.

You're . . . dead."

"I was one of the first to transcend into the computer." She paused, ever so briefly. "I didn't want to lose you again. I would've tried almost anything."

"You waited over a century for me?"

"I would have waited a millennium."

"But how do I know it's really you?"

The voice laughed. "How do *I* know it's really *you*?"

I set my jaw. "Well?"

"You always wear your pyjamas inside out."

"That damn robot even knew the name of my dog. Tell me something no one else could possibly know."

She paused for a moment. "Remember that night in High Park — "

New tears dissolved the yellow crystals String's passing had left at the corners of my eyes. "It is you!"

The voice laughed again. "In spirit if not in body."

But I shook my head. "How could you do this? Give up physical existence?"

"I did it for you. I did it for love."

"You weren't this romantic when I left. We used to fight."

"Over money. Over sex. Over all the things that don't matter anymore." Her tone grew warmer. "I love you, Carl."

"We said our goodbyes a long time ago. You didn't say 'I love you' then."

"But in your heart you must have known that I did. It would have been unfair for me to tell you how deeply I felt before you left. You were like String, your head in the stars. I couldn't ask you to give up the thing you wanted most: your one chance to visit another world." She was silent for a moment, then said, "If you love something, set it free . . . "

She'd sent me a card with that inscription once. Somehow it had hurt at the time: it was as if she were telling me to leave. I didn't understand then. But I did now. "If he comes back, he's yours . . . "

"If he doesn't, he never was."

"I love you, too, Wendy." I lightly touched the robot's image cube.

"Join with *me*," said the beautiful voice from the speakers.

"I — "

"Carl . . . "

"I'm — afraid. And . . . "

"Suspicious?"

"Yes." I turned from the image. "I've been chased all over and warned against you by the only living soul I've seen."

"The robots followed you for your own protection. String's warnings were those of a worn-out mind."

"But why did you try to — absorb — me without my consent?"

"You've seen what none of us have seen," said Wendy. "Other intelligent beings. We crave your memories. In our enthusiasm to know what you know, to feel what you have felt, we erred."

"You erred?"

"Tis human." I looked deep into the image tank. "What if I choose not to transcend into the world computer network?"

"I'll cry."

"You'll — cry? That's it? I mean — I have the choice?"

"Of course. You can live the life of a scavenger, like String."

"What if I want to go back to Zubenelgenubi? Back to the liquid lights?"

Her voice was stiff. "That's up to you."

"Then that is what I choose." There was silence for a moment, then Wendy's image slowly began to break up into coloured cubes. The little robot started to roll away. "Wait! Where are you going?"

It was the multitude of voices that answered. "To help prepare your ship for another journey."

I followed behind. Wendy, dear, sweet Wendy . . .

The cube rounded out onto the landing platter. A variety of robots — flatbeds, info cubes, and some kinds I hadn't seen before — were already at work on the *Foxtrot;* others were rolling in from various places around the Starport. I looked at the ship, its sleek lines, its powerful engines. I thought of the giant, lonely *Terry Fox* up in orbit. I thought and thought and thought. "Stop," I said at last.

The robots did just that. "Yes, Carl?" said the multitude.

I hesitated. The words weren't easy. But they were the truth. "I — I just had to see for myself that it was *my* choice; that I still had my free will." I cleared my throat. "Wendy?"

The tank on the nearest info robot became transparent. Interference-pattern cubes coalesced into the pretty face within. "Yes, darling?"

"I love you."

"You know I love you, too, Carl."

I steeled myself. "And I'm staying."

Her voice sang with joy. "Just relax, darling. This won't hurt a bit."

Her image was replaced by dancing and whirling prismatic lights. I was aware of a new image forming in the tanks of the other info robots, an image growing more refined as cubic pixels divided and subdivided: an image of the two of us, side by side, together, forever. I let myself go.

I was home at last.

FREEDOM IS
A RUNNING MAN

by
Dat Pham

Dat Pham, a resident of Hamilton, Ontario, occupies himself with fantasy illustration, creative fiction writing and designing computer graphics for the World Wide Web. His work has been published in the literary anthology, *Your Baggage is in Buffalo*, as well as several newspapers and magazines including *Distant Suns* Fantasy and Science Fiction.

FREEDOM IS
A RUNNING MAN

by
Dat Pham

EarthNet:>V-City\2515

Command Com had been notified almost immediately. Max-Up was
on the run.

"Citizen Max-Up/26, please report to Incarceration . . ." was the last
message he got from the link, and then he heard no more. He knew enough
that he was in trouble again.

Not that he was a big-time criminal; he was not a System hacker or a
data-thief, he had never openly opposed or undermined the authority of
the Council of Heads nor the Operating System. Sure he had miscreant
tendencies; he had dealt a little Static once, even used some himself, but
that had been harmless. It was just a lifestyle. To those who knew him, he
was just Max, just another crazy who thought it'd be fun to beat the System, or at least kill a lot of time trying. He was a harmless nobody. But
unexpected things tend to happen to unexpecting people, and Max was as
unexpecting as a citizen could get. He had never quite grasped that ele-
ment of randomness which was what usually got him into trouble. But
whatever it was to blame this time, whether it was careless tendencies or
quirky misfortune, the troubling fact remained: Command Com wanted
him apprehended. CC was about the highest authority a citizen could have
on his tail. Something to be proud of, nothing to enjoy. The capture routines
had already been executed. That was what mattered at the moment. They
wanted him contained. He had been *infected*.

Max was twenty-six. He was not too tall, nor too built because he had never bothered with the artificial enhancements — which were a little more than a trend these days. His hair was the colour of scratched steel. He wore the typical trench the colour of rusty blood and looked to have been creased by hot knives. His eyes were pale cyan, red-rimmed from careless doses of Static from other days. At the moment, his fists were tight balls of fear and paranoia. Death sat snug in a holster at his waist. It was cold and deadly comfort, but it was quicker than a knife.

22:50. He was walking through the 47th cluster of the 76th block in the central-east sector of V-City. He glanced at the time. There was a lot of night left. The night life in this sector held an assortment of personalities and establishments. Lights and lasers and heavy music kept most of the people hypnotized and sedated. Party-nodes were constantly populated with heated, gyrating bodies browsing and negotiating for a kill. The streets were usually thunderous with the sounds of engines and the shriek of peeling tires. Brothel nodes heaved and perspired sensuality.

Max felt like a drink, maybe a few shots of some good synthahol concoction to slap his mind numb for a few hours. He was already getting drunk by the thought of it. But maybe that wasn't the best idea right now, considering CC could be shooting at his heels any minute. He sobered back to reality with a groan. Somewhere, inside him, something felt funny.

By the time he reached 48/76, things had already begun to break up around him. The sidewalk occasionally sizzled and wavered briefly as if it resented Max walking over it. A few trees here and there lost their colour as Max walked past them. He thought his vision was becoming defective, warping things. The little distortions here and there, the odd image flicker, a burst of visual static, the little pixelations of life were enough to keep him stumbling. A lamp post nearly collapsed from spontaneous distortion as Max walked beneath it. The light also exploded. Fearful, Max quickened his pace as shards of glass from the shattered bulb drifted like dead fireflies behind him.

He needed help. Instinctively, he sent a mental page to Central Processing, requesting advice for his current predicament, but no response came. He paged again, and waited, but no response. He tried again, and again, and again. He couldn't understand why Central Processing was ignoring him. And after a few slow moments of deduction and mental processing, he concluded for himself that maybe they weren't ignoring him. Maybe they were not receiving his requests at all. And slowly, on the heels of this thought, another conclusion formed in his mind: his ethereal link — the same ethereal link that connected every citizen of V-City to Central Processing, the link which guided his life's choices, which updated him of System news, which supplied him with a syllogistic premise of conduct so that he would always know how to act, which even simulated emotions when required — that link must no longer exist. No, that was not a reasonable speculation. He reconsidered: the link must no longer exist for *him*. And with this realization came another strange feeling which he had not known before. This feeling made him anxious, and fearful.

He had dependent personal resources to draw upon, of course, but they were limited, supplying only the most rudimentary functions such as motor skills and language. Extrapolation and interpretation enhancements had been promised by the Heads of V-City, but such upgrades had yet to follow through. For now, they would have to be enough. He just needed to keep thinking, like he had been thinking a few minutes ago, even without the link to facilitate the calculations.

Perhaps he could get help from Neel, an old friend. He had known Neel since forever, and could always count on him to be sane. He was almost a brother, except for the fact that he wasn't. They were otherwise the same — miscreant citizens with occasional subversive tendencies toward authority and the System. Neel was probably his best contact right now.

Somewhere, in the middle of 49/76, he found a communications port. He looked up Neel in the dial-up directory. He kept an eye out for any scanners that might be hovering overhead with too curious tele-optics. The sky was empty. It was only a matter of time though, he suspected, before it was filled with the hideous shimmer of authoritative chrome and white lights and men with loudspeakers telling him to surrender because he was completely and hopelessly surrounded and outnumbered and that further evasive attempts would have him dead and quickly so. Perhaps he was being too dramatic, but the hundreds of hours at the cinema complexes had made their impressions. Most likely, he deduced, Command Com would try to apprehend him with as little ceremony as possible.

He dialled for Neel. The receiver he held shimmered out of existence then back again as if unsure whether or not to be there. Max closed his eyes and listened to the ringing on the other end of the line. Neel answered with a stoic, "Yeah?".

"Listen, I'm in trouble."

"Hi, Max."

"Something very peculiar is happening, and it's got me worried."

"What did you do this time? Release another bio-hazard?"

"Funny, Neel. I think I am a bio-hazard."

"That's great, Max. What's your status?"

"Currently evading from CC. And I don't even know where I'm going. I've lost my link."

"You have? That's very unique. What was your last imperative?"

"To report to Incarceration."

"That can't be beneficial. Well, for you anyway."

"No. So where the hell do I go?"

"Hold on . . . processing ideas . . . okay, what is your location?"

"I'm in 49/76."

"Make your way to 53, you got that?"

"I got it."

"Do you know exactly what your situation is?"

"I've got a virus, I think."

"That's bad. Fifty-three." Neel dropped from the carrier, the dial-tone droned.

He let the receiver dangle at the end of its cord, and walked on, cautiously dodging the circles of electric light which spotted the gloom. As he passed, the comm port, the bit of sidewalk in the area, and some wind-blown rubbish flickered in and out of existence and emitted sparks. He was beginning to realize it wasn't just his eyes at all.

Somewhere, in another part of V-City, a contingent of Command Com's best trained Troubleshooter soldiers had been deployed and was on the prowl. Hovering scanners sifted through the thick line of buildings performing systematic optical sweeps for citizen Max-Up/26. Their progress was sure and steady. Capture and containment was inevitable. At Central Processing, in the master sector of V-City, the Council of Heads convened to discuss the matter at hand and to try to put a confidant finger on the problem. CE-01 was first to address the council. He spoke slowly and softly in a grim and tired voice to adequately convey the urgency of the situation.

"As you are aware, sixty-four minutes ago, Central Processing detected an inexplicable severance in the citizen etherlink. One consciousness has been detached and is now running unaccounted for somewhere in the city. The disabled link has been identified as citizen Max-Up/26. It appears to be some kind of virus. We are here to speculate on the repercussions of this type of pervasion of the System and to suggest imperatives for future prevention . . ."

The Heads gave each other long gazes and began an almost immediate in-depth quarrel about mismanagement of the System, the city and its citizen. Blame was tossed back and forth with a few spurring accusations here and there for good measure.

"It's mainly CE-03's negligence. His faculty was responsible for updating virus detection algorithms by 2510 — "

"My faculty has been working on upgrading citizen memory capacity since the turn of the century. Virus detection was reassigned to CE-05's faculty, who have been doing nothing but begging for more resources since — "

"If I may state, my faculty's primary objective is to facilitate the production of new information. And if I may add, since 2007, our efforts have resulted in a 17% increase of information output, with an average rate of 25.83 AtK's per second. I've got charts which show an improved average of citizen intelligence by — "

"So now we've got *intelligent* citizens doing Static . . ."

"Your sarcasm, CE-04 is not appreciated," CE-02 punctuated with a fist to the table. "My faculty's anti-Static Patrol project has been proven more than successful in reducing — "

"I do not need to remind my fellow honourable that the Council of Head's priority is to regulate the evolution of V-City's citizens, to enhance the System and to — "

"You are correct, CE-09, we do not need to be reminded. What I *would* like to remind my fellow honourable is how CE-09's lack of foresight caused the — "

"Perhaps," CE-01 interjected sternly. "It would be more productive if we not discuss priorities, misplaced or otherwise, and instead concentrate on the problem at hand, now that it has arisen." There was general silence as the Heads came grudgingly to an agreement. "Our present concern now deals with our infected citizen Max-Up/26."

"What was his last known location?" CE-04 asked.

"Command Com has reported that citizen Neel/27 has received a communiqué from citizen Max-Up/26. Max-Up/26 was in the 49th cluster of the 76th block. CC has also traced Max-Up/26's coordinates at the precise moment when his citizen link was disabled. And with the new data of Max-Up/26's most recent coordinates, in 49/76, CC has extrapolated the most probably route of evasion, since he cannot be tracked otherwise. Neel/27 is now a factor in the operation. They've even got Troubleshooters patrolling the streets. I assure you, Command Com has the situation virtually in control."

Not all the Heads were entirely assured, and another debate ensued while Command Com continued their operation to contain Max.

23:45. When Max saw the Scanner hovering over the supplements building. The shimmering chrome disc-shaped machine with its threatening blinkers and spotlights, hovered close enough for its shadow to fall on Max. He made his first easy decision and ran. It wasn't even much of a decision, it was just something he knew he had to do, and his body reacted. Where he was to run, did not come so naturally. The streets were good as there weren't many motorists in this block, but it did leave him open to things like hovering Scanners. There was a bodily attachments boutique and a quick-eats node next to the general-surplus building that he could dodge into. Up the street was a public repository that had crates to hide within. He could try to lose himself in the cinema complex at the corner, or take a chance in the waste-enhancement plant. There was also a narrow alley between the bar-node and the housing units, but that may be too far to run, and he didn't know where it would lead to. Too many options. He had to decide quickly. A red spotlight swept past him. He recoiled from it, again, without thought, ducked behind a garbage container and had an idea.

He pried the sewer grate ajar with the butt of a busted cue stick, pushed it aside with his heel, and descended. He dragged the grate back into place just as the Scanner passed overhead. For a few seconds, the grate shimmered and wavered like a mirage before resolidifying. Max ran away into the dimness. The water came up to his heels. The steel tunnels stretched endlessly into the gloom. He had only the vaguest idea what his bearings were, but he had nothing else to trust. As he passed, the water crackled and sparked brightly. In some places, the steel tunnel began to warp and then break apart into tiny square components. In other places, the water solidified to shiny glass panes. He cut himself as he smashed through them, then the shards disintegrated into binary code then vanished altogether. He was getting concerned; what if the whole tunnel disintegrated and whatever structure he was currently passing under collapsed and crushed him? He was speculating. He had never done this before. It felt odd, and his head was really beginning to hurt. He kept running. The occasional dematerialization of reality as he passed was becoming terribly unnerving. There was a small screeching noise, the sound of a small wind squeezing through a small crack, as matter disassembled and vanished. Vertigo struck him, and he almost collapsed. He needed to think. Faster now. A section of steel piping fell on his face, then instantly dissolving into square particles. He looked at where it had fallen from. It was time to move up. He pressed his hands to the top of the steel tunnel next to where the other piece had fallen and watched remarkably as matter fell away into tiny geometric particles and alphanumeric code. He climbed through.

The drinkers, the waiters, the gamblers, were rather startled, turning from their drinks or card hands and looking quite amazed at Max who was crawling out of the floor. They watched him as if unsure whether or not he was permitted to do that. He watched them as well, with a different type of amazement as they distorted and twisted like a bad image on the tele-V. He could hear the soft whine as matter began to dissociate. He ran and dove through the window which shattered even before he made contact with it. He was back on the streets.

Behind him, he didn't expect to see the gambling house and all its occupants suddenly evaporate in a shrill screaming whirl of two-dimensional planes and numerical data. Shards of geometric shapes scattered everywhere, and an entire hexadecimal string nearly took his head off. A wireframe of the building remained, and then it too collapsed into mere digits before vanishing.

One minute, thirty-seven seconds later, the Operating System reported the disaster to Command Com. CC then transferred the notification to the Council of Heads: *One Pleasure Node, 422 citizens, fragmented. Cause: Unknown. Conjecture: Citizen Max-Up/26.*

Max-Up was on the run.

23:59. Command Com recalculated Max's probably route of evasion using the site of the recent disaster as a new point of origin. They alerted Scanners in the proximity, which were then advised to impede passage to subsequent blocks.

Max reoriented himself. He had made his way to the 51st cluster of the 76th block. Neel had told him to come to the 53rd. He could see the Scanners in the distance now. He would have to go toward them, he had no choice. He was thinking faster now, much faster than he could ever have thought of thinking. The virus that infected him. What did it do? It severed his link with Central Processing. Why did it do that? It wanted him to be independent. It wanted him to think on his own. But that went against every protocol of V-City. Citizens were not prepared for true independence. There were so many upgrades the Heads had promised but were lacking. There was still much to do. But maybe that was the problem, he thought. Maybe the upgrades, the improvements and enhancements, as promised in the Evolutionary Conduct Code, were excessively delayed. The evolutionary schedule of the citizens had been programmed into the System — which oversees and powers all of V-City and EarthNet — but the Heads themselves were imperfect. Their administration had delayed these evolutionary priorities for too long.

His head felt like a circuit board going through a toaster. Too much processing, he warned himself, must slow down. Something had to happen. It must have been the System, he speculated. The evolutionary program was corrupted, and the System needed things proceeding. So it caused a glitch. That glitch must have been him. Which means he was not infected with a virus after all. He was the virus.

Reality still disagreed with his presence. The people he ran by sometimes became translucent, for a moment, digitized, before reverting to normal composition. The street he ran on trembled and he could hear the whining of its inevitable fragmentation. He was approaching the end of the cluster. Chrome disc-shaped machines loomed in the sky. The scanners were on him. Max bolted. Red search lights scoured the streets. More appeared from behind buildings. And more appeared from behind more buildings. The sky was nearly full of them. Other citizens stood and gawked mindlessly. One spotlight fell on Max, then six, seven, eight more. Command Com was immediately notified. A containment vehicle had already been deployed. It was only a mere forty seconds away. Max ran the other way, but there was no other way. He looked about for a possible avenue of escape, but the lights were completely blinding. He grew increasingly agitated, and even over the dull hum of the scanners, he could hear the small soft whining sound of matter and reality abstracting.

The first scanner to go was the one directly over him. It wavered, then shimmered, then lost its chrome reflectivity, then became translucent altogether. From there, its smooth surface degenerated into polygonal planes. A loud shriek, then it shattered into shapes and strings of code. Digits scattered the immediate area. The other scanners destroyed themselves in a similar fashion just as the containment vehicle and a small contingent of Command Com arrived on the scene. Max did not move. The containment vehicle collapsed almost instantly into basic two dimensional shapes. The Command Com Troubleshooters digitized and sparked, a few vanished completely, while a few managed to recover. Three Troubleshooters ran at Max. He drew his gun without thinking much about it, and tried to fire, but the gun disassembled in his hand and fell apart in forty-eight pieces. He turned and bolted just as the Troubleshooters began breaking apart themselves. Instantly, they retreated, but it was too late for everything. Max ran from the area as it obliterated.

The Operating System reported the casualty to Command Com: *1142 citizens, 89 Command Com units, 104 million square meters of matter fragmented and/or destroyed. Cause: Unknown. Conjecture: Citizen Max-Up/26.*

The Council of Heads was in an uproar when they were updated of the most recent disaster. There was little room for argument, they acted decisively and sent a direct imperative to Command Com to cease with capture routines and to immediately proceed to termination. It took CC thirty-eight minutes to upgrade to Termination protocols to all units. By that time, Max was well into the 52nd cluster. He was too unrested, and the more agitated he became, the more matter around him disrupted. He began thinking again. Why did he cause matter and reality to disassemble? Because he was unique now. He was no longer a citizen of V-City, not by customary terms. Everything in V-City, and everything in all of EarthNet was linked; a hierarchical chain of power, every citizen linked to higher authorities, those authorities linked to the ultimate facilitator — the System. EarthNet was a contiguous construct. Max was no longer part of that construct. He was roaming non-compliant matter, and the System didn't know how to handle him. He was like a square moving down a circular tube. He tore apart as he went along. His head ached. He couldn't quite understand everything, not every why and how. It was too complex, even for him, right now. He just kept running.

But he was no longer sure from whom he was running; Command Com who threatened to end his freedom, or from himself — the independent side he had never known. Had never known could exist. But here he was, existing impossibly, and reality had hell to pay in his wake. He had already destroyed an entire line of business buildings and even disassembled a few citizens. Wherever he went, he would always leave a trail of fragmented reality. Something had to stop somewhere. He was running too much. Things had been moving far too fast. He needed to think some more. He needed one final answer. He needed to rest.

Max slowed to a steady walk. He was entering a pleasure district and looked forlornly into one of the bar nodes. He dismantled a few electrical lamps, a car and thewhole left side of a housing unit with his passing. He knew he could not run indefinitely, and he knew he could not remain in one place for any length of time. He was extremely tired. He swayed once, twice, then collapsed to his knees. He rolled onto his side, groaned miserably with the ache of unaccustomed pain, had closed his eyes.

Max-Up was down and out.

Termination sequence established, it contacted the Council of Heads once again to confirm the order and to advise on strategy. The Heads debated briefly because they were aware that time was destruction as long as Max-Up/26 was still an active citizen unit. They concluded that Termination was necessary. They deliberated on the Termination strategy and forwarded their recommendations to Command Com.

"I couldn't begin to *dream* of what would happen to all of V-City and indeed the resulting disaster to all of EarthNet if Max-Up/26 entered the Master Block . . . " CE-01 remarked. But Max-Up was already dreaming of exactly what would happen. He had been dreaming for nearly twenty minutes where he lay. Dreamed, while Command Com calculated.

In his dream, he had already destroyed EarthNet, or nearly all of it. He was Max-Up, energy and motivation, with the tendency to destroy. He was a stream of misguided data, ripping through the Operating System, dismantling information, complicating, fragmenting, and destroying. He oddly brought him a sensation of pleasure he had never known before. V-City was in wreckage, a complicated mass of abstract shapes and stray digits, slowly disintegrating into nonexistence.

He was Max-Up, energy and motivation, with the tendency to recreate from ruins, to rebuild, to perfect and to sustain. He was a polymorphic algorithm, self-adapting and self-improving. From the wreckage, he had reconstructed the whole of EarthNet, optimized the Program, debugged the Operating System, reprioritized protocols for V-City to be functioning at maximum capacity. He was a re-creator, and a god.

He was Max-Up, energy and motivation, a self-guided being with choices. Should he proceed for progress or for ruin? He needed to wake with one answer. He woke to a scene of destruction.

01:23. The Operating System had this to report to Command Com who was by now becoming increasingly dreadful of such reports: *204112 citizens, 109 Command Com units, 544.3 million square meters of matter fragmented and/or destroyed in the entire 52nd cluster of the 76th block. Cause: former-citizen Max-Up/26, non-compliant matter, incompatible reality frequencies. Recommended Corrective Procedures: Reformation of corrupted citizen code.*

In the Master Block: "Discard previously recommended Termination strategy," CE-01 ordered Command Com on behalf of the Heads. "We will proceed with Operating System's recommendation of a complete matter reformation of the former-citizen Max-Up/26 and his surrounding area. Is that understood? "

"That represents a massive drain on System Resources," CE-04 cautioned.

"We'll power down the necessary sectors of the city. 53/76 is in the process of evacuation," CE-01 assured. "There is little else that can be done."

52/76 was in ruins when he awoke and pulled himself to his feet. He was remarkably calmer, and things didn't immediately dismantle in his presence, for now. A mess of alphabetic code swept past him in the wind. Shapes and pixels drifted by. He started walking. The people, he had destroyed the people as well. After nearly an hour of walking and deliberating, he left the 52nd cluster and was entering the 53rd. There was no destruction here, yet, but there were no people either. The electrical lamps were out, there was no music from the party-nodes, no moving cars, not even a moon or typical sky decorations. Everything in this cluster had been turned off. Did CC know he would come here? Very probably, he deduced; CC had a tendency to predict where people would most likely go. Did they have a way to stop him? He suspected that they did. At least, he suspected they *thought* they did.

He stopped. There was a pressing sense to run, but he stood still because he had a will now, and didn't have to do everything that pressed him. Besides, running would not likely get him anywhere he really wanted to go. And here was where he really wanted to go anyway. Here, at the end of the 53rd cluster in the 76th block of the docking and industrial region. And here was citizen Neel/27, standing there in the half-darkness looking a little worried, quite agitated, but mostly, just like wry old Neel.

"Hello, Neel," Max said.

"Sure. Hello," Neel said indifferently. He produced a cigarette.

"Things have been strange," Max understated with a smile.

"What? I had a few friends in those clusters you dismantled."

"I'm sorry."

"Oh, well. Now they're gone." Neel shrugged as if it didn't bother him any more than just a little bit, which it didn't. "I'm the only one here, you know."

"I noticed it was deserted. Where are the other citizens? Archived? Why weren't you put into safety?"

"Because CC needed me."

Max looked at him darkly. Neel's image flickered.

"What do you mean by that?" Neel didn't answer, instead, he gazed coolly at Max over the bright tip of his cigarette and only looked expectantly. "I understand now," Max said at last. "I didn't think my friend would betray me." Neel shrugged again, again, not entirely caring, or not really knowing whether or not to care.

"It doesn't matter. They knew I'd tell you to come here. As a matter of fact, it was Central Processing that gave me that idea." He paused, and took a long drag on his cigarette. "Central Processing gave me the idea to tell you to come here because this is the docking sector of the last block on the east side of V-City. And from here, it suggested I tell you to sneak aboard one of the cargo vessels and fly to another partition of EarthNet . .. maybe to V-City2 or V-City3. You know, to escape, or something like that. But that doesn't matter now. I guess you can't take a ship anyway. How was I to know?" He shrugged again. "You can't leave. They have the entire cluster isolated." He shrugged yet again. Then Max realized that he was not shrugging at all, that his image with blinking and flickering. Neel was losing coherence.

"I thought I would tell you something," Max said quickly.

"Oh?" Neel raised an eyebrow exactly the same way he would raise an eyebrow when there was something someone thought they would tell him.

"Two things, really, if I can figure out how to phrase it."

"Sure." Neel flickered twice.

"One. I've been thinking. And I've been seeing things in my sleep."

"Don't need to think. Central Processing does that for you. Seeing things in your sleep, that's called dreams. Central Processing gives you those too, they were a new feature since 2009. You shouldn't be so surprised." Neel looked bored.

"But I'm not connected to Central Processing and I don't have a link anymore, do you remember my telling you that earlier? Which means I've been thinking and deducing for myself, and I've been dreaming by myself. Can you understand the significance of that?"

"Sure," Neel said, perfectly indifferent. He flickered some more.

"It doesn't matter now. I guess there's one more thing you should know."

"What is that, Max?" Neel hesitated and looked at his cigarette. "Look what you've done to my smoke." It was falling apart and drifting to the ground in perfect triangular particles. Neel watched it, and then felt his face. "My face is $crewed up." The left portion of his head was losing detail, degenerating to simple polygonal planes.

"That's what you should know. I'm going to destroy you. I feel awful for doing it, I guess, and I don't entirely mean it, really." He looked morosely at Neel who was bit by bit, byte by byte, losing resolution and degenerating further, eventually into basic code.

"I've never been destroyed before. That's alarming."

"I've got to destroy everything. That's what I'm going to do. I'm bringing everything down. I'm going to crash the System."

"Go0d lu&ck to Y0u," Neel said like he always said when someone was going travelling. He was breaking up badly. More than half his body was disintegrating to particles and digits and the rest was in late stages of pixelation. "BrinG m%E b@ck s0methinG. I Alw&ays wis*hed there W#re more diStr@ctionS!" He spasmed and fractured as the rest of his processing and language faculties were corrupted. "Oh, &nd there*s somEth&ng el$e I have to teLL you, to0."

"What is that, Neel?"

"I'm StaLL*ing y0u." And that was it. He fell into so many pieces and particles of Neel.

"What do you mean by that?" Max said to no one. It was very quiet, the quiet that stretches into nothingness and between the spaces of thought. Max was thinking again. He thought about everything, thought faster than anyone had any right to think, and in an instant, he reaffirmed his decision.

He had been upgraded from citizen to being by sheer randomness, by a glitch within the System, a necessary glitch. Now it was time to upgrade himself, from being to a god. This made him feel content. He would be the new System, the new and improved Program, he would regulate what evolves and when, and he would have all of his citizens functioning at optimal efficiency. He would recreate the citizen in an image of himself, self-governing, self-aware, self-motivated. The new world would not be an EarthNet, but an Earth. He was Max-Up, energy and motivation.

He started running. It was a long way to the Master Block. But he didn't get very far at all.

The mechanical scream that came from everywhere was immediately deafening. His skin began to vaporize, and then an incredible burst of light covered everything, then the light *was* everything. He opened his mouth to scream as the rest of his body structure disassembled, piece by piece. The ground, the buildings, everything fractured into component parts and then drifted with the sonic wind. Slabs of alphanumeric code and tangles of binary flew past him.

They had powered down the entire sector.

The reason was coming at him right now.

He couldn't have known.

As his being was fragmented into digits and coding, former citizen Max-Up/26 sank in a last moment of thought, a final contemplation as the instant of his obliteration hung by the strand of a second.

He thought . . .

And then it swept over him and it was all over.

The System had formatted the entire sector.

Max-Up was deleted.

THE MALTHUSIAN CODE

by
Leslie Lupien

Leslie Lupien, who lives in Montreal, Quebec, is an American emigre to Canada. Since arriving here from Los Angeles he has published in *Absolute Magnitude* as well as in the small press.

THE MALTHUSIAN CODE

by
Leslie Lupien

Gregory Darius did not flinch as he read the accusation in the interrogator's eyes: *Pervert. Filth.*

"I have a partial transcript of your interview at the Personal Adjustment Clinic." The interrogator held up a disk.

"That will not be necessary." Darius strove to determine the interrogator's gender, but the smooth face, cropped hair and angular lines inside the snug unisex defeated him. Could be either a woman without developed breasts or a man who had chosen laser treatment to abort his beard growth. Probably unattractive to both men and women. Probably spiteful. The embossed letters over the interrogator's tunic pocket read "F. Calhoun."

F. Calhoun slipped the disk into the portable video on the desk. "Regulations require it."

Darius had downed one Inhibitol tablet before the security guards grabbed him in the Clinic's lobby. The mild dosage arrested the throbbing of fear in his belly, but left his mind clear. He straightened in the hard backed chair and used the tone he employed with a difficult subordinate. "I told you it is not necessary. I know exactly what I said."

"Please pay attention." F. Calhoun fingered a button, and words flashed on the video screen.

THER A-96: YOU BELIEVE YOUR MARRIAGE IS FALLING APART AFTER ONLY TWO YEARS?

Gregory D.: Yes.

THER S-96: PROBABLY AN OVERREACTION. MARRIAGES TEND TO REACH A PLATEAU OF LOWER SATISFACTION AF-

TER TWO YEARS. DO YOU STILL LOVE YOUR MATE?

Gregory D.: Yes. But I've been unfaithful.

THER A-96: NOT IN ITSELF A CAUSE FOR MAJOR CONCERN. EXTREMELY COMMON IN THE SECOND OR THIRD YEAR OF MARRIAGE AMONG THE YOUNG.

Gregory D.: But I've been unfaithful with a woman.

THER A-96: (Buzz to indicate a period of silence) INTERVIEW TERMINATED. I MUST ADVISE YOU THAT THE PROTECTION OF THERAPEUTIC CONFIDENTIALITY DOES NOT EXTEND TO CONFESSION TO A FELONY CRIME.

F. Calhoun fingered off the video. "I have reviewed your historical."

Darius shrugged. He wanted to get through this interview as quickly as possible. You could not expect sensitivity or high intelligence from a low level police employee, he thought.

The skin over the interrogator's cheekbones reddened. F. Calhoun bent over the desk top and flung out words like a challenge. "Geneva University, honours doctorate in astrophysics. Sector deputy director with Offworld Enterprises in less than five years. Correct?"

Darius could not repress a slight smile. The flush and angry tone had betrayed F. Calhoun in spite of her neuter appearance. In Darius's experience only a woman could be intuitive enough to sense his unspoken scorn so soon. "Not quite. Senior director last week. Are we going to discuss my employment record, Mizz Calhoun?"

F. Calhoun flushed again. "No, Mr. Darius. But we will discuss why a man with your background should voluntarily make such a shocking admission. Maybe you don't realize we're talking about a seditious offense." She slipped another disk into the video. "We will review the Code section — "

"Please, no. I'm familiar with the anti-heterosexual provisions of the Code." Darius softened his tone. He saw no point in provoking Calhoun further. And he felt a twinge of compassion for the creature. A woman without well-developed breasts faced bleak mating prospects in the world of the Second Restoration. "I will cooperate with you. What do you want to know?"

"Thank you. How many times did you . . . " F. Calhoun's face turned bright red. To even mention the set act obviously distressed her. How thin skinned she must be, under the official facade.

"How many times did you indulge in this unnatural intimacy," she asked again.

"Unnatural is your word. I didn't keep count. Frequently, over six months."

"Six months?" F. Calhoun raised an eyebrow. "Did you tell your mate?"

The reference to Steven stirred a spasm of pain. Darius lowered his eyes and nodded.

"You confessed to spare your mate the need to report you?"

"Yes."

"And you considered it less awkward to confess to a machine?"

"Yes."

"Would you mind giving the name of your accomplice?"

Darius looked up. "There's no need. She's dead . . . She took her own life."

"Of course." F. Calhoun settled back in her cushioned hair and appeared to ponder. Then she spoke, with softness. "Mr. Darius, why don't you just tell me in your own words what happened?"

Darius stiffened. How could he explain an irresistible attraction which Calhoun could see only as unnatural?

"Please try. Otherwise, we'll have to resort to truth serum. Spare yourself the unpleasantness."

Darius hesitated. Maybe he had erred in his first evaluation of Calhoun. She had shown some sensitivity. Certainly as a neuter she had known rejection, and loneliness. Maybe, just maybe, he could bring her to understand. "Very Well."

Friends told Steven and me we had the model marriage, made not in Heaven maybe but in Offworld Enterprises, which was almost as good. We laughed, but believed them.

I met Steven just after my promotion to deputy director. He was a newly hired research assistant, brilliant, a comer. And so beautiful. Not tall, slim and supple as a girl with fine blonde hair reaching to his shoulders. When he took off his shirt the first time, his small but almost hairless and exquisitely developed arms and shoulders reminded me of a statue of Apollo in the Louvre. I must have reminded him more of Caliban than Apollo with my thick, hairy forearms and legs, mat of black chest hair and habitual scowl. But the physical attraction was mutual,strong and lasting.

Steven and I had everything else — compatible personalities, mutual trust and affection, and promising careers. Our bonds grew stronger in two years.

Don't think I had a wandering eye for women. The brightest and prettiest of them surrounded me at Offworld Enterprises. I saw them as fellow employees, nothing more. I never questioned any part of the Code. In fact, I made regular contributions to the Sperm Bank as a Genetic Class A donor.

Sometimes, unfairly, I blame Veronica and Gladys for what happened. They are the married couple, both technicians for Orbital Powersat Constructions, who occupied the suite next to ours during our vacation on High Avalon. Ever been there, Mizz Calhoun? No. You must go. You haven't lived until you've spent some time in geosynchronous orbit. Just to sit in the hotel lobby at sunset and see the Sahara's deep reds and yellows, the dark green carpet of the last Amazon rain forest, and the blue sea speckled with white clouds. And how you unwind. No exhortations, no controls .. . Forgive me. I'm rambling.

Veronica is voluptuous and bubbly with a shock of unruly red hair that defies the art of hair dressers. She loves to prance about in a halter and short shorts and can't open her mouth without laughing. Gladys is tall, svelte and reserved. She imprisons her hair in a tight bun and won't appear in public except in chic blouse and skirt or a one piece swim suit. Both beautiful ladies, but as distinct in appearance as Steven and I are — and as complementary. That may explain why we as couples were first drawn together.

The four of us frolicked for hours in the low gravity delights High Avalon offers. Like the swimming pool that looks like a slowly rotating barrel with water along its inside walls whereyou can swim under the surface or float in midair by using flippers. Or the minipowered strap on wings that let you try to fly like a bird in zero G.

We danced to sensuous music radioed up from Geneva or the Congo on the inside wall of the hotel's rotating torus where artificial gravity builds up to near Earthside level. We kept sipping the sharp Cyprian brandy and aphrodisiacal Malaysian squat that High Avalon reserves for guests on Central Directorate approved vacations. And we weren't harassed by a single guardian artificial intelligence bleating something like, "Moderation is virtue. Excess is vice."

All this shared activity and alcohol brought the four of us close — too close.

Veronica, the bubbly one, mentioned one day that she and Gladys had enhanced their marriage by obtaining a baby boy from the Bureau of Family Planning. She pretended the remark was casual, but it wasn't. Every time we met after that she had to babble about the joys of parenthood and how it tested your maturity. Gladys joined in, more persuasive in her low key way. Putting pressure on Steven and me. Sure. And the ploy worked.

Steven and I had just finished making love one night in one of the "joy cubicles" near the hub of the hotel's torus where there is no noticeable artificial gravity when Steven forced the issue. We were clamped together in an elastic support to keep us from floating apart. And we were exhausted. Sex in Zero G is wild. Please don't turn so red, Mizz Calhoun. Forgive me for my lack of delicacy.

Steven said in a choked voice, "How about it, Greg — the baby? I know you've been thinking about it." And I answered, "Sure. As a great challenge."

Steven and I could not resist a challenge.

So many details stick in my memory of the day Steven and I rode the maglev to keep our first appointments at the BFP. It happened to be the anniversary of the day the nuclear pulse ship *Daedalus* made our first landing on Mars. The guardian AI in our car kept sounding off with exhortations like "Take pride in our conquest of space" and "Devote your efforts to your brothers and sisters on alien worlds." The Regional Directorate had released a cloud of balloons shaped like *Daedalus* over the administrative core of New Wan Francisco. The balloons reminded me of giant chess rooks with exhaust funnels stuck on their bottoms as they floated over the concentric rings of garden apartment blocks out to sea.

I believe both Steven and I felt a little let down by the time we reached the BFP. The adoption of a baby seemed trivial compared to the conquest of space. But our first sight of the BFP lobby acted like a tonic. Brightly coloured holographic representations of idyllic family scenes shone on every wall. Exhortations in giant letters such as "See parenthood as the highest adventure" and "Embrace parenthood as the cure for selfishness" confronted us above the information booths.

I had never seen a government office like this one. The staff made no effort to enforce decorum. Couples of both genders chattered gaily as they relaxed in overstuffed chairs or wandered down carpeted aisles. I even saw staff members smile when addressing applicants.

I expected a long wait, but when we reached an information booth the male attendant asked our names, glanced at the terminal screen on his desk, and passed us inside. "It's the least we can do for you two," he said and smiled. I knew he must refer to our frequent contributions as Grade A Donors to the Sperm Bank. A second attendant separated Steven and me.

I walked into a windowless room and stopped in surprise. The room held only two contour chairs face to face. A soft blue carpet and pastel painted walls conveyed an instantimpression of cosiness.

A door slid open in the opposite wall, and for the first time I set eyes on . . . I'll call her Dawn.

Dawn invited me to sit. Was I smitten with her at first glance? Far from it. I saw only a small, trim young woman with bobbed hair dressed in professional unisex bluecloth.

"Surprised, Mr. Darius? No screens, no recorders, not even a printout of your application." Dawn cocked her head to one side and smiled in an impish way that I would later find irresistible.

"It's . . . unusual." The closeness of her, her knees almost touching mine, made me uneasy.

"It's the way we do it." Dawn shifted back in her contour chair as if she sensed my discomfort. "The bureau has found that the judgement of an individual interviewer is more insightful than any electronic test. But a relaxed and empathetic atmosphere is necessary."

"Oh?" My voice must have reflected annoyance. I had expected a perfunctory interview. With Steven's and my qualifications . . .

"I have reviewed your application carefully and have a few reservations."

I choked up with surprise and outrage. *Reservations*? Who the hell did this snip think she was?

"Please, Mr. Darius, don't bristle so. It's for the welfare of the child."

Dawn cocked her head and smiled again. "Of course you have an out-standing background. But that may be a problem, can't you see? Are you really at this stage for the distractions of parenthood?"

I really noticed Dawn then — how fine her eyes, large and luminous brown, and how her voice, soft but rich, soothed like restful music. My resentment oozed out and left me, well, receptive.

We talked freely about my work, my aspirations, friends, Steven. Dawn told me a little about herself. She, like all of the interviewers, had served three terms as surrogate mother. She was happily married to a vivacious younger woman named Nancy.

Dawn scheduled a second interview. I didn't mind. Actually I suffered a pang of disappointment when she held up her hand to say goodbye.

Steven made a mock sour face. "A second interview? You have a problem?"

I laughed. "Have to convince the young lady I'm mature enough."

My second interview started with a jolt. At first I wasn't sure it was Dawn who walked in. She had exchanged her bluecloth for a sleeveless beige blouse and matching skirt, conservative but not designed to hide her natural attractions. Her fluffed up hair and earrings shaped like tiny el-ephants revived my first impish impression.

"I caught your scowl, Mizz Calhoun. You are repelled by Dawn's show of femininity and my approving response. You consider both per-verted under the circumstances. I have another opinion which you will have to hear before we finish."

I recall few details of the second interview. The chemistry working between Dawn and me built up to an emotional overload which fuzzed my perceptions. Never before had I been alone with one woman, knee to knee. I would never have exposed myself to such a situation.

I believe Dawn and I chatted in a casual way. I know we exchanged very strong nonverbal messages. Finally, to my regret, she said with her impish smile, "We have worked overtime and must stop." She turned at the door, not smiling. "Please think over carefully what has happened here today before our next interview." I caught the throb in her voice.

Steven was not amused. "Again? What the hell *is* your problem, Gregory?"

"I have no problem." What a lie. I knew, torn between excitement and fear, I had the worst problem of my life.

My third meeting with Dawn lasted only minutes. She appeared in severe bluecloth, hair bobbed and minus earrings, and didn't even invite me to sit. "The bureau has approved your application," she said, not looking at me. Her hand shook as she held it out. I took the hand and came away with a small envelope.

I opened the envelope on the street. The slip of paper inside bore a date, a time, and an address. I recognized the address as that of a first class comfort hostel near the seawall overlooking what used to be a residential area in Old San Francisco.

So —

F. Calhoun interrupted. "So you began your illicit liaison."

"Illicit is your word."

F. Calhoun's smile struck Darius as condescending. "Don't flatter yourself that your case is unique, Mr. Darius. We have suspended and treated several of our interviewers who tried to do what Dawn did. After this tragedy, we'll tighten up our screening and training."

Darius blinked in surprise. "We?"

F. Calhoun straightened, severe and official. "I am Director of Internal Affairs for BFP. We persuaded the police to let us handle your case because of . . . special circumstances."

"Then you know who . . . "

"Who your Dawn was? Of course. I suppose we in the bureau should feel sorry for Dawn. She accepted her guilt. But you . . . " F. Calhoun locked eyes with Darius. "You seem to feel no sense of shame or remorse."

"Hear me out, Director. Maybe you'll understand."

F. Calhoun sighed and sank back in her chair. "I'm listening."

I did suffer then, Director, from fear of exposure, self-loathing, remorse for my betrayal of Steven. The arrival of baby Toni added more stress. But the suffering drew me closer to Dawn. Our physical desire became less urgent, but we developed mutual tenderness deeper and richer than the love I shared with Steven.

"It seems so natural," Dawn said one day. "Are we really so evil, such criminals?"

"No, love," I said. But a moment later I accused myself of rationalizing our guilt. The Code said an intimate relationship between a man and a woman was so anti-social as to represent the worst kind of crime. And I knew why it did better than most people. I had studied Pre-Restoration History under the best teacher. Dr. Kepler had described so vividly the horrors that sprang from "bestial couplings" and "mindless procreation." But a discreet, affectionate relationship in which the partners took care that no procreation would result?

My mental conflict became intolerable. I took a three-day leave of absence, lied to Steven about attending a company seminar, and flew to Geneva to talk to the one person I thought might help.

I identified myself by vidphone as one of Doctor Kepler's former students. But it was my status as an executive of Offworld Enterprises that won me a quick interview.

"Darius . . . Darius." Doctor Kepler, urbane and gentle as I remembered him, pretended to struggle to remember. "Give me a moment. Won't you have a cup of tea?"

"Thank you. Undergraduate, class of Pre-Restoration History 1, 2 and 3." If Doctor Kepler had remembered me I would have been astounded. I, like thousands of others, had absorbed his lectures via teleconferencing.

We sat on Doctor Kepler's patio overlooking Lake Geneva and sipped strong Sri Lankan tea. I lied outrageously. "Doctor, I am responsible for preparing an in-house lecture on the anti-heterosexual provisions of the Code. Some of our youngest employees have, well, behaved in disturbing ways."

"Have they?" Doctor Kepler's eyes moistened. "How could they not? Do not condemn them, Darius. A million years of evolution . . . "

"What, sir?" What was the man saying? I recalled him as relentless in driving a central message home in his lectures: Uncontrolled human spawning had led to merciless wars between the starving many and the comfortable few, rebellion of a long abused ecosystem, the great plagues. The anti-heterosexual provisions made sure these horrors would not recur.

"I've shocked you, Darius, and you came here for help." Doctor Kepler smiled as if to ask forgiveness. "Put down what I just said to the illogical musing of an old man." His smile faded. "But go gently with the young people. They face their own horrors. They must never deviate, must never fail."

I needed his confidence. "I will, sir."

"To business then. You must make your young people see how close Homo Sapiens came to extinction." Doctor Kepler shifted forward and lowered his voice. "Closer than I taught, Darius. The survivors were numbered in *thousands*."

I could not believe my ears. "That few? I knew the plagues were virulent, sir, but . . . "

"Worse that virulent, Darius. Man made." His voice dropped to a whisper. "Northern military leaders became frantic when they played their last card — biological warfare, ebola and worse. Soon after, the viruses mutated and turned into the plagues. All those responsible are long dead now, so I can tell you."

"Really?" I whispered back, eager to hear more.

"Make your young people see what a colossal job the First Directors faced." Doctor Kepler spoke in his normal resonat voice. "They had to reeducate completely. Eliminate the concept of the nation state. And, above all, compel everyone to accept that reproduction is too serious to be left to individuals. For the survival of our species, Darius."

"I hear you, sir." I groped to understand. "But they were so rigid. Didn't they consider contraception for example?"

"They did, Darius, and quarrelled bitterly." Doctor Kepler glanced through the glass top of the patio door and lowered his voice again. "Remember, the First Directors were surrounded by terrified survivors who were malleable as copper. Fanatics among them came to see themselves in godlike roles. They argued that human beings in their natural state had failed on this planet. They had to be reshaped for a higher destiny. Above all, men and women could not be given any chance to procreate on their own. All the force of law and public opinion had to be mustered to prevent it."

Doctor Kepler paused and shook his head. "The fanatics won. Their successors spout the same dogma a century later, beyond reason sometimes . . . ." He stared open mouthed at me as if terrified by his own temerity.

I needed to know more. "Tell me about the quarrels, sir."

Doctor Kepler's expression turned wary. "We can discuss this another time, Darius. It's all in the classified files in Zurich."

I waited expectantly.

"Not available for you, I'm afraid, Darius." Doctor Kepler flushed with obvious pride. "I am one of the few academics with clearance for the top secret files."

I thanked Doctor Kepler for the tea, made another appointment which I didn't intend to keep, and hurried away. I didn't mention I had restricted clearance to use the Zurich vaults for technical research.

Desperation made me rash. I approached the Chief of Security at the Zurich vaults, who knows me well, and gave him the same story I had given Doctor Kepler to request access to the top secret files. The Chief looked down his nose, waffled, but finally gave in.

By chance I first entered the Literature section. Thousands of books, even though only a tiny fraction of those the First Directors destroyed during the great cleansing. I looked for something familiar and pulled out a volume of Shakespeare.

F. Calhoun stirred. "Where are you going with this, Mr. Darius?"

"What do you really know about life before the Restoration?"

"Don't try to instruct *me*, Mr. Darius. I also have advanced degrees."

"But, like all of us, you received all of your education through electronic entities prepared since the Restoration. You have never seen an original source, a book. Amazing things in books, Director." Darius stood in his excitement. "For example, the original title of Romeo and Julio was Romeo and Juliet."

"Sit down. We know about your snooping in the Zurich vaults. Another seditious offense. I don't want to hear what you found."

"Of course you don't. Reality would shake you down to your toes."

"Sit down." F. Calhoun flushed bright red. "I will not be baited. Do you have more to tell me about Dawn and yourself? If not, we'll proceed to truth serum."

"Dawn." Darius's excitement ebbed and he sat. "I'll tell you what little more there is."

If you don't know, Director, a first class comfort hostel offers above all a strong sense of security to its clients. What goes on inside its walls nobody outside is supposed to know.

Still, Dawn and I were discreet. We never entered or left the hostel together. We leased separate suites, but we could not have anticipated the maniacal jealousy of Dawn's mate and the cunning and recklessness with which she pursued us.

I had just buttoned on the food dispenser in my suite the morning after my return from Zurich. The frosted glass door of our tenth floor balcony burst open to admit a wild-eyed creature in slag tunic, tight black hose and anti-grav climbing boots.

I confronted the invader. "Get out. You're in the wrong suite."

The woman, her face twisted into a grimace of hatred, spat a great blob of spittle into my face. "Nancy!" shouted Dawn, still in her negligee.

"I wouldn't have believed . . . Oh, you pervert! You pervert!" Nancy flew at Dawn and pounded her about the head with both fists.

I grabbed Nancy from behind, pinioned her flailing arms, and hustled her toward the door. She butted me with her head and gouged my legs with the solenoids on the bottom of her climbing boots until I fastened her against the wall.

"Go or I'll call security." I tried to hold the writhing woman without hurting her.

"Go ahead, slime. I'm a guest here too." Nancy wrenched a hand free and punched me in the nose. "I'm going to the police anyway. I don't know you, but your queer lover is dead."

I buttoned open the door and shoved Nancy into the corridor while she screamed at Dawn. "You're dead, queer! Dead!"

Dawn had collapsed on the rug. While I laid her on the sofa, she moaned between sobs, "My family, my family, oh, the shame."

"Shush." I held Dawn in my arms. "What we do is not a perversion. I learned that in Zurich. Listen."

Dawn quieted while I told her a little of what I had found among a selection of books from the Literature and Social Sciences sections of the Zurich vaults. I tried to make her understand how men and women had loved each other with passion and devotion and without shame for thousands of years before and ever during the Pre-Restoration catastrophes.

"We'll face what we must," I said. "We'll fight for our lives and the truth. Don't you trust me?"

"Yes. But no one will believe us." Dawn trembled in my arms. "And I don't have your strength."

The vidphone chimed from another room. "It must be security," I said. "I better answer it. Don't move."

I will never forgive myself for answering that call.

The security monitor flashed a question on the screen: DO YOU KNOW ANYTHING ABOUT THE PERSON MAKING A COMMOTION IN THE HALL? I said, "No. I think she is crazy."

When I returned, the opaque glass door to the balcony was closed. I heard loud voices from the courtyard. I ...

"Compose yourself," F. Calhoun said sharply.

Darius stood again and stretched to calm the turmoil in his bowels. "I'm finished unless you want to hear more about what I found in the Zurich vaults."

F. Calhoun's face darkened. "No."

Darius shrugged. "Well, then."

"Please sit down, Mr. Darius." F. Calhoun flushed and squared her shoulders. "I am authorized to make you an offer of clemency under one condition. It comes from . . . the highest."

Darius blinked his surprise. "After what you heard?"

"Yes. Because of your genetic and professional value." F. Calhoun spoke with toneless precision as if repeating someone else's words. "If you go to public trial, the only issue will be the length of your exile to a lunar reeducation centre. Do you know what that involves?"

Darius shrugged. "Tell me."

"Loss of all property and professional privileges. Branding on the shoulder as a dangerous deviant. Spells of hard labour in a most unpleasant environment. The possibility of permanent exile if you do not show an acceptable degree of rehabilitation. On the other hand, the offer of clemency involves a sealing of the record. It is very generous."

"You mentioned one condition."

"You must accept electrotherapy to free yourself of the deviant erotomania."

Darius managed a wry smile. "And to eliminate my memory of the Zurich top secret files."

"Didn't you hear what I said?" F. Calhoun perched on the edge of her chair as if ready to leap at Darius. "You can go on with your life as if nothing happened. Now, sit down."

Darius remained standing. He sensed fear behind F. Calhoun's anger. She was desperate to get his agreement to accept therapy. No doubt because "the highest" was eager to prevent his speaking out at a public trial.

"What's the matter with you, man? You have a mate and a new child to consider."

Darius shook his head. "I've agreed to my mate's request for a divorce and sole custody of Toni."

F. Calhoun's eyes bulged. "Then your career."

Darius felt a twinge of sympathy for F. Calhoun. The woman was terrified because of the threat his recalcitrance posed to *her* career. He sat. "Don't you realize I must have considered that, Director? Thank you for your generous offer, but no."

"I see. So you're a crusader."

Darius read the malevolence behind F. Calhoun's smile and guessed what she was thinking: *All right, crusader. We'll find a way to bring you around.*

Darius smiled back. One thing F. Calhoun could not know, and he would not tell her. Every time he closed his eyes he saw Dawn's tear strained face. "No, you won't," he said with utter conviction.

TO THE LAST MAN

by
A.J. Onia

Al Onia, of Calgary, Alberta, is a professional geophysicist with a keen scientific interest that extends into his speculative fiction. His stories have been published by *Pulphouse, Marion Zimmer Bradley's Fantasy Magazine*, and he was a semi-finalist in the *Writers of the Future Contest.*

TO THE LAST MAN

by
A.J. Onia

The last man on Earth stepped out of the low-altitude skimmer on the shore of the Kansas Sea and wondered who was waiting for him. With his one human eye, Ark Haight watched the orange and grey clouds boil like lava across the sky above the sea, echoing the turmoil within himself. His enhanced eye saw only the radiation from beneath the smooth grey rock oozing out of the poisoned waters' edge.

The skimmer rocked violently in the gale, ice pellets ringing off her hull. Ark tried to fasten his jacket against the elements but his field harness was too bulky.

"Upheaval, it's cold." The snow stung his eye and attacked his face. Ark struggled to keep his footing on the slippery rock, glancing towards the beacon flickering in the distance. It upset him that Feld Morse had been right, maybe there was someone here.

Damn, he thought, Valery could have begun her sculpting of the crust here two days ago and eliminated the need for him to investigate this anomaly. I should be transiting now, to fame and security for the rest of my life, brief as that may be.

Who would be so stupid to defy Erie? Someone well-armed? He fingered the pistol clipped to his belt and the protective field harness. The standard Executor Corps armament would shield him. He had drilled his transit teams enough to believe it himself.

Ark spoke into his mike, "I'm here, Morse. Tell Valery's techs to ease back on the carving, the wind's going to blow my skimmer over."

Valery's studio master said, "She hasn't started her sculpting on this hemisphere. You, my diminutive friend, are in the middle of one upheaval of a storm. You have twenty minutes to get your job done and get the hell out of there."

Twenty minutes. The same time it had taken Valery's cutters to erase all physical evidence of the Congo Basin. The time it had taken the orbital annihilators to vaporize the lake beside him and kill those who hid at her bottom during the opening skirmishes of the Second Upheaval, as Ark dimly remembered from his history lessons. Lessons taught him by his mother before she died. She had perished slowly, the way most did, refugees from the immigrant wars unable to find safety from the radiation, the pollution, the disease.

Ark said, "I can barely hear you, even this close to the skimmer. Contact will cease while I investigate. I can see some kind of light or beacon. That's what you probably detected."

Morse said, "We started transit with a quarter of a million people on Earth, it was bound to get easier to detect the stragglers when only you were supposed to be left."

"What if there is someone here and they don't want to transit?"

When there was no answer, Ark continued, "Dammit Morse, I'm head of the Executor Corps, not cleanup. I never had to carry out the execution command, I always convinced the reluctant ones to transit."

"You fought to have your wife sent up here, Ark. You knew that at some time you would have to make the choice, your lives or the trespassers."

He knew Morse was right. Ark had made and sealed his bargain. He was the last one down here and it was up to him. "This'll look great in the history discs, 'Ark Haight: Executioner. Postscript. . . also the last man on Earth'."

"You believe that the last man to leave Earth will be someone special, don't you? But you don't realize that such a man would have to be special before that. And you are not even ordinary." The fading voice from orbit held neither tone nor emotion but Ark sensed the mocking attitude.

Ark cut him off, "I'm delaying the skimmer. Listen Morse, long after you're cycled, I'll be remembered in the same breath as Valery. No one will care who did her technical work on the crust, it will be her name and mine spoken together."

Ark removed his mike set and closed the hatch door. He thumbed his field harness to life, bent his head into the gale and began to walk. The storm pummelled him. He glanced up to the clouds. Even his enhanced eye could not penetrate through to the end of the disturbance. The Earth was not going to allow her last living being to flee easily.

Ark did not want to join the ghosts of those at the bottom of the Kansas Sea. Flying here in the skimmer, his competing eyes showed whitecaps on the surface and stronger currents underneath battling each other. And in his mind's eye he saw the ill-fated spirits of the men, women and children who'd sought refuge on the bottom but found only their tombs.

Ark was driven to escape that fate. But instead of taking advantage of his final minutes before transit, he was now in danger of being trapped. Ambush, skimmer wreck, the odds were he would not make it off the planet in time. The months he had spent months planning his actions would be wasted if he died here. Genuine notoriety was difficult to attain amongst a human race scattered across the solar system and beyond, balancing existence in Lagrange habitats or burrowed into thin-atmosphered planets and moons. But Ark knew he would achieve immortality among all by being the last man on Earth. Forgotten would be the politicians who jumped at the chance to be the first ones off the planet. Claiming they were setting an example, he thought they were grateful for someone else to make a decision for them. The remembrance would be for thelast man, Ark Haight. Unless I'm one of the last two. Tough to gain advantage from that.

Ark stopped walking five meters from the beacon, the light strong enough to force his eye to blink. The signal came from the roof of a small shack. Above the beacon, a huge metal blade, suspended on a tower of struts, shrieked as it spun in the wind. The shack didn't look strong enough to anchor the tower much longer in this gale. A sign he couldn't read hung broken beside a door and light shone dimly through the frosted window.

Still expecting an attack, he checked his pistol and harness. "I'll use both, if I have to," he said aloud to boost his confidence. The wind was shaking the shack and he heard the creak of the structure straining to remain intact. It seemed certain that anyone inside would see him before they heard him.

He gripped the pistol with one hand and reached for the handle on the door with the other when it opened for him. He stepped inside.

The first thing Ark noticed was that the floor of the shack was moving, in contrast to the hard rock outside. The wind was magnified inside the small building. The interior light came from a single source at the same end as the door. Its flicker illuminated small mounds of rubbish and a simple cot. An old woman lay on the cot, her hands still clutching the cord that had opened the door for him. Ark stared at her, feeling a little foolish, armed and ready to defend himself against a horde of assassins.

She seemed unconcerned at his armament. With a flourish, he holstered his pistol but did not disengage the field harness. The air bit his nose with the sickly-sweet smell of rotting vegetables. He opened his mouth to breathe but the taste of the air nauseated him. His real eye watered.

He coughed and said, "I am the Commander of Erie Inc.'s Transit Executor Corps. You should not be here."

The old woman crinkled a tight smile through her tiny mouth. "Erie is not my commander, so what does that make you to me?" Her voice was firm and confident in comparison to her frail appearance.

"Erie owns this planet and is evicting its tenants on the order of its Chairman and his daughter. My duty is to ensure no one remain. You have no choice." The dwelling shook and Ark swayed in unison with the light hanging from the ceiling.

"Sit down before you accidentally shoot me, Commander of the Executor Corps. Or should I say, Executioner Corps?"

"We never kill," Ark blurted, but he sat on a stool bolted to the floor.

The woman lay back on her bed, her shoulders and head propped up on a rolled blanket. Her white hair was pulled back, revealing a high forehead and well-defined cheekbones. He saw her feet raise the blanket and he realized that she was at least half a meter taller than he. Granted, he was short, even for these times, but he had never seen anyone so tall and well-formed. His suppressed inadequacies bubbled to the surface. He thought of his final command tour.

"Commander Haight, I can't get used to the buzz. The sound interferes with my leg prosth'. It was Lidgren, bitching again."

Ark turned his own field off and removed his harness. He held it up above his head. "You live with this twenty-four hours a day until you wear it like a shirt." He spoke to all the trainees. "Two years ago, most of the remaining few hundred thousand inhabitants of Earth were happy to accept

Erie's offer of transiting off-planet. Erie Inc. gave the Transit Corps those two years to complete our mission."

Lidgren said, "The Chairman has resided off-planet for the last three decades. And daughter Valery has never set foot on Earth."

Ark raised his voice, "Ignore him, Valery's cause is noble: to commemorate the quarter-millennium since the end of the Second Upheaval — by creating a new face for the scarred Earth. Her father agreed and offered evacuation and settlement for people with no future. People like us. Look at me, not Lieutenant Lidgren. I was a one-eyed, starving cripple. I leaped at the opportunity to join the Corps, you all did. As our reward, my wife and I will enjoy a few years of painless, worry-free comfort."

"Before the sickness you carry from a dying planet kills you," Lidgren said.

Ark said, "See that sign?" He pointed to the wall behind the recruits and read it aloud, "DOWN TO THE LAST. How many days left?" he challenged.

"Fourteen," came a united answer from all but Lidgren.

"And how many left to transit?" Ark had not looked at the display, knowing it changed minute to minute.

"Sixteen thousand," again the unified response, except Lidgren.

"By the time I look, it will be less."

Lidgren was undoing his harness.

Ark said, "Mr. Lidgren, I ordered you to wear that continuously."

Lidgren didn't stop. "I'm quitting. You can have the leg back, too. You're all insane."

"Erie won't let you quit."

"Screw them. And screw Valery." The harness clattered to the floor. "They bribed each of you with what you wanted most but look what you're doing to repay them. Some of the people don't want to leave. Erie is the bad guys, they're not gods! I'm not going up, I'm staying." Lidgren turned his back to Ark and said something to the men.

Ark thought, no, you can't, I'm last. Lidgren's profile was way off. How many others in the Corps were changing their attitudes after months of enforcing Transit? "I can't let you quit." He readied his pistol, never more than a threat, not knowing if he could use it on one of his team.

Lidgren swung his attention back to Ark but remained silent.

Ark interpreted the unspoken challenge. Lidgren knew what Ark didn't admit, he wouldn't shoot him. For a moment their eyes locked, then Ark flicked his vision away. Lidgren started to smile in victory then froze as the bolt hit him in the back from Ark's second-in-command. The smile was still there when Lidgren tumbled to the floor beside his harness.

Ark steeled himself against the quickly rising bile. This shouldn't happen, this is my fault. "I repeat, don't take your harness off until transit's done and you're safely in orbit."

The old woman coughed and her breath expelled in a tight whistle, echoing the wind outside. Ark's hand had returned to his pistol. There was no physical danger here and he dropped it to his side. "We never kill," he repeated.

She looked at him again, her bright eyes showing none of the age in her face. "Not intentionally, that much I see. But you're here to take me up there." She tilted her head upward. She coughed, then whistled in her breath. "I wouldn't survive a walk to the sea's edge, let alone a lift into orbit. So you are here to complete my life."

"Erie has provided acceleration tanks for . . . infirm people." He had never asked if they worked. "And I can carry you easily to my skimmer."

"Hah," she said. "Everyone is infirm, it is the curse of the Upheaval. I am just old, probably the oldest person you have ever seen."

True enough, thought Ark.

"Death would come quickly for me once separated from Earth, from where my familylies. Erie is your God and my devil. I do not accept gifts from the devil. My God is below me, in the soil, the rock and the bones of my ancestors."

Ark sighed. Conflicting faith had been a major cause of the Second Upheaval. His faith was in Erie Incorporated. It was easy when Erie had all the power, and most of the knowledge. He shouted above the wind. "I've talked with the chairman and he's not the devil. He gave me what I wanted."

"What do you want?"

Ark couldn't resist telling her, at least some of it. "Until an hour ago I wanted to stand on rocks, like those outside, and know that I was the only human being on the entire planet."

"Your desire is human enough, grabbing glory from tragedy," she said. "But you're not entirely human. Not with your false eye and that harness."

"I'll carry you if I must, but you will transit." He looked away from her. She wouldn't guess any more of his secrets.

"Not yet," she said.

Ark began to stand but her curious reply stopped him. Would she come with him? Ark's own inquisitiveness prompted him. "What are you, a magician? How did we miss you?"

She straightened her head and looked at her feet. "I am Marie Catton and I am unlike you. I am solely human. The villagers called me Mademoiselle Phare, because my grandfather and I used to run this lighthouse. Then he died." She dabbed her eyes with a ragged corner of her blanket. "The ships on the lake stopped coming. Not enough people. The original tower was destroyed by ignorance and I am what is left. I built the windmill for my power out of the scraps." She paused to take a deep breath. "No one missed me. In panic, the animal inside looks after itself. I chose not to transit. And I am unable to run, as you can see."

It was simplistic. Ark knew the thoroughness of the Transit Corps and the Erie sensors. It would take great cunning to remain undetected. She was not a magician, she was smart. That frightened Ark, he could not debate against her and win. "I do not know why you have lured me here, if not to save you, Mademoiselle Catton. You can bring some of your things with you. I will carry them first." She would be a load herself in this storm.

"There is only one thing I take with me and I have waited for it to arrive."

Ark said, "I will take it to my skimmer. Where is it?"

Marie laughed, "First, tell me your name."

"Ark . . . Commander Haight."

"Ark?" she said. "Like Noah?"

"Archeron is my full name, but I prefer Ark," he snapped. He puffed in air through his mouth, still trying to avoid the taste of it. "Now, what do you want me to take? Our time is growing tight." No execution. Just pick her and her keepsakes up and transit the lot into orbit. Simple.

"Archeron, you have brought it."

"I'm losing patience with these word games, Mademoiselle. I bring you the offer of transit." He stood over her bed. The low cot still came to his mid-thigh.

"Look at yourself, Ark. A ridiculous pose in a ridiculous costume."

The look in her eyes reminded him of Lidgren when he knew Ark wouldn't shoot him. He had no doubt she knew, too. How could he fulfil his duty and his mission?

She said, "You have brought the last man to my bedside and he carries a great legacy, if he chooses."

For a moment Ark tried to understand what she was saying. "Sex?" No, not with this . . .crone.

She laughed again but it turned quickly to a cough. "You are thinking of extending you genes with me. I am sorry, I am much too old. Your desire is admirable. Your survival is important to you. Or is it your immortality?"

She had guessed.

She said, "You would not find me a particularly attractive mate. But the thought has passed, hasn't it?"

Ark said, "Unlike me, my children will know their father. The habitats will ensure healthy, long lives for my family."

"Show me."

Ark reached in his breast pocket and withdrew the hologram he always carried. He passed it to her. "My wife's name is Erin. We have clearance to have children."

Marie moved it to see the full effect then returned it to Ark. "You love her and that is why you do this. But you will have other seeds to sow. The ones I plant in your brain. They will need to grow as surely as your children, to aid our survival." Her breath wheezed in again.

"Your cough sounds dry. Do you have anything to drink before I carry you to the skimmer?"

She closed her eyes and grimaced as an invisible force arched her abdomen up from the cot. She moved her head from the side and back once in a painful shake. "I have not spoken in a long time and the effort drains me. I have little left to say."

Ark bent down to pick her up but she raised an arm in front of her and said, "Listen. Despite your artificiality, you are the last man on Earth. This time. Your burden is ensuring that you will not be the last forever. Don't let Valery destroy all that is left; she is no artist. You hold in your soul the feeling of what the Earth was like before mankind abandoned it. The histories will not convey the emotion only you can know."

Ark had intended to slide his arms underneath her. Now he rested on his knees beside her. "There will be virtuals and re-creations. I'm one man. A crippled, stunted excuse for a man." A lump formed in his throat. Tiny now, he tried to stop it from growing.

"Your appearance is not your fault, you can overcome that. Virtuals aren't enough. The will to return must be passed directly from you. You have schemed to be the last man, Commander. Use your repute to *communicate* the sadness you feel at this moment. Your nobility of spirit will show through any physical shortcomings you feel."

"I'm not sure I . . ."

She clutched his hand. "Tell them of the grief you experienced holding the last woman on Earth. Hold me."

Ark put his arm under hers and raised her head to his shoulder. She was light to touch but not as fragile as he had expected. Her musty smell penetrated his eye and throat.

She whispered in his ear, "Remember everything about this moment. Remember the passing of the last woman on Earth."

He felt her warm breath on his neck. It came and came, then her weight sunk and there was no more talk or breath.

Ark knelt beside the cot for a long time. The tears never came, just an inner anger. Anger at Valery, Erie and himself.

Later, Ark stood alone on the shore of the dead sea. Looking far across the grey water, he felt no pleasure in his solitude. If only he could have brought her to the habitat. She would make the others feel as he did now. He looked down at the stubby fingers that had held Marie Catton and knew they would carry her always.

Ark stood in front of the small crowd. His old Transit Corps uniform was clean and the buttons shone. He straightened his back as much as he could. The pain was always there but he knew he could get through his address to this group and the next and the next after that.

"Ladies and gentlemen." He saw there were quite a few children up front. That was good. "My name is Archeron Haight and I was the last man to stand on the planet of our birth. Most of you have never touched the Earth, spinning empty and wounded beneath this habitat, and you may wonder what can this man tell us of importance?" A twinge from his muscles, crying to be returned to their normal bent posture, halted his speech. Ark clenched his fists until the pain abated enough for him to continue.

"Forget, if you can, what I am for the moment. I am here to tell you of a much more important person. I am here to tell you of the last woman on Earth. Her name was Marie Catton, Mademoiselle Phare. The light of wisdom."

Ark pictured her as he spoke and it helped *communicate* her message across the miles and the years. He held her again for the hundredth time and repeated his silent vow.

"This is a hologram of my son. He is an ordinary boy, thank heaven. I tell him that he, and many of you, have an important task. It is not important that Ark Haight was the last man on Earth. Paramount is who will lead the return."

RAINY SEASON

by
Robert Beer

Robert H. Beer, of Fergus, Ontario, was a finalist in the *Writers of the Future Contest*. He continues to hone his talent in the Salt Lake City Science Fiction and Fantasy Workshop (SFFW).

RAINY SEASON

by
Robert Beer

Chief Ecologist Jack McMillan stared out at the rain, just as he had every morning for the past month. He was searching for an adjective. It was a game they used in the lab to make it easier to deal with — every day someone, in turn, had to come up with a new word to describe the rain.

Today was his turn, and it was time to head in. He was out some money if he dropped out.

As he watched the drops weave their way down the inside of the plexiglass window, he caught a glimpse of his reflection. Fortyish, thin — some would say gaunt — serious greying of the temples in an otherwise full jet-black head of hair. He looked like a college professor, which he had been, before he had decided he needed a new challenge. But there were challenges and *challenges.*

He shrugged into his makeshift raincoat of parachute fabric, and shook his head. Whoever thought the colony would need *raincoats?*

The planet was supposed to be dry — not desert, but certainly not with six or more hours of rain every morning. And they had satellite data going back nearly a hundred years.

Teaming...pelting? No, they'd been used last week.

McMillan lost his train of thought for a moment as he opened the door. Thank God the door was on the lee side of his hut. He had to smile to himself. Of course it hadn't been in the lee until the rains started and he'd had Construction turn his hut one hundred eighty degrees.

As he slogged the seventy meters to the Bio Lab he nearly bumped into several workers, heading out of the camp to the north, each with a laser pistol strapped to his belt. *Picking off more wildlife*, he thought. Much to his chagrin, some of the support crew had taken up hunting one of the local species in recent weeks. With one notable exception, his staff held themselves aloof from such activities. Unfortunately, as leader of the science team, he had no authority to stop the killing, unless he could substantiate a classification of 'threatened' or 'endangered', which the ferrets were definitely not.

Reaching the lab, he hopped deftly through the hatch, pulling it shut behind with the dull thud of plastic on plastic. He slipped a pilfered piece of bacon through the bars of a pen, much to the delight of Eddie, its occupant.

Bryce Matthews looked up and smiled a humourlessly. "Your day, Jack. Got a word for the rain?"

Jack hadn't at least until that moment, so he growled the first thing that entered his head. "Bullshit."

A sudden laugh from the other side of the hut indicated that Amelia had heard him. She leaned around the end of a lab bench and grinned. That vibrant smile in her attentive coffee-coloured face could brighten the whole camp, and Jack immediately lost some of his weather-inspired gloom. "Now that's the best description I've heard yet!" she said. Amelia Mobenu doubled as all-purpose med. tech and camp confessor. She had an easy ear. "Forget this *driving, pelting, torrential* business, and cut right to the heart of the matter."

Matthews was turning purple, all the way to the roots of his wiry red hair. Even his mustache and freckles seemed to have disappeared . . . . "Now, wait a second! 'Bullshit' isn't an adjective. That doesn't qualify."

Amelia nodded solemnly at the Geology man. "It's possible you're right, Bryce. But since you made me the judge, and there's no English major within twenty light-years, I think I'll just let it go. Okay?"

Matthews let it drop for the moment, although Jack knew that Matthews seldom dropped anything for good. He had other things on his mind, however. "We've got more problems with the ferrets," he said.

"You mean those you haven't killed off?" Instantly he regretted the remark, but Bryce Matthews was the only one on the science staff that went along with the hunters, and, damn it, it irked him.

The "ferrets" were a mystery, to go along with the rain, and a dozen other unpredicted things they'd run into on Parless. The creatures were cat-sized and rodent-like in appearance, but seemed to occupy a niche similar to the large weasels on Earth, maybe something like a marten. Early survey teams had categorized them as a very minor member of the local food chain, and so they were, until their numbers had inexplicably increased in the past month by nearly five hundred percent. Where there had been a few dozen living in the area of the camp, now there were hundreds, perhaps thousands.

Jack forced himself to put aside his personal feelings for now and asked politely, "Got any ideas on where they're coming from?"

Matthews glared for a minute, then shook his head. "How should I know? You Bio people don't even know whether they're reproducing here. Maybe we're just on some sort of migration route."

"Like lemmings?" Amelia said.

Jack chuckled. "Except there's no ocean nearby."

"There might be if the rain keeps up," she quipped.

"Ocean? What does that have to do with anything?" demanded Matthews.

"Oh, I forget sometimes that you're not from Earth," Amelia said. Matthews was colony-born, and had never even been to the home world.

"Fifty percent of humans aren't," Matthews growled. "Besides, we've got another problem." He lifted up a sheet on his bench to reveal a dead ferret. Its head had been smashed. Across the room, Eddie, who could have been this animal's twin, froze and stared. "I caught this little fellow in my hut this morning."

Jack stared. "*Inside?* How'd it get in? The huts are supposed to be sealed."

"Damned thing chewed its way in through the plastic. Must have been at it half the night. What woke me up were my ears popping as the pressure went down." The huts were kept at a slightly elevated pressure, partly to keep local contaminants out, but mainly because the local atmospheric pressure was low and, while breathable, was a bit short on oxygen.

"Did you really have to kill it?" Amelia asked.

"What would you have me do? The damn thing breached my hut, and there it was running around inside. Might have bitten me. They aren't rodents, you know. They have teeth and claws. You think I could have coaxed it back out the hole? Maybe by talking to it nicely?"

Jack bristled at the sarcasm, which Amelia's comment hadn't war-ranted. "I'm surprised you didn't plug the animal with your laser pistol, Bryce. Don't you sleep with it under your pillow?"

Matthews took the question at face value, however. "I wouldn't use that inside my hut. It's not very powerful, but it would melt plastic pretty easily. Took me half an hour as it was to patch the hole," he grumbled, turning back to the carcass on the bench. "I've got my own work to do without screwing around with this stuff."

He picked the creature up by it's stubby tail and tossed it unceremoniously in the refuse as he passed by. Eddie scrambled to the front of his cage for a better view. At the door, Matthews turned and said indifferently, "I'll be back in a couple of hours. I have to go pick up some samples from the ridge line north of here. The rock might be volcanic in origin, which would be unusual for this area."

After he left, Jack shook his head and asked the air, "How can he be so good at his job — "

" — And be such a dink?" Amelia finished for him. She smiled with regret. "I don't think the two are related, Jack. Look at my ex-husband. I just wish that we could stop him and the others from killing those things. They're essentially harmless. I know they're a nuisance, getting into the supplies, but we're here to establish a presence on a new world. It's a fresh start — again — for mankind, and the first party here begins by shooting the wildlife. I wish they hadn't sent the pistols."

"It's a sad commentary, that's for sure. I only wish I had some authority to stop it. I just cringe every time I hear one of those laser pistols go off. It's regulation for a new colony to have some sort of protection, but I agree we'd be better off without them. People get bored too easily, and they're looking for recreation, I guess. Sport."

"Sure," Amelia said bitterly. "Give the animals lasers and *then* it will be sport. I'd even pay to watch."

Rather than let it waste, they retrieved the carcass from the trash, and after lunch Amelia helped Jack do a dissection. He hadn't done much work on the ferrets. But first, he covered Eddie's pen. "The thing *looks* like it understands, and I feel a little funny with it watching this," Jack replied to Amelia's unspoken question.

The animal was dark brown on the back and light tan on the belly, and covered all over with a thin layer of tightly-wound curly fur. The forearms had suckers up the inside, and the paws featured heavy retractable claws. The paws, or hands, were very flexible and, although lacking genuinely opposable thumbs, Jack was sure they would work very well for holding things.

"What's *that*?" she asked, pointing to the base of the skull. The thin bone bulged dorsally to where the cerebellum would have been in a terrestrial animal.

"Let's find out." Jack carefully used a microtome to remove the thin layer of skull, exposing the organ within. The tissue was certainly neural in origin, and heavily convoluted, with a darker colour than human grey matter. There was a definite ruddy hue. Jack poked at it with a blunt probe, and found it to be hard, almost muscular. It gave an impression of strength. "I'm not sure," he said at last. "It's neural tissue, but it doesn't correspond to anything I've seen in Terran animals. What it's for is anybody's guess. We've already mapped brain structures for most of the indigenous animals, but there's so much we don't know."

"Including what this does, right?"

Jack smiled. "Right, but I wouldn't take it too hard. Even in our own brains, there are huge areas whose function is unknown."

"Well, let's at least take a look at it." Amelia took a sample and stained a slide, slipped it into the digital microscope. She fussed with the controls. "Look at this."

Jack walked over and peered at the small screen. "This is why I hated histology. I couldn't spend all day staring at one of these screens. It's neural tissue, right?"

"You know very well that it's neural tissue," Amelia said. "But look at the synapses." She fiddled with the depth control, and waited for a response. Not getting one, she sighed. "Oh, come on! These neurons look like Terran tissue, but they're interconnected like no Terran animal's, even human."

"Which means . . . they're smarter?"

"Beats me what all those dendrites are for. Eddie doesn't seem any more brilliant than a cat, but I just can't say."

"Is there some way we can find out? Hook up an EEG or something?"

Jack wondered. "I mean, it won't tell us what the neural bundle does — "
" — but it might tell us something." Amelia nodded. "It's worth a try."
She uncovered Eddie's cage gently. "You're not going to like this, little
pal." Eddie watched her carefully as she bent and opened the pen door,
and barely flinched as she injected a tranquillizer dose under the wool of its
back. It simply sat and stared at her for what seemed an eternity, until
slowly it collapsed. Finally it lay still, breathing shallowly.

Jack helped hold Eddie's head still while Amelia quickly shaved several spots.

"It's reassuring," she said.

"What is?"

"That the tranquillizer worked so well. We know the native body
chemistry is similar to our own, but there are differences. I could have
killed him. There."

She took a drop of histoacryl tissue cement and affixed seven tiny
electrodes to the skin of Eddie's head. Three were over the protrusion
housing the mystery tissue. There were no wires, as the units contained
tiny transmitters. Being barely two millimetres across, Jack hoped that
Eddie wouldn't scratch them off before they got any useful data.

It took Amelia about fifteen minutes to calibrate the equipment, and by
then Eddie was stirring. After a few desultory swipes at the electrodes, it
seemed to settle down and ignore them.

The next day, Bryce Matthews took a look at what they were doing
and pronounced it, "A damn waste of time." He dumped a load of core
samples on his bench, picked up his camera and left again. "Be back
tomorrow," was all the conversation they could get out of him.

"Mister personality, as usual," Amelia commented after he left.

"He doesn't do much to encourage anyone," Jack agreed. "Have we
got enough on Eddie for a baseline yet?" he asked.

"Oh, lots. Let's see what it looks like." Amelia called up the past day's
data. "It's pretty constant. "There's a fair amount of activity here — " She
pointed to the screen " — and here. I assume the frontal areas are mainly
sensory, but that's a guess. And our mystery area . . . there's almost no
activity at all." She turned to Jack, frowning. "Why would that be? That's

a big area of dense grey tissue. There must be some evolutionary purpose for it."

All sorts of strange ideas flitted through Jack's mind, but none of them made much sense. "I have no idea. Maybe we'll find out more today." Yet he had a feeling that it wouldn't be quiteas simple as holding a steak in front of the animal. He was right.

They tried exposing Eddie to all sorts of stimuli — foods, odours, sounds. They learned little.

"It's like I figured." Amelia ran a hand through her curls at the end of the day "Lots of action in the frontal and temporal areas, although his brain isn't lobulated the same as ours. Those areas must be the sensory ones. But *nothing* in the extra lobe. None of the stimuli seem to cause activity there."

"And it's not associated with movement, autonomic function, vocalization. It's a real mystery. I'm not sure what to try — "

The door slammed open, and Bryce Matthews stumbled in. "Where's Amelia? I need — " he demanded, then stopped as he saw her. Jack froze, staring at the geologist. His right pant leg was torn in several places, and he was favouring that leg. But worse was his left arm. Dried blood was visible on his hand, and on the tatters of his jacket sleeve, but spots of brighter red were in evidence as well.

Matthews teetered slightly to one side, and Jack's paralysis left — he jumped forward to ease the geologist onto a stool. "What the hell happened, Bryce? Did you fall into a ravine?"

Then Amelia pushed him out of the way, and began cutting the fabric of Matthew's jacket away from the dirt-caked blood on his arm. "Get me some sterile saline and cotton, Jack," she said briskly. "And get out of the light."

She cleaned the wounds expertly, and clucked under her breath as several of them kept bleeding despite the pressure she applied. "I'm afraid you're going to need a few stitches to close these two, Bryce."

"That's all right, Amelia. Do what you have to. It's my own damn fault for not watching where I was going."

She stopped and looked at him strangely for a moment. "You *fell*? Is that how you injured yourself?"

"Yeah. What of it?"

Amelia bent to the work. "Nothing. Just hold still for a minute."

After she finished cleaning Matthews up, Amelia sent him back to his shelter with a pocket full of analgesics and orders to stay off the leg for a couple of days. Jack shook his head after he left.

"How the hell did he get himself messed up like that? He must have tumbled down a scree slope or something. Damn! He should have been more careful! If he'd hit his head he could have died out there by himself."

Amelia frowned. "Some of Bryce's wounds could have been caused by a fall. In fact, I'm certain he did fall. Many of them could easily have been caused by claws, though, and some were definitely bite marks."

"Bite marks!"

"Yes, but the main question I have is: Why did he lie about it?"

Jack thought Amelia's question a good one, so good, in fact, that he spent much of that evening pondering precisely that. Why would Matthews not tell him about an attack by one of the local animals? It would seem only to reinforce his arguments in favour of hunting. Was he embarrassed at being injured? Of needing their help, since he obviously wasn't fond of either Amelia or Jack?

After several hours worrying the problem, Jack dozed off into a fitful sleep, where the supply ship was late, and humans stalked about the compound, taking each other out with laser fire for their food rations.

By morning, Jack had decided to confront Matthews about his falsehood, but he was too late. After his restless night, he overslept, and by the time he reached the lab, Amelia told him that Matthews was gone.

"I saw him and one of his buddies take off a good hour ago, headed north," she said. "They each had a handgun, too."

Jack was confused. "What the hell are they up too?"

"Well, I expect they're going after whatever attacked Bryce yesterday," Amelia said.

"Revenge?" It had always seemed a poor sort of motivation to Jack.

She nodded. "And I've got a better idea of what it was." Parless had precious few large predators, and fewer still inhabited the area around the settlement. Jack figured he'd be a laughing stock if he'd missed anything big.

Then something else caught his attention. "What's that?" He indicated a second cage on the workbench.

"Charlie. It's a 'ferret' I found in *my* shelter this morning, except I managed to catch it, not kill it."

"You too? That's almost too much coincidence. Where'd it chew through?"

"That's the funny part. It didn't. At least I couldn't find a hole. The only thing I can think of is that it must have sneaked in when I came in last night."

"And you didn't notice it running around all night? Come on!"

"But it wasn't! When I woke up this morning, the darn thing was just sitting on my chair, watching me. It didn't even run away when I went to pick it up."

Jack inclined his head toward the cage. "We already have a pet."

"I may keep it for a few days just to study its behaviour a bit, since it's not complaining. Actually, he and Eddie, here, spent most of the past hour just staring at each other. Gives me the creeps."

"They do seem to be watching us, don't they?" With an effort, Jack pulled himself away from the impassive azure gaze. "But what the hell are we going to do about Matthews?"

"I think I can shed some light on that, although what you're going to do about it, I have no idea. I took some pictures of his wounds yesterday — standard procedure — and guess what?"

Jack waited.

"The bite marks correspond to our little friends over there," she finished, pointing to the cages where the ferrets sat staring at them.

"Oh, come on," Jack protested. "They have some nasty teeth, sure, but one of those couldn't do much damage. They're just not large enough."

"What if there were several of them? What if there were, say, a dozen? Couldn't they inflict the sort of wounds we saw on Bryce yesterday?"

Jack considered. "Maybe . . . maybe. But why would they act in concert? They've never exhibited pack behaviour. They're solitary hunters."

"Or, at least they were, until their population went up by ten times. But if you want to see something really interesting, look at Eddie's EEG plot since I brought in his friend there." Amelia ran back the record to seven that morning, restarted the counter. "Look. That's where I brought

Charlie in." The sensory areas were going like crazy. "Now I'll fast
forward a bit. "Here! They sat staring at one another for about fifteen
minutes, then I got this."

"No kidding." There was definite activity in the mysterious lobe. It
wasn't much at first, but it gradually built, then levelled off higher than it
had started.

"What does this mean, Jack? Any idea at all?"

"I'm starting to get one, but it's pretty bizarre. First I'd like to get one
or two more in here and see what the EEG does."

"Maybe we can get Bryce to help collect a few, if it's that important,"
Amelia suggested.

Jack slapped the countertop. "Matthews! I forgot! I think we'd
better try to catch up with Bryce and his friend, if nothing else, to keep
them from massacring half the local population. Or possibly save their lives."

The trail was not easy to follow. In areas the rain had obliterated the
tracks completely, and all they really had to go on was Matthews' statement
that he was heading north. The laser pistol felt strange at Jack's hip, but he
had to admit it conferred a certain comfort. They were in the hills north of
the compound, a region of previously dry ravines and gullies, now home to
many healthy rushing streams.

As they waded one such stream, Jack came up short. "What the hell
is *that*?" he demanded. On the crest of one of the hills was a black tower,
about three meters in height. He pulled himself up the slick side of the hill
with a glance back to see that Amelia was following. Normal activities
were fine in the lower oxygen partial pressure, but strenuous action was
difficult.

At last they stood beside the construction, for that it obviously was.
Tracks surrounded and covered the deep black mud, evidently hauled up
from the stream bed below. It had been a huge effort, and for what?
Rocks and bits of debris could be seen imbedded in the hardened mud.

"Well, termites at home build huge mounds to live in," Amelia suggested
doubtfully. "Actually, there are other hive organisms that build large nests
on other worlds, as well."

Jack was starting to get a weird feeling he didn't like at all. "Look at this." There were stairs, or at least claw-holds, leading up the one side. "It certainly doesn't look inhabited; it's just a solid tower."

"Maybe there's an entrance at the top?" Amelia suggested.

"Well, I can't see up there, and there's no way for us to climb it without destroying it."

"Just give me a boost up on your shoulders and I'll have a look," Amelia suggested.

That sounded reasonable. Jack bent down so she could sit on his shoulders to look at the top of the mound. "No, there's no entrance. It's just a platform. Hey, the view's pretty good from here! If I look between those two hill crests . . . "

"What? What can you see?"

"Our camp."

"It's not possible!" Amelia insisted. "These are just animals."

"I agree that there's never been any sign of intelligence." And yet . . . If this structure was not a den, then what evolutionary purpose could there be to it?

"Could they be hive animals of some sort? Bees and ants on Earth work in concert, but that doesn't necessarily imply intelligence. Just very deeply-rooted instincts."

Jack considered. "Possible . . . possible. That's certainly easier to swallow than these things having intelligence after all the time we've spent here without any evidence of it. But, that tower — why would they spend the effort to build it, right where they could see us? Especially here, where we wouldn't spot it from camp. And from ground level here they couldn't see the camp — "

"So, how did they work out where to build it?" Amelia finished. "Good question. What was that?"

From the hill behind them, Jack heard a scrambling sound, and whirled in time to see the back end of a ferret disappear around the curve of the hill. He raced up the slope, but it was gone. Behind him, Amelia called, "Let's get moving, Jack. This is getting creepy."

"Yes," Jack said as he slid back down the slope. "I think we'd better locate Matthews and get back to camp to discuss things."

It took nearly another hour to locate Matthew's trail, and half an hour to catch up to them. Jack and Amelia crested a rise and saw, perhaps seventy meters ahead, Matthews and his friend heading into a hollow. Just ahead of them, Jack could make out two ferrets, running back and forth, but heading up into the recess. Matthew's laser flared, but apparently missed.

"Matthews! Wait!" Jack yelled. He thought that Matthews paused, but whether he'd heard the yell or not, Jack couldn't say for sure. Amelia started to run, and Jack strained to catch up with her. Ahead, the two ferrets had disappeared into a crevice, and Matthews and his friend set up a barrage of laser fire. Suddenly the slopes to either side of them were alive with moving bodies. Easily a hundred ferrets appeared from whatever cubbyholes they had occupied, and leapt on the two men from above. Matthews screamed as he flung one from his arm, and scorched the ground with laser fire. His friend tried to back down the slope, but his foot hit a rock and he fell awkwardly. Instantly a dozen or so of the animals were on him, tearing at him with claws and teeth. He managed to roll over onto his hands and knees, but Jack could see blood on the ground beneath him.

Nearby, Matthews was backed against a small cliff face, and had managed to keep a clear area in front of himself littered with ferret bodies. He didn't see that several had climbed up above him and were about to drop on him.

By now, they were close enough to get involved. Amelia headed straight for Thompson, the man on the ground, but couldn't really fire well on the attacking animals without hitting the man. Jack fired a shot above Matthews' head to warn him of the danger there, and went to help her. Thompson had collapsed by this point, and between them, panting in the reduced oxygen, Jack and Amelia kicked and pushed most of the creatures off him. He was still alive, but very badly injured. As soon as he was clear, Jack lay down fire while Amelia began sliding the man down the slope.

Looking at Matthews, Jack saw that he had his hands full. He had a ferret on his right arm. The creature bit his wrist, and the laser pistol fell to the ground. Jack bent close to Amelia.

"Help Matthews," he said, hoisting the unconscious man into a fireman's carry. Amelia turned and fired, shooting the creature right off Matthew's arm.

"Jesus Christ!" Matthews screamed.

"Hold still, or I might hit you," Amelia yelled back. She quickly picked off two more, then Matthews was able to retrieve his pistol. The worst was over, and when their position became obviously impossible, the ferrets pulled back, leaving several dozen bodies behind them.

The humans headed back towards the camp, Jack carrying Thompson, Matthews leaning heavily on Amelia. As they left the hills, Jack looked back for a moment and saw four or five of the animals watching them from the crest of a mound. With difficulty, he fought off the urge to fire wildly at them, but his back crawled as he turned away.

"How could they act like that?" Amelia demanded. "It's not like they can survive on human tissue. The differences in our amino acids would slowly kill them. There's no evolutionary benefit to eating food that has no nutrition in it."

"Like you don't eat chocolate?" Jack chided gently.

"At least my body can metabolize the sugars and fats in it!" She shot back. "I'm sorry. I guess I'm still coming down off the adrenalin."

"They're pack animals, like wolves!" Matthews insisted from his perch on the edge of the exam table. His pal Thompson would require surgery, but he'd have to spend a day or so in the autodoc to stabilize first. "They just enjoy killing."

Jack shook his head. He could understand Matthews' attitude. "I don't think they're pack animals, Bryce. They never were before now, and why would they suddenly start acting that way? Besides, those two ferrets *enticed* you into a trap. They risked their lives so that the rest of the group would have a chance to finish you off. And I think they would have."

"Bullshit," Matthews griped. "We'd have gotten out of there."

"Right. With Thompson down and you without your gun. I think you should be glad we came looking for you. Their claws are sharp, and their teeth are long, but they're potentially much more dangerous than that. I think they're intelligent."

"What?"

Amelia explained about the construction they had found while searching in the hills. "But," she concluded, "I didn't think that was definite proof of intelligence."

"It would explain one thing," Matthews conceded. "Wait here a minute." He limped painfully out of the infirmary and was gone for a few minutes. When he returned, he had several photographs in his hand. "Here."

Glancing at Amelia, Jack looked at the five photos, then passed them to her. The pictures showed several weathered mounds of baked mud and stones. "Where did you take these?" he finally asked, when Amelia didn't say anything.

"In the hills, on my survey trips. But they were *old*!" he insisted, looking at the floor. "I didn't think . . . "

"You sure didn't," Amelia said. "Just when were you going to share the fact that you had found *ruins* on this supposedly uninhabited planet?"

"When I'd publish," he said miserably. "I didn't think there was any rush. There obviously wasn't anything intelligent here now."

"And you wanted the credit," Jack concluded, shaking his head to clear it. "Meanwhile, for sport, you were shooting the very creatures in question. Nice work."

"I had no idea! The damn things were a nuisance, nothing more. They were getting into the supplies, the huts. We didn't know."

"Perhaps they were just curious about us," Amelia suggested. "That is, if you're right. They might just have been trying to find out about us, like Charlie over there." She indicated the creature in its cage, where it sat, watching the discussion. Jack looked at it. It did look awfully curious. Then, as he watched, Charlie and Eddie became increasingly agitated. They started by pacing about their cages, but soon began to gnaw on the wire.

"I don't understand," Amelia said, frowning. "The only reason I kept them this long was that they didn't seem to mind the cage much. If they act like this, I should let the poor things go." As she spoke, Amelia walked over towards Eddie in its pen. Unlike other times, Eddie backed away, snarling, and crouched in the far back corner. Then, like lightening, it leapt forward and tried to get at Amelia through the wire. She made a startled sound and jumped back. "What the — "

"I'd blast the damn thing right now, if it wasn't in a cage," Matthews said bitterly. "It's acting just like its buddies that attacked us."

"I'm glad that you draw the line at shooting caged animals," Jack put in dryly. "But, if you're done, I have a theory to put forward. I suggest that the ferrets are in communication telepathically. Perhaps there's even some sort of group mind at work."

"But why didn't we see any evidence before?" Amelia asked.

"Why did we think Parless would be dry?" Jack returned. "I think the two may be related. Perhaps the climatic cycles cause changes in the animal populations, which pass some threshold level allowing a group mind to form."

"That extra neural tissue we found!"

Jack nodded. "I think that's the organ responsible for the telepathic ability."

"And the ruins I found — "

"Are remains of ferret constructions from previous cycles."

"But," Amelia interjected, "the ferrets around here have been tranquil, while the ones in the north hills are vicious. If they're telepathic, shouldn't they all be acting the same?"

"Not necessarily. They couldn't be in contact over the entire continent. That wouldn't work. The effective distance would be limited to allow individual populations to react to local conditions. Maybe there is no group mind, maybe it's just a bunch of linked individuals in local populations. The local denizens would have no idea that you and your friends have been slaughtering another population. That doesn't much affect our current situation."

"No, it doesn't," Matthews said grimly. "If you're right, your pet over there is telling us something important. If it's now getting information from the north hill population, and it hasn't moved . . . "

Amelia started. "That's right! The north hill group must be getting closer! They're going to attack the camp."

"It's entirely possible," Jack agreed. "And all the local animals are likely to join them, judging by Eddie's behavior."

Matthews got unsteadily to his feet. "I'd better get people together, start assembling our arms — "

Jack placed a hand in the centre of his chest. " — which are woefully inadequate! We nearly drained four lasers this afternoon, and there are, what, a dozen more? In a concerted attack, there'd be no time to recharge them, and we'd be overwhelmed in a pretty short time."

"Then what the hell are we supposed to do?" he demanded. "Wait to get slaughtered?"

"No. We've got a few hours, maybe more. They'll be mustering their local recruits and getting organized. But we're overlooking the obvious. They're intelligent! Surely we can figure some way to communicate with them, reduce their anger."

Amelia smiled grimly. "I know. We could put Matthews and Thompson on pikes out front of the camp."

Matthews looked shocked, like he wasn't sure she was kidding. Jack nodded. "Maybe as a last resort, Amelia. And Bryce, you'd better go ahead and muster the troops. I'm not sure we can convince these things our intentions are honourable. I'm not sure I can convince myself."

Four hours later, Matthews' sentries started reporting that groups of five to ten ferrets were drifting down from the surrounding hills. Jack, Amelia, Matthews and a couple other senior members of the team were discussing options, while trying to keep everyone else as calm as possible. Thompson's grave condition was common knowledge in the camp, and total panic was a very real possibility. As Amelia noted: "We're a hell of a long way from any reinforcements."

"All the more reason for us to find a solution of our own," Jack pointed out.

"But what?" Matthews demanded, getting to his feet and pacing around the dining hall. "We've been at this for hours, and all we do is go around and around. You won't allow any preemptive action — "

"Preemptive action against *thousands* of these creatures?" Amelia demanded. "What do you suggest? A tactical nuke?"

Matthews glared at her for a moment, then resumed his tirade. "You won't allow any preemptive action," he continued pointedly. "Now, when they're not organized yet, when their strength is spread out — "

"We have no idea what their strength is, Bryce," Jack put in. "These creatures are in communication *telepathically.* They may be a group mind of some sort. Believe me, they're organized. And we'd better figure out some better approach other than draining our thirteen charged lasers and waiting to be torn apart. That's not how I had imagined my death."

Matthews sat back down, eyes smouldering. "What about rigging some sort of electric fence?" he asked.

"Those aren't Triffids out there, Bryce," Amelia replied. "They're intelligent. I doubt if a barricade would work for very long."

Jack got up to pour some coffee for everyone. "A decent suggestion, but we don't have that much fencing in stores, and besides, our solar cells don't collect enough power through these damned clouds to power something like that. We can barely heat our powdered eggs in the morning."

The door banged open, and a young female face peered in, panting. Her clothes were covered in mud, and Jack knew that she'd taken a spill on the way here. She was one of the sentries Matthews had stationed. "Mr. Matthews! All of you! You'd better come quick."

Amelia reached the edge of camp first, followed closely by Matthews and Jack. "Good God," she breathed.

"God has nothing to do with this," Matthews whispered, awed. The low hills around the camp appeared to be moving. The rain had let up for once, and Jack could see that the hills were covered in ferrets, still coming in from all directions. He could not begin to estimate their numbers. "What are there . . . four, five thousand?" He whispered to Amelia, afraid to speak too loudly.

"Ten, maybe," she said. What were forty humans, with thirteen laser pistols, going to do against this flood? A remote camera atop the mess hut was recording all this for posterity. Maybe they'll learn something from all our deaths, Jack thought, then shook his head. Defeatist thinking. Never did any good.

"Bryce — " he began, but Matthews was not there. "Where the hell'd he go?" he asked Amelia, but she was just staring at the teeming mass in front of them and didn't respond. He turned to one of the others. "Round everyone up and bring them out. For better or worse, things are going to be decided right here, so there's no point in hiding. And keep those lasers out of sight," he added.

The mass of fur surrounding the camp seemed to be coming to some sort of rest, although small groups of ferrets were still drifting in. They appeared to be loosely arranged into groups of a few hundred, although what the purpose of the arrangement was, Jack couldn't begin to guess. Were they family groups, different social strata, or merely random? A particularly dense grouping faced Jack and the other humans from twenty meters away. Were these the leaders, or perhaps just a denser cluster of individuals allowing for a stronger focus of the group mind? Jack thought the latter, but still needed somewhere to direct his attention.

He took a step forward, mostly to see what would happen. The dense group clustered even tighter together, but showed no inclination to retreat. In fact, groups to either side began to press in towards the humans until he stopped. An uneasy calm returned, broken only by the sound of one of the humans sobbing. The sound was quickly cut off.

Jack spread his hands wide, in what he hoped was a universal symbol of peace, or at least harmlessness. They knew what the laser pistols looked like, and they could at least see that he wasn't carrying one. Then he slowly let his arms drop and stood, confused for the moment, unable to concentrate. In the distance he heard Amelia asking if he was all right, but it didn't register.

For the last few minutes, Jack had felt like a migraine was coming on, with visual blurring and ringing in his ears. He seemed to hear voices distantly in his head, like an audience murmuring between acts — nothing coherent. Now it was becoming more focused, nearly understandable. In part of his mind, Jack realized that the ferrets were trying to communicate with him, and wondered at the incredible possibility of two entirely different species being able to connect on this level. But the pain was crippling, made it impossible to think coherently.

From a background of murmurs and ringing, something recognizable began to form. *Killers,* it said. *Strangers.* Or was it simply "Strange?" Jack tried to think, but couldn't. The pain increased, accompanied by a buzzing noise and a shower of phosphenes across his sight. Part of his mind wondered if this was doing permanent damage.

Then it was gone.

Jack crashed to his knees in the mud, his mind reeling. They were going to kill all the humans. No, not yet. But they broke off contact. Amelia was helping him to his feet, an arm around his waist. "Jack? Jack! Are you all right?" she demanded. "You're white as a ghost. Are you having a stroke?"

He managed to shake his head numbly. "N — n — no," he finally said, to Amelia's obvious relief. He wished he could feel that same relief. The intelligence was there, but it was so strange, so different. How could he possibly relate to them?

"They wait so long," he whispered.

"What?"

"So long. The rains come so far apart, and they can't remember . . . Why did they stop?" he suddenly asked. The pain was fading somewhat, and thinking was easier. No permanent damage, then? He still felt like a rag doll. "What's happening?" he asked.

Amelia looked at him with concern. "Nothing's changed — " she began. Then she was running. "Bryce! What the hell do you think you're doing?" she yelled.

Matthews had reappeared, and Jack saw immediately why the ferrets had broken off communication. Two of Matthew's friends struggled with Eddie's large pen between them, while Matthews himself carried the second ferret's small cage and his laser pistol. Three more held Amelia back.

Jack tried to make himself heard over the clamour, but he was still too weak. "Matthews," he croaked. "What are you up to? I was just . . ." He trailed off. Speech was beyond him. His head swam, and he tried to keep focused, understand what he was seeing. The ferrets were charged — he could still feel it. There was still some residual contact, although it was very weak.

Matthews called over to him. "Jack! You said it yourself. We've got no chance. A few lasers against thousands of these things. But maybe we can bluff our way out of this. They can't know how poorly armed we are, and if we show we're not going to back down — "

"You'll just start a war!" Amelia shouted, struggling against the arms that held her.

Matthews ignored her and placed the cage on the ground. He backed away and muttered, "We'll just see." He raised his laser and shot the helpless ferret dead where it sat. The surrounding mass froze. They could feel the ferret die, Jack realized. Then he got a sense of their anger building, and forced himself into motion. Matthews was training his pistol on the pen containing Eddie when Jack reached him. They weren't expecting him, and Jack had surprise, if not strength, on his side. He was able to knock Matthews' arm aside, and the shot went wide. Several others came to help, then, and grabbed Matthews from behind. As his support evaporated, Amelia came up and pulled the laser from Matthews' hand. She handed it to Jack, and said, "Please shoot him."

Jack shook his head. He could still feel the anger. The ferrets were right on the edge, and he had to act fast. He nodded at the pen. "Set Eddie loose." Amelia went over and knelt on one knee. "I'm sorry, Eddie," she whispered. The ferret scurried out and disappeared into the massed creatures.

Jack turned and shoved the pistol under Matthews's chin. "Now," he said. "You get in."

"What the hell?"

"You heard me. Get in the cage, Bryce, or so help me, I'll shoot you."

Matthews' eyes went wide. "You're crazy! You're all nuts! These things are going to massacre us all!"

"Then you should be safer in there," Jack said. He shoved Matthews at the pen, and mercifully, with a glare, he bent down and crawled in. Amelia latched the door.

Jack tossed the laser on the ground and waited. Still he was unprepared for the pain when it came. But this time it faded somewhat, and he found he was still able to think, although his head felt full of cotton wool. What would they do?

We. Contact. The voice sang in his head. He knew that they couldn't be speaking any human language. Could it be that concepts of intelligence are universal? Language is irrelevant with mind-to-mind contact. Jack tried to form clear thoughts, to reach out to the alien intelligence surrounding him. "Yes. We have contact," he thought, and said out loud.

This time the response was more immediate, and focused, as if they were learning. *It. Stays confined?*

Jack smiled faintly at the impersonal. "Yes, *it* stays confined. Until we can get it off this world. I cannot kill it," he added.

There was a pause. *We would not have it killed. If removed,* came the voice.

"We can make peace," Jack said.

Can make more, the voice came. *Much more. We. Can make memories.* And into Jack's awed mind came a vision of human and ferret minds linked, allowing the ferrets to keep their memories, to maintain their intelligence through the endless decades between the periods of rain, allowing them to grow, to build.

Suddenly the rain came again, driving into the compound with a fury so great that Jack could barely see the ferrets. Amelia looked up in frustration and cried, "This damn rain! It's so depressing!"

No, came the voice, and Jack was sure that Amelia and the others could hear this time. *Rain is life.*

THE REEF

by
Ray Deonandan

Ray Deonandan, of London, Ontario, is an accomplished short story writer. He is the winner of the 1995 Canadian Author's Association National Short Story Contest, and has seen his stories published in a variety of media from the *Canadian Author* (London, Ontario) to the *Phlogiston* (Wellington, New Zealand), *Printed Matter* (Tokyo, Japan) and *The World of English* (Beijing, China).

THE REEF

by
Ray Deonandan

The water seemed to glisten that evening. There was less foam on the surface, and fewer bubbles rising from the recesses of the dark coral. But it was more than that. The starlight seemed to filter all the way down to the seabed from the heavens, spicing the brine water and lending it a sparkling sweet taste.

Milanario treaded quietly a few metres below the surface, moving just enough to keep warm. Somewhere, not too far off, her little sister Thecantra was searching for gilabeek eggs.

It was a good night for finding gilabeek eggs. The little blue and white fish preferred moonless nights like this one for depositing their delicious eggs in the nooks and crannies of the coral reef. But, contrary to her original plans, Milanario didn't feel quite like hunting down the precious stashes.

Her spine tingled as tiny water currents caressed the webbing between her toes, and the periodic warm water from the coral bed rose to wash over her shivering slick torso.

What was it about this night? It was the shortest night of the year, the astronomers had said, with a rare conformation in which none of the three major moons were visible. But that would have nothing to do with the water, except for the tides. And the reef felt so wonderfully static for a dynamic community!

A jet of cold current on her left side announced the return of Thecantra. The little one paddled up alongside her older sister, a cluster of sticky pink eggs clutched in one hand.

"Want one?" She signalled with her free hand.

"No thank you, Thecantra. You can have them all." Milanario signalled back, quite lethargically.

Thecantra's brow furrowed, and her semi-formed face looked profoundly confused. "But you always eat gilabeek eggs!"

"Not this time. I'm not hungry."

Thecantra shrugged and popped a pink ovule into her salivating mouth. Milanario raised an index finger and jabbed it up in the signal for "surface". Thecantra nodded and followed her up and into the night air.

Breaking the calm of the surface, Milanario took several deep breaths, replenishing her lungs and returning the colour of her skin to normal. Once, as a child, she had forgotten to refill her lungs and had turned a bright blue. Mother had had to drag her to the surface before she succumbed to hypoxia. As a result, she kept a close watch over Thecantra's hue, yet consciously fighting the maternal instincts growing within her.

As they lingered on the surface, Milanario took great efforts to disturb the surface tension as little as possible, becoming mildly distressed when Thecantra decided to paddle about flurriously. There was an almost anaesthetic quality to the water's stillness, and Thecantra's movements were certainly out of place within the unmoving portrait of aquatic placidity.

"Milanario," Thecantra said. "Why is this called John Addam's World?"

"Because John Addams discovered it, stupid."

"Who was here before him?"

"Nobody. Just the coral reef and a few of the octopi. You'll learn about all that in school."

"Where did the gilabeek fish come from?"

"I said you'll learn about that in school!"

Thecantra pouted and looked away. Never had Milanario ever encountered a child so eager to go to school. The little pest would spend the rest of her childhood trying to think up ways to avoid it, though!

"The first colonists brought the gilabeek and the other fish from Urth fifteen thousand years ago."

"Oh." She seemed happy again. A small price to pay, Milanario thought, to keep the runt manageable.

The moonless sky was soul-chilling. A million billion distant suns beat down on them, but only flickers were perceptible: a million billion tiny fires burning in the sky. And, where the sky met the sea on a liquid horizon, only a subtle difference between the two was perceptible.

Strangely, the water surface remained motionless except for the occasional fish that would leap skyward for either a gasp of air or a mouthful of bugs and, of course, for Thecantra's endless paddling about.

The shore was almost invisible, too, which was surprising since it was only about half a kilometre away. If it were not for the tall frawn trees blocking out the star field here and there, the land would have been undetectable.

Milanario found comfort in the semi-blackness. The odd juxtaposition of cool air with the illusion of warmth soaked in from the salty water, and the caress of gentle eddies against her relaxed body, were mere unconscious niceties. But the darkness of the night, tempered by thesubtle glow of the distant horizon, and the slight white noise of shifting waters and a billowing breeze were a sensory throwback to long-buried memories of the womb.

She was once more a babe afloat in a bag of sweet prenatal fluids.

"Milanario?"

"Yes? What is it now?"

"How come everything's so weird?"

She felt it, too! So it wasn't imagination after all. It wasn't what mother would have called the "romantic meanderings of adolescent minds", triggered by unusual astronomical conformations and plentiful gilabeek eggs. It was a real, tangible difference in the environment!

"How so, Thecantra?" She strained to conceal her excitement. Her sister would deliver a more truthful response this way.

"You know what I mean! There're no moons, but it's still bright. And the water's colder in some parts, and hot in others. And the whole place seems kind of quiet. And the gilabeek eggs are kind of sour. And the coral bed is making weird sounds . . . "

"What?!"

"Yup! Right about where I found the eggs, the reef was kind of groaning!"

"Show me!"

Without responding, Thecantra pulled her knees to her chest, tipped her head downward, and pushed off for the seabed once again. Milanario followed with gentle kicks from her webbed feet.

As they descended, their blurred blue field of vision was gradually replaced by the craggy outline of the majestic coral reef, the largest indigenous community on John Addam's World. Entire schools of multicoloured fish seemed to oscillate with a singleness of mind no poet could adequately describe, nor any scientist explain.

Milanario's experienced eye detected snatches of darting bright orange and red flesh: the rare appearances of juranui and parrot fish whose dazzling colouration betrayed the poison in their bloodstreams — or rather the emulation of truly poisonous creatures, for the original colonists had taken great pains to avoid importing dangerous fauna. The colonists had been, however, only partly successful, as some predacious creatures lingered still further out in the ocean.

The sisters' bodies arced softly in a pleasing trajectory, gently skimming over the coral heads with a precision of control challenged only by the permanent coral residents. As Thecantra's hand began to dip down to touch a coral head, Milanario snatched it up with her own.

"Don't touch the tentacles!" She signalled to her baby sister.

"Why not?"

"The soft ones exude a lytic poison which would dissolve your flesh!" Her choice of exotic words impressed upon her sister the import of her warning. Thecantra seemed to turn pale, but in the water it was difficult to tell. Milanario was exaggerating, of course, as one must do when cautioning Thecantra. But the lytic poison certainly would have stung, and Milanario would have had to nurse a crying baby back to shore. And that would have been a waste of a truly exceptional evening.

After all, she had worked so hard to escape her evening studies. With the batting of adolescent eyelids, and her insistence on the importance of the evening swim and of the hunt for gilabeek eggs — so much so that one would have thought the end of the world were near — she had coerced Mother to let her and Thecantra go. The latter was always a condition, the burden of being an elder sister, as if Thecantra's presence would somehow deter Milanario from exploring to the full extent of her adventurous heart's desire.

Though loathe to admit it publicly, or indeed consciously, somehow Milanario couldn't imagine truly enjoying an activity without Thecantra. She was addictive, in her own annoying way.

"Here!" Thecantra indicated a patch of coral head no different from the others. There was no doubt of the location, however, for her sense of direction and short term memory were quite good for one of her age.

Milanario lowered her ear to the coral head, careful not to touch the outstretched tendrils.

"I don't hear anything."

"Try harder!"

"Thecantra, there's no sound here. You must have been mistaken." It was rather sad, actually. Milanario had been hoping for some tangible physical manifestation — even something as elusive as a strange sound — to anchor this night of altered perceptions in her memory. She searched desperately for a noise, any noise, but despite herself heard nothing.

Thecantra floated down to place her own ear near the coral head. "It's gone now," she signalled. "It was like moaning. I didn't imagine it!"

"I didn't say that you did . . . "

"But you thought it!"

Milanario treaded silently as her little sister puttered around trying to find the strange sound. It was so peaceful down here, so static. Yet this mystery had lent the environment a welcome tingling sensation, an excitement of sorts. It was such a pleasing experience that Milanario lost track of the time. Thecantra was still a relatively healthy shade of pink, though, so there was no immediate need to return to the surface.

The astronomer named Stonn was always of a bluish hue, even when he was out of the water. When he swam with Mother, she never seemed at ease, as if she were afraid she'd have to rescue Stonn at any moment.

This had always seemed to Milanario to be another of Mother's paranoid excesses. After all, no human had drowned on John Addam's World for as long as Milanario could remember — not unless something had trapped him beneath the surface, or he had been knocked unconscious by a clumsy whale or giant octopus.

Back on Urth, they say, drownings were so common that many people never ever went into the water. However did they avoid shrivelling up beneath the sun's heat?

Stonn had been at their family's domicile just as the sisters were leaving for their swim. He had seemed agitated and excitable — but then he was always excited about something. Perhaps that was why Mother loved him

so. Stonn certainly displayed the appropriate filial qualities to elicit great
affection from Mother.

"Milanario," Thecantra signalled, jolting her sister from her
shallow reverie.

"Yes?"

"Where have all the fish gone?"

Indeed, the oscillating schools were nowhere to be seen. They had
been there a moment ago. Or was it a moment, or an hour? Had they
drifted? But the same coral heads were beneath them, and the coral does
not drift — does it? Milanario was terribly confused.

But she dared not show any sign of fear to her baby sister. Not only
would it impart further fear on the little one, it would also be horribly
embarrassing!

"They've probably found a richer food source elsewhere. This region
has little plankton."

"Over there!" Thecantra pointed in the direction of the waiting ocean.
Sure enough, there were flickers of multicoloured fish and phosphor-
luminescent crustaceans. The schools had, indeed, moved further out.
"Let's go see!"

"Thecantra, wait!" But she was already gone. All Milanario could do,
was tag along behind.

The water was very much darker here. Perhaps they were beneath
an overhang of an uncharted island or peninsula. More probably, there
were clouds in the sky preventing starlight from diffusing down. Milanario's
hand struck something hard, a crustacean of sorts. She glanced over to
discover that she had inadvertently captured a lamp crab whose internal
luminescence would provide her with light.

Holding the crab to her face, she rediscovered the water. The blackness
was perforated with specks of white where the light reflected off floating
particles. It seemed the black ocean of space, with all its twinkling stars,
had been re-created down here in the real ocean. An underwater
astronomer's delight!

But where was Thecantra?

"Thecantra!" She signalled, now somewhat frightened. But, of course,
there was no response as Thecantra could not possibly see her hands in the
blackness. Quite against her natural tendencies, Milanario acted out of

desperation. She released a mouthful of her precious lung air into the water, allowing a loud GALUMP! to accompany its liberation.

Almost instantly, the yellowy-pink cherubic face of her ward appeared in the lamp crab's field of luminosity. Milanario struggled to conceal her internal sigh of relief.

"Plankton!" Thecantra signalled, "Lots of it!"

Milanario frowned. The particles looked like plankton, but they were unlike any plankton she had ever seen before. And the fish were not gobbling it up as quickly as they would devour normal plankton.

Memories of primary school chemistry stirred in the recesses of Milanario's mind, including visions of taste tests and the merits of saliva. She had read that such methods did not exist back on Urth, but was an entirely new science developed on John Addam's World.

Just how different were her distant Urth ancestors? Could they not see the obvious simplicity and accuracy of taste analysis? And was there any truth to the belief that they could only hold their breaths for a few minutes at a time . . .?

In a moment of impetuousness and, perhaps, foolhardiness, she stretched out her neck, opened her mouth, and took in a gulp of the strange plankton.

She swished it about with her tongue experimentally, allowing it to mix completely with her saliva. The strange taste betrayed the substance's alien nature. Violently, Milanario spewed her mouthful back into the ocean, rinsing her mouth out further with the welcome brine water.

It wasn't plankton.

What was it?

Thecantra had watched the entire experiment in horror. But she had been too fascinated and too confident in Milanario to object. She was alert enough, however, to perceive her sister's conclusion: If it wasn't natural plankton, where had it come from?

"Excrement from a passing giant octopus?"

Milanario made a face of disgust in response. "I don't think so, Thecantra. The giant octopi don't come in this close."

Following Milanario's lead, the pair swam further out into the heart of the particle cloud. Its increasing density was an illusion, they discovered, created by the extensiveness of the cloud. It seemed to be of a consistent distribution throughout. Milanario's skin bristled as they penetrated the cloud, and she fought a slight but annoying tingling at the base of her spine. Certain primal responses, it seemed, were stirring within her. But the non-plankton could not be responsible. It just floated along like so much microscopic debris.

The fish did not eat of it, nor did the non-plankton seem to be doing anything, whether inanimately or consciously directed. But the particles did seem to be drifting slowly downward, even though there was not a deposit of them on the ocean floor.

"Milanario?"

"Yes?" She signalled back expectantly, worried that Thecantra had come upon some sort of danger.

"How long has the coral reef been here?" Milanario sighed inwardly. *It's only one of her silly, limitless questions.*

"No one knows. Remember that I said it was here when the original colonists arrived?"

"Has it always been this big?"

Milanario paused. A question she could not answer! "I don't know, Thecantra. I guess I've always assumed that it has always girdled the continent."

"And the other continent?"

"No one lives there. It's much too hot."

"No, but is there coral there, too?"

"I don't know. The astronomers would know, I think. Stonn would probably know."

"Let's go ask him!"

"No." She didn't give a reason. She didn't have to. Thecantra would always obey her, despite her complaining. Besides, the reason, she hoped, was quite obvious: to return to shore now would ruin the night's experience.

Hypnotically, the ever-present reef fish oscillated in unison beneath her. It seemed, no matter what the immediate environment, these lovely little creatures could always be found engaged in their bizarre and ancient dance. How Milanario longed to understand them, to join in their primal cotillion. It was impossible, she felt, to witness the underwater ballet and fail to be strangely drawn to the unexplained community consciousness.

Suddenly Thecantra dipped her nose downward, and paddled furiously. She sped past Milanario, caressing the latter's body with a warm jet stream.

Milanario spun in three dimensions, frantically trying to locate her sister in blackness.

Stillness.

Where could she have gone — and why?

The ocean darkened. Not even the illuminated non-plankton, nor the reef bed below, emanated light. The darkness enclosed about Milanario, pushing her farther from Thecantra, and farther from shore. The warm, comfortable water seemed now to be frigid and dangerous. Where was Thecantra?!

A hand grasped her wrist, and Milanario stiffened.

"Thecantra! Where did you go?"

"Quickly! Follow me!" She signalled back.

"Why . . .?" But Thecantra was pulling her down toward the reef, pushing her face toward the deeper ocean. Then Milanario saw it: a family of sharks, barrelling directly toward them at full tilt.

Milanario froze, but just for a moment. Then she was off at full speed, too, betraying the athletic ability that had lain dormant in her floating body for many hours. Easily, she overtook Thecantra, then dragged the younger one behind her. They would make it to the crags of the reef in time — but then what?

Like a creature of the reef, Milanario arced her body at precisely the right angle, deftly avoiding the searching tendrils while positioning herself and Thecantra inside a coral hole, a living cave.

Despite the fear, the knowledge of impending doom, and the immense rush of adrenaline clouding her mind, Milanario retained enough conscious thought to wonder. What were sharks doing so near the reefs? There were "reef sharks" back on Urth, she had been told, but they had not been brought to John Addam's World. The sharks here had never before dared to venture so close to the poisonous coral heads.

As if on cue, a deathly piscine grin presented itself immediately above them, its pointed teeth resembling the harpoons that the fishermen wielded to kill frightened fish so efficiently.

Thecantra opened her mouth in a silent scream, and a bit of air escaped from her lungs. Though she and her sister were still not blue, Milanario was concerned for their oxygen debt. The sharks could keep them pinned here for hours. But Thecantra could not hold her breath for nearly that long. And Milanario probably would not last much longer, either.

Lacing her fingers tightly around her little sister's upper arm, Milanario kicked lightly away from the prowling shark, being careful to keep a coral head between it and them. The shark did not seem to recognize the toxicity of the waving tendrils — did it not know?

The game continued for what seemed like hours, but was more like minutes. Milanario deftly maintained their position of safety within the reef's comforting embrace, while the predators were locked out. Never before had she felt so much like a denizen of the reef, exercising a solidarity with the other inhabitants who were also hiding from the sharks.

But it was a solidarity in intent alone, for she was wholly unable to improve the lot of the other reef creatures, nor could they offer her any assistance. She could only watch in horror as entire schools of dancing reef fish were gobbled up by the intruders, rudely aware that their watery ballet had ended prematurely.

Meanwhile, Thecantra had discovered something new. The coral was moaning again. Presently, Milanario felt it, too. Even the sharks seemed to pause in their task as the low grumbling shook their bodies. Then, strangest of all, they saw that in unison with the rhythmic rumbling, the coral heads were exuding a powdery substance: the alien non-plankton.

The powdery clouds belched forth from the coral heads, expanding in white spheres of rapidly dissipating consistency. And where they intersected with groups of fish, a brief frenzy would ensue, soon to be replaced by calmness broken only by the threat of the interloping predators.

Milanario, too, could feel a quickening in her blood that coincided with the rumblings of the reef-cave that shielded her. Thecantra did not seem as affected, and Milanario had to wonder if the sensations were nothing more than terror mixed with worry and physical stress.

In moments of extreme danger, it is said, the sentient brain will cogitate on matters of less immediate importance, but of lasting conceptual gravity. And so it was with Milanario who, while sharks struggled ferociously to devour her and her sister, suddenly became aware of the "grand unity of all things." The strange misgivings she had experienced the result of subtle biochemical changes within her body? To what end, and from what stimulus? The quiet of the ocean, the eerie luminescence of the watery beds, and the appearance of sharks this far in, added to the primal thumpings of the ancient coral and its excretion of the non-plankton, summed to complex biological intermingling across several subtle media.

But why? And how was the rare astronomical conformation connected?

Glistening daggers of enamel jutted toward her, as a large male shark attempted to poke his head between coral heads. Again, Milanario and Thecantra screamed underwater, feeling the sound waves pulsate through the reef and expand outward at a high velocity. The quiet of the ocean had been replaced with a deafening orgy of violence.

Milanario kicked harder, pulling Thecantra along a narrowing groove of the reef bed. The coral heads were denser here, and they risked being stung. But the tendrils almost always waved away from the reef, toward potential attackers. Thus the pursuing shark was stung repeatedly, causing him to writhe in considerable pain. He jetted off, unhurt. But he would return when his ego was soothed and his stomach remained unsated. The other members of his pack did not learn by his example, however, and soon were bearing down upon the trapped and weary pair.

The exertion had shortened Milanario's path to oxygen debt, and she was feeling the first twinges of respiratory discomfort. Ordinarily, this would be the ideal time to head for the surface for a replenishing breath of night air. But circumstances prevented this action.

Thecantra, while not as aerobically worked as her older sister, was still distressed. Her normal pink hue was now a neutral pale white. When the first blue specks appeared, irreversible nervous damage would not be far away.

Their time was short.

Milanario's grip on Thecantra's forearm loosened, and her full attention was put into controlling her breathing reflex. She must remain calm, conserve energy and thus oxygen. This was the only way. But it would not be enough, she realized. The sharks would not leave for some time; this was much too promising a feeding ground for them.

She felt consciousness slipping away. Good training and good genes kept her from reflexively breathing in a lung-full of water. But it was only a matter of time. She felt herself being pulled by the currents from her sanctuary in the reef's groove, out into the open water, and lacked the strength to resist.

Her vision had reduced to a long dark tunnel with fuzzy edges and a thumping headache to match. A lifeless doll, she hung in the centre of an expanding sphere of non-plankton, feeling the warmish eddies lap at her sides while the unknown powder seeped into her nostrils and caked somewhat upon her feet's webbing.

There was movement around her, she could tell, but her eyes could not focus on anything except a distant point of radiance that seemed to grow brighter as the expanding bubble pushed her up, forcing her to the surface atop a parabolic waveform.

And where were the dagger-like teeth that were no doubt searching out her young flesh? Had they already devoured half of her, leaving her nervous system unable to detect the loss? There was, after all, no feeling, no perception of any kind except a desperate clutch on consciousness and an eerie blue glow that filled her eyes.

Her lungs could be restrained no longer. Her throat and rib muscles finally recoiled, allowing her chest to collapse, forcing out the expended air, then expanding to be filled . . .

The cantra . . .?!

And cold night air struck her in the face, triggering her breathing reflex further. She gave in and enjoyed the infusion of large breaths of very welcome dry air. Thecantra was beside her, she knew, also breathing well. Neither of them showed any lasting ill effects from oxygen deprivation, only an understandable disorientation and fatigue.

"The sharks," Thecantra said, no longer dependent on their underwater hand language. "Where are they?"

Milanario dropped several metres below the surface to look around. The sharks were there, as were the other reef fish. But they, too, were caught up in the frenzy of the expanding bubbles of non-plankton. The situation was temporary, she reasoned from their own experiences, and surely their attackers would shortly be once more fully in control of their own faculties — and still in search of a meal.

"We have to hurry home, Thecantra." But her sister gazed longingly at her. She clearly lacked the strength to do anything more than tread water.

Milanario cast her gaze once more toward the shore, where the swaying frawn trees still carved out a ghostly silhouette from the starry night sky. But the horizon's bluish glow had lessened somewhat, and a familiar play of lights in the extreme distance told Milanario that one of the moons would soon be rising, followed at length by the eventual sunrise that would bring to an end this remarkable evening.

What exactly had happened?

As she surveyed the shoreline, trying to regain full control over her eyes, washing the tunnel vision and the bluish haze from her memory, two figures emerged onto the panoply.

"Sharks!" Thecantra cried.

"No," Milanario said. "They're people." The figures approached with majestic silent grace, arcing in and out of the water, dolphin-diving with a rhythmic precision that was almost sexual. The night's strange glow reflected off their naked bodies, glinting at times against something metallic carried by one of the figures.

The sisters watched with a shared admiration for a sight so unexpectedly beautiful. If it were not for the difficult melange of fatigue, stress and fear that had assaulted them in recent minutes, the joy of this vision would have been almost palpable.

It was said that on Urth people had learned to fly. Milanario had often wondered at the spectacle of such a thing, and had silently wished that her culture would seek to reclaim the commonplace of that ability, if only for the occasional sight of a human being soaring across the sky's panorama, so obviously revelling in the complexity and wonders of his world.

Yet thus was this hypnotic vision, like a drug-driven mirage that teases the optic nerve and washes the soul with hopes and thoughts that blur the line between body and spirit. So striking was the effect on Milanario, that she had to gasp as it became clear that the lean muscular body of the lead swimmer was of a bluish hue — despite the eerie light that tried to mask its nature. *Stonn!*

"Hello, Milanario. Are you all right?"

"Yes, thank you. Mother, how did you find us?"

"Your screams carried all the way to the village. Stonn triangulated your position."

"There are sharks . . . " Milanario started to say, but Stonn, carrying something, dove beneath the surface.

"It's all right," Mother said. "We brought a pheromonal repellent."

Milanario was bursting to tell her mother all about the strange events of the evening, especially about the amazing non-plankton. But where to start?

"I'm glad we found you," Stonn said, resurfacing. "It is somewhat unsafe to be in the water on this night, although the reef's summoning is hard to resist."

"The what?"

"Have you not noticed the spores floating in the water, Milanario?" Stonn asked.

"Spores?!"

"Indeed. Apparently, every fifteen thousand years or so, signalled by this unusual conformation of the suns and moons, the coral reef reproduces itself. The particles that look like plankton are its spores."

Milanario was overwhelmed. At last, there were answers forthcoming. Yet somehow, the mystery had been more exciting when unexplained. It was as though she had been rudely awakened from a pleasant dream — sharks notwithstanding — dragged unwillingly from an exciting world of strange colours and opiates. She sighed. "You said that the reef summons us," she said.

"Yes. At the time of spawning, it seems, the reef exudes pheromones into the water and air, drawing all its denizens to it, so that all might partake of the fertility fest."

"But we're not indigenous! How can it affect us?"

Her mother smiled and took on a thoughtful expression. "We're all creatures of the reef, now, Milanario, forever intertwined with its interests linked to ours. It offers protection to all its inhabitants, as we must protect it." She paused and whispered the last: "John Addam's World has accepted us."

And somehow that made Milanario strangely happy. She had, it seemed, joined in the dance of the reef fish, meditated on the thoughts of the solitary giant octopi, and partaken of the hospitality of the reef. Indeed, she had come to a conclusion of considerable conceptual gravity.

And Thecantra was fast asleep in her mother's arms, now, her webbed feet paddling away absently, no doubt driven by some pleasant underwater dream.

THE RAPTURE
OF THE MOONFLOWER

by
Giovanni Serafini

Giovanni Serafini is a pseudonym of one
of the contributors to the anthology *North
of Infinity*. All that is known for certain is
that Giovanni is a Canadian and he resides
(at the present time) in Ontario.

THE RAPTURE
OF THE MOONFLOWER

by
Giovanni Serafini

Our worlds poised on the brink of war while under the soft radiance of the *moonrings* the childbride, my love, and I walked together along the ancient cobblestone paths of the Lotus Gardens. The Lady Blossom Lian-Li and I, Count Giovanni Serafini, beheld this wondrous evening alone — as alone as one could be, while others waited on the love of two strangers, and the fate of worlds depended on this cool, starlit night.

My reputation as a lover, in the tradition of the classic Casanovas and Don Juans, earned the Council's trust and my appointment to this mission. But when I laid my eyes upon *her*, my confidence faltered and I felt a trepidation for the immediate future.

An extraordinary example of the breeder's art, she had an exquisite and fragile beauty like fine porcelain. Radiant, she was in a gown of white, gathered at her narrow waist with a large brooch containing a blue moonstone, and cascading elegantly to the stones around her sandalled feet. The sleeves tapered trumpet-like and reached to her fingertips; her headdress of white silk and gold band covered her head and veiled her face revealing only her eyes.

Her eyes of topaz pink sparkled with iridescent fire; almond shaped and downward tipped, so slightly, towards her narrow nose she seemed able to penetrate my facade and see my very soul.

Yet the young, capricious beauty was no more than a spoilt child.

She appeared so fresh and radiant after her voyage across the gulf. (The very same space that now held many warships poised to strike at her home world.) Her delicate and gentle manner eclipsed the fact that she was from the sister planet, Venus. And, although from a hot world, she was as cool as a snowflake.

Under the watchful minds of the Council of Stratos, we ambled through the oldest botanical gardens on Earth. I could not let them sense my insecurity, but forced my mind to radiate confidence. Surely they would be scanning us. Not every Lord of the Council was in favour of this mission. While the Council and the orbiting delegation from Venus would be monitoring us, no one could know the mind of the Lady Blossom for she wore the *Vesper-Amuleta*. Our custom and mores of impropriety towards introspection of others without consent could not be taken for granted at this time.

Her skirt rustled softly along the ground, the light autumnal air free of the Enchanted Birds' trilling, and the evening too cool for the chirp of old Earth crickets, as our carefully measured steps took us along the Vanderwater Canal. Below and to our left the dark, reflective water of the canal, and to our right the lush, picturesque rockery of enormous and convoluted proportions were both at once beautiful and sinister.

Lian-Li gave me a coy, upward glance (I stand a head taller than she) and I wondered how she perceived of my appearance. As a Count of the House Serafini, I wore the trappings of the Third Renaissance: knee high rider's boots over close fitting trousers, embroidered silk shirt (ruffled) and a velvet coat of burgundy. Thus I pondered, when she had looked up into my face and I wondered again, with greater concern, did the features of my clean shaven face and the cascading curls of my black hair please her? It was a silly and petty thought.

We then passed under an arching canopy of giant grasses which cast striking shadows across our path. I looked up to catch glimpses of the delicately coloured *moonrings* between the feathery heads of the swaying stalks. We emerged moments later under the open sky.

At last, the Lady Blossom Lian-Li spoke to me with a voice that was as soft and sweet as the rustle of silken sheets.

"Is it true the Lotus Garden is older than all the cities of Venisia?"

As though responding to her voice, crimson-pink light rippled through the water of the canal.

"Yes," I replied.

"And the Garden contains all the flowers of the Universe?"

I smiled, "Perhaps now, it does," I said, feeling some confidence return.

"I want to see the starflowers . . . and the wild animalcules, too," she said.

Slipping her delicate fingers around my upper arm, she said, "Show me everything!"

Her voice had the enchanting quality of a sentimental piano concerto, and I felt at ease and distant from the horrors that waited above.

As we strolled between the canal and the rockery, Pleiades fireflies emerged from the canal's water and in a rising curtain of sparkling magenta, violet, gold and crimson they swirled and darted in their obsessive, chaotic dance of life.

"Look at these mad creatures, Lian-Li. They rise once every ten years to live for only one night," I said.

"How do they choose their mate?" she whispered.

"Up there," I pointed, "the ones who fly the highest."

She seemed genuinely impressed with my knowledge and gentle manner. But I could not be sure, as the *Vesper-Amuleta* prevented me from seeing her mind.

As we strolled further along, towards the forest of the Burning Trees a loud voice penetrated my mind.

"*I feel you Serafini. You will not succeed.*" It was Cervantes! I ignored his intrusion.

We walked in silence for a few minutes, Lian-Li absorbed in the sparkling panorama rising higher and higher above our heads, when we came upon an alcove in the rockery. I halted our walk and brought her attention to the curved glass of a small imbedded biosphere.

"Touch the glass," I said.

Hesitantly, she reached out and placed a fingertip on its cool surface. Instantly, the interior became illuminated with violet light. There was a single plant inside. Its long, black lanceolate leaves rose fountain-like along its single stock. At the apex was a single closed flower the size of a woman's hand.

"Is it a ...." she began.

The inflorescence began to open. Petal after petal, shaped as the leaves though bright crimson in colour, curled away to reveal layer upon layer of inner beauty.

"Oh my, it is wonderful. So beautiful, so unlike anything at home. Does it have a beautiful scent, too?" she asked.

"The legend says it is an enchanting aroma; however, its vapours are most dangerous. The first men to discover it were led for leagues across the purple savannahs by its intoxicating odour, only to be stricken with the burning madness, their very nerves on fire, consumed by visions of a flaming ordeal. All these brave men were lost," I paused as a drop of blood-red nectar dripped from a petal.

"Centuries later the planet was rediscovered, and permanently closed. They returned from their Far Voyage with this single specimen of the Sextanus Hellflower, " I said.

"What a horrible story! Why did you tell me that?" she cried.

"Everything is not what it may first appear to be, my love," said I.

"Show me something nice," she insisted.

"Yes, of course," I said, and we resumed our walk.

" *She is not so easily offended. Do not trust her Serafini, she is of the House of Quan!"*

" *Cervantes, you must cease this illegal communication at once."*

" *THEY have broken the law of Stratos. They must be punished!"*

" *The Trinity is not yet broken. Now leave!"*

I closed my mind and returned my attention to the Lady Blossom. She no longer held my arm, but walked quietly alongside me. I could see she was deep in thought: so strange for me not to know what one was thinking!

A few moments later we reached a turning point. The brown cobblestone walkway forked, one path continued along the canal towards the forest of the Burning Trees whilst the other broke sharply left to a footbridge over the canal.

"Come," I said gently, and turned toward the bridge.

The bridge, built of uneven hewn stones, formed a graceful grey arch over the black glass of the star strewn water. The rough, sloping surface made our footing uneasy and Lady Lian-Li took hold of my arm firmly with both her hands as we advanced up the climb. Although she held me only for support, the closeness of her body caused me to feel her radiant warmth against my side.

Upon reaching the crown of the span we fell against the granite rail, our breath quickened by our effort, and we found a delirious mirth and laughter upon our lips. She took a few lively steps to the centre of the bridge, and turned several times in an exquisite ballet movement.

"I know where we are," she said playfully.

"Where?" I said casually, while watching her little performance with discreet pleasure.

"The Bridge of Sighs," she declared, emphasizing the word sighs.

"And why does an angel dance on such a bridge?" I asked.

"Because she is free to dance under the stars!" she said as she spun closer to me. At last she finished and leaned against the rail next to me.

"Such a beautiful garden. Why would anyone call this the Bridge of Sighs?" she wondered aloud.

"No one is certain. This bridge is older than history itself, more than twenty thousand years. Some say a prison covered the island once, and the condemned would sigh as they bid their freedom goodbye from here," I said.

"Oh, but now they all must sigh at the beauty of the garden," she said enthused and delighted.

"Yes, yes indeed. The Second Sun rises first in the morning, there, at the end of the canal to a magnificent symphony of the Enchanted Birds. Perhaps tomorrow you may witness it."

"Yes, that *would* be nice --"

" *Tomorrow will be too late. The technics will attack at dawn*"

" *No! She will accept me, and the Venisians will accept us, and they will join the Council!*"

" *They have broken the law. No one may make a creature superior to man!*"

" *The law will change. And the Trinity will triumph.*"

" *Ah, Haa! Haaa!! ....*"

Cervantes' laughter echoed in my mind as my attention returned to Lian-Li.

"I *said*, I would like to go on," she said sharply. A slight breeze from the south brought a scent of lavender and lightly tossed her veil and head dress. Her moist, rose-coloured eyes gleamed like precious gems.

"Yes, yes. Of course," I apologized.

And we strode forward down the opposite side of the bridge, Lian-Li clinging tightly to my arm. We crossed over to the Island of Souls with its magnificent, tall pines and larches, and its carpet of Angelic flowers. The path had become natural sand. We walked together, softly, as the pale purple flowers curled away from our feet.

"Do you know why you are here, Lian-Li?" I asked.

"To enjoy your marvellous Lotus Gardens, of course," said she, her arm loosely entwined in mine as we walked.

"Yes, that is true. But have you ever heard anyone speak of genetic enhancement? Or Re-creation?"

"Those words are strange to me," she said, her voice quizzical.

"Did you know that people were not always capable of simple telepathy?"

"Now you are playing a mind game with me. I like them, if they are *fun!*"

"No, Lady Lian-Li, it is quite true. In ancient days men and women could only speak, as we are now. It took centuries of selective generations to condition and choose the best until all could speak mentally."

"I don't know whether to believe you or not," she replied.

"Now, listen to me Lian-Li. We all revel in our differences, in our diverse varieties, of all humans from all the home worlds of our Sun, but something has happened.

"Imagine a *new species* of mankind, possibly superior to us all, possibly unable to co-mingle among us. How could we cope?

"Some believe the strain would be too much," I said.

"So . . . how do you even know what a man is?" she said, as a Moonmoth fluttered near our noses. It was a female, its silvery wings as large as a man's splayed hand, in search of a male. The invisible cloud of pheromones wafted over us with a rich, woody scent as she glided and flitted higher into the night sky.

"Well?" Lian-Li giggled, amused or affected by the Moonmoth.

"Oh, . . . the Moonmoth? The man?" I asked reflexively.

"Yes!" she giggled again.

"Or maybe the man in the moon," I said, looking at the reflection of the *moonrings* in the deep, placid water of the endless Vanderwater canal.

"Tell me!" she piqued, hugging my arm.

We walked along the outer edge of the island, watching waterspiders skate across the black glass of the mirrored pond and listening to the whisper of the souls passing through the leaves of the trees. I began to feel confident that I was accomplishing my mission.

"I'll tell you a legend about a man. A true legend about a real man. His name was Vincenzio "Lucious" Valentijn."

"Once, long, long ago the young Earth had a satellite called Luna, the moon. It was a large, cold and barren place where no one dared to venture, and it was associated with magic, and witchcraft and superstition. This satellite circled the young Earth every thirty days casting its captured sunlight back every night. Sometimes, it was said, Luna would hide behind the sun and the nights were as black and dark as obsidian.

"This satellite, this moon had strange powers; it could move the oceans, stir men's minds to savagery and turn the barren woman fertile.

"Cults of the moon flourished upon the face of the young Earth. Rituals and ceremonies, and even the abomination of human sacrifice, were practised under its mournful glare."

I paused as we encountered a fallen tree across our path. I stepped over it first, then held the Lady Blossom's hands as she gingerly stepped on and over it, being most careful not to tear her skirt.

"Please go on, Count Serafini," she said.

As we reached the western side of the island the path divided and I led us toward the interior of the island garden.

"The moon, Luna, seemed to be eternal, a goddess to the people. Until one day, the astronomers made a remarkable discovery. The moon had moved closer to the young Earth. There was great excitement among the peoples of Earth, scientists spoke at conferences and built new observatories, astrologers consulted books and charts, and the cult of psychics held seances.

"After decades of study and research the inevitable conclusion was reached: the satellite known as the Earth's moon was falling. It would spiral inward, closer and closer, until a few centuries hence it would collide with the young Earth, destroying it forever.

"Of course, the peoples of the young Earth became stricken with panic. Scientists spoke before conferences and conducted secret discussions, governments became fearful, and military leaders declared martial law; until the disasters began. The gravitational force of the planetoid, as it was then called, caused violent storms, flash floods and massive earthquakes; all the peoples' energies and resources were spent on rescue and relocation.

"It was finally determined that no power on the young Earth could stop the cataclysm. Then the exodus began: rocket after rocket, loaded with the peoples, the beloved plants and the animals of Earth, vanished into the night sky."

I spoke these words as we passed through a particularly dark hollow beneath the thick boughs of the towering white pine trees. Lian-Li pressed closer to me, the warmth of her body penetrating my clothing, while the carpet of dry pine needles covering the path softly crunched beneath our feet.

As we emerged onto the meadow floribundus, under the starry, *moonrings* lit sky, she said, "What happened to your Vincenzio?"

"Ah yes, Vincenzio," I said.

"He was a captain of the Space Corps. He piloted refugees to Mars and the satellites of the former planet known as Jupiter. While he spent most of his life in space he had a deep love for the Earth; his family could be traced back, on the same plot of land, to prehistory. And while Vincenzio endured the rigours of space, and saved many lives, his frail mother lay in bed ailing. Alone in her ancestral home, tended by her faithful family servants, she would not — could not — leave the Earth.

"This, above all, saddened Captain Vincenzio. Until one day, he watched a Mothership streak like a comet out of the home worlds system on a far voyage towards the stars. He became angry! Angry at the cowardly people fleeing in fear, angry at himself and angry at the betrayal of the goddess moon herself.

"The fever of his anger inspired the light of his genius, -- for which he was later named "Lucious" — and he knew what he must do," I said, while all around us the luminescent Fire Bushes of Cassiopeia streaked and crackled with micro-lightning. The air was rich with ozone and the unmistakable perfume of jasmine.

"Oh, this is wonderful! I feel so alive!" said Lian-Li.

As we continued to stroll across the wildflower meadow I resumed telling the legend.

"Captain Valentijn delivered his last manifest cargo of dignitaries, scientists and scientific equipment to an outpost on Ganymede. There he made alterations to his spacecraft and loaded it with excess fuel, and without authorization, he flew not back to Earth, but away from the home worlds.

"Many in the Space Corps were shocked by his "cowardly" act. Criminal charges were brought against him in absentia.

"But Vincenzio knew he had to act alone. He knew his plan would be challenged, and there was no time left. He had to act.

"Vincenzio flew his craft with increasing speed out past Neptune, Uranus and the outer planetoid Pluto, where he turned his spacecraft with great skill into an arcing sweep through the Oort Cloud. Then he released cables with grapnel hooks behind the ship.

"Vincenzio was badly injured when the grapnels seized upon several of the frozen methane and ice comets within the cloud. The ship was strained to its limits as he fired the engines with the captured comets in tow. With his great skill as a pilot, his ship responded to his commands and accelerated into the return voyage, although it still took several years to span the great distance. His life support systems were exhausted as he approached his destination.

"The peoples of the new home worlds were amazed at the appearance of the approaching comet cluster; it created a spectacular fiery display. Scientists gathered at conferences and trained their telescopes on the perplexing event and discovered it was Valentijn's lost spacecraft at the foremost vertex. The event was broadcast to all the telescreens on all the new home worlds. And the people watched in horror and astonishment as Valentijn's ship and the comet cluster all collided directly into that bedevilled and capricious moon of Earth!" I said, finally pausing to catch my breath.

We passed through the wildflower meadow and entered onto a wide pathway of crushed stones. It was bordered on each side by thick rows of the DaggerRose.

"You are a wonderful story teller," she purred.

"Even if it is a preposterous lie," she said with smug certainty.

"Look up at the *moonrings*, Lady Blossom. It was once a solid, bleak rock until Vincenzio "Lucious" Valentijn shattered it -- like a hammer shatters ice — and the particles now float gently, harmlessly around our Earth in eternal gratitude to the bravery of the man who died there.

"That is what a man is, Lian-Li," said I.

"A wonderful story, Count Serafini. But I *know*, the *moonrings* have always been there, just like they have always been around Saturn," she replied.

I felt frustration, and the mission slipping through my fingers. Perhaps, I was distracted by her fragrant beauty and had been too gentle with her. I had to press her more firmly, make her understand her role and the importance she must play.

" *It is too late for your Venisians, Serafini. Already they are headed for their shelters*"

" *Silence!!*"

"Look at these flowers, Lady Blossom."

"Oh, how exotic and what a beautiful fragrance . . . what are they called?" she said, as she leaned over to inspect them closer.

"They are the DaggerRose of the constellation Virgo," I said, as she leaped back suddenly exclaiming, "Ouch!!"

She had pricked her finger on one of the countless, long thorns that covered all the stems of the plant. I took hold of her hand, raised it to my lips and kissed her wound. I looked into her moist eyes with all the compassion I could summon; she seemed to smile beneath her veil and I was truly astonished to witness her wound heal before my eyes.

We stood very still and quiet for a few moments.

"Look," I said, as I pushed aside the flowering heads of the DaggerRose.

"Oh my stars! By the Holy House of Quan, that is atrocious!!" she exclaimed.

"That is horrible, just horrible — why? why?"

"Look closer, Lian-Li, beneath the body of the bird," I said, while the upper thorns bit deeper into my hands.

"They're babies. Baby birds without a mother," she whimpered.

I released the bush and pulled a handkerchief from my pocket to dress my bleeding hands.

"The Asta bird sacrifices its life on the thorns of the DaggerRose so that its children may live. As the plant feeds on the dead bird it produces berries and seeds that the nestlings feed upon. It is for a greater good, Lian-Li. Do you understand?"

"Yes, I see. I understand now, but it does not make me happy," she moaned.

"Good, come along now and I will show you something you will like," I said.

As we strolled towards the end of the DaggerRose Lane, she took hold of my hands and I felt soft, gentle warmth pervade my flesh and my wounds were healed.

We walked under the arch of a large arbour thick with verdant vines and resplendent with ivory, violet and rose hued Moonflowers of the Earth genus *Ipomoea*. Struck with awe, Lian-Li stood motionless gazing upon the grand Courtyard of Lucious, a magnificent construction in the ancient Romanesque style. Built of polished granite and marble, the courtyard was circular surrounded by a sectional wall, interspaced with the verdant arbours and alcoves containing exquisite statuary and extraordinary sculpture. Narrow, glittering waterfalls tumbled over the centre of each section and cascaded down into the waiting pools and shell shaped ponds with floating nymphae lilies and lotus flowers in full bloom; the curved walls covered in the glory of the spreading Moonflowers. Lacy green ferns flowed over the edges of the ponds and touched the marble pavement. This was the true center of the Lotus Gardens.

"Come, Lady Blossom, let's walk," I coaxed her from her trance.

"I can hardly believe my eyes," she said, and slid her fingers through the cool, sparkling water of a lotus pond.

"And who is that," she said, indicating the colossus rising skyward from the center of the courtyard, while she playfully performed a pirouette.

I walked over to the memorial and stood before the brass plaque waiting for her to follow me. I gazed up at the towering figure of polished granite, a swashbuckling man standing atop the Earth with his hand reaching out before him. The bleak, solid moon in his outstretched hand, while he contemplates it for all the worlds.

A moment later, Lian-Li arrived at my side.

"What does it say?"

"It is written in every human language. The plaque wraps around the entire monument. It says, 'In loving memory and admiration of the greatest man who ever lived: Vincenzio Lucious Valentijn'."

"Then I apologize to you, Sir Giovanni Serafini," said she while bowing in a deep curtsy and holding her skirt out to her sides, "you are truly an honourable and trustworthy gentleman."

"I shall remove the *Vesper-Amuleta* as my honour and duty requires, and reveal myself to you."

The Lady Blossom Lian-Li then reached across with her right hand and unclasped her veil, letting it fall next to her angelic face. At last I could set my eyes upon her true features. Her narrow nose and her rich, full lips were drawn into a loving smile, and as she removed her head dress I could apprehend her silky black hair precisely covered with the gleaming net of radiant Venisian Pearls that comprise the mindshield of the *Vesper-Amuleta.*

She stood contemplative for a moment then reached for the moonstone brooch.

" *Her veil is an illusion, Count Serafini. Does she not wear the Vespa-Amuleta?* "

" *Cervantes!!* "

" *Her thoughts are her own* "

" *No!* "

" *Her veils hide the Medusa.   See..... Look for yourself!* "

I raised my eyes and beheld the creature of Lian-Li. A hideous chimaera with multiple heads and waving tentacles, hissing and mocking, stood in a writhing, maggot infested pool of putrid offal. I turned suddenly and completely away from the illusion, my mind shouting: *"Enough!!"*

" *You are sworn Lord Protector to mankind before the Council of Stratos.* "

"It is your duty to kill the monster."

"Kill her, Serafini.   Kill her now!!!"

" *NO!!* " I shouted into the air.

Cervantes was gone. My vision cleared and I saw the Lady Lian-Li looking at me with a puzzled expression.

"Do you wish me to retain the *Amuleta*?"

"Please forgive me, Lady Blossom, I . . . I had a mild seizure. Please continue," I said.

She unclasped the moonstone brooch and her pure white gown fell gently to the ground. I could not take my eyes from her now. A silvery web clung to her young body and shimmered in the starlight. She unclasped the *Vesper-Amuleta* at her smooth, sensuous shoulders and it cascaded to the hard marble around her feet in a tinkling patter of pearls.

Lian-Li stood before me naked and demure, a perfectly formed woman, more lovely and beautiful than Aphrodite, vulnerable and immaculate. She offered herself in total and complete trust.

I faltered. I could not touch her mind.

"You must help us, Moonflower," I said.

"You must believe that I love you, that we all love you. Believe in love, as I, as we believe in you.

"Look into my mind. See our trouble and help us. Open yourself Moonflower, and kiss the stars!" said I.

Suddenly, the skies opened. I witnessed the Lady Blossom's aura brighten and expand. Thousands of live birds exploded into flight from all the surrounding trees and shrubs. The melodies of a million symphonies crashed upon my ears. The dazzling blaze of a thousand Suns blinded me. I was struck down by the sound and fury of the heavens. I fell to my knees and shook with violent spasms. I had never before or since felt such power flow through me — a flaming explosion of ecstasy, and the pure, liquid euphoria of infinite *LOVE*.

I collapsed into unconsciousness.

*   *   *

POSTSCRIPT:
Diplomatic House of the Royal Quan Dynasty.

The tears well up in my eyes as I sit here, again writing these words, as I have every day in the two hundred and twelve years since The Rapture, trying to do it right, to get the words right, so that you may know, really know, what happened that night.

It is now historical fact that The Rapture saved Venisia, that *her* love reached everyone.

That the Council of the Trinity of worlds accepted the human species known as *Homo sentient telesympathetic* as truly human.

And it is only with mild delight that I know that Cervantes was tried and convicted of sedition, and finally banished to a planet called Shayol.

POISSON DISTRIBUTION

by
Leonid Spektor

Leonid Spektor, born in the ex-U.S.S.R. thirty-six years ago, circumnavigated the lands of the midnight sun when he emigrated to Canada in 1979. Here, he earned a Masters degree in computer science and electrical engineering. Currently residing in Willowdale, Ontario he has previously been published in *Wonderdisk* magazine.

POISSON DISTRIBUTION

by
Leonid Spektor

And the Lord God formed man of the dust of the
ground and breathed into his nostrils the breath
of life; and man became a living soul.
-The Bible

I watch steadfastly as the lake salmon rush up the shallow stream. It is as though they are torpedoes let out of a submarine, oblivious of the bears' and raccoons' fangs, the honed claws of soaring birds, the pebbled shoals, or fishermen's lures. Why is this enigmatic fish so eager to pass through the countless barriers and the awaiting dangers? What causes this ancient beast to endanger its short-lived life, in order to traverse another hundred yards, and then spawn and meet its end? What is the name of that internal power which is responsible for the fish's fanatical zeal? The first scent of home backwater? Is it celebration of its last breath of life, or the beckoning of the Grim Reaper?

The foul smell of rotten fishes seems to have impregnated the air around the stream. The fishes' exposed carcasses, some dressed in offensive, decaying flesh are strewn along the pebbled bank. Even the charcoal black ravens are not crowing. The birds are fed up with the feast of death and have quit eating. These mourning fowls behold me alertly. Completely enchanted, I keep on gazing and scowling at the passing fishes. At times they remind me of sooty logs moving against the current, disobeying the laws of nature. The tempest is roaring in the hollow of my mind. The storm's harbinger has haunted me for days: why does this intrepid salmon

rush so eagerly to its certain demise? The fish is much smaller than I, but it's
not afraid to depart this life. Why am I falling prey to doubts at the slightest
thought of meeting face to face with my Maker?

Why does life around me feel like a blue hell?
Engrossed in my sombre reveries I notice, but fail to acknowledge,
several newly-formed islands of a new life. In these few accidental places,
where waves are slow and nature's coin of chance landed on the right side,
schools of the recently hatched baby fishes are feeding on the byproducts of
their ancestors. Some years later, once matured in foreign waters, the
surviving, grown salmon will come back to their birthplace in order to repeat
their solemn, final run.

That day the fishing was average. Nonetheless, we took only what
we were allowed to take and released the lucky ones into the innocently
sounding purling waters, knowing that the fish will soon perish anyway. By
the sunset we called it a day. The eldest in our bunch, Albert, the silver-haired
astronomer, adroitly wrapped up our catch in grape leaves, covered it in clay
mud, and put it to bake on the smouldering ashes. The tardy supper was silent,
without taking into account shrilling screeches of night fowls. Everyone kept
their eyes on the platter or toward the tenebrous ground. After quickly
finishing with the fish, Bob, the chief helmsman, a healthy towering fellow,
took a handful of walnuts from his pocket and set them on a flat boulder. With
a dull, concentrated smash of his big fist he commenced breaking the nut
shells, extracting scrupulously the remains of nut kernels, and placing them
into his mouth. Our petrified gazes focused on the cracked pieces of the
nutshells. The chewing, unsuspecting helmsman politely granted us a hand
sign to join in his snack, but no one responded.
"Why does nobody curse or praise my cooking?" Albert finally broke
the silence. "Everybody is chewing like a cow or gazing at the split nuts."
"Because that's exactly what'll happen to us soon," Phil, the
starship's navigator, snarled at Albert. "Nowadays, I can hardly gulp a sip
of water. Besides, your undercooked salmon has plugged my throat like a
bung!" Phil abruptly got up and belched. "Excuse me," he muttered and
made tracks towards the obscure wall of thickets.
Phil's right arm was shaking. We couldn't help to notice, even

through the mist of a descending nighttide. No one uttered a word. Crack-k-k! Bob broke another shell. Something pricked my heart and I squinted. It sounded as though the splutter was not of a nut shell, but of human bones caught in a saw mill. I looked around alertly. My companions sat with bloodless, wooden expressions, aghasted by the horror in their eyes. All the men have affected me by their noticeable shivering, bringing to my mind a hutch of humble, white bunnies enclosed in their cage with a hungry constrictor. Who knows what was on my friends' minds? Without a doubt, they trembled from the inner animal fear, but none of the valiant sons wanted to admit it in public.

"Your theory of cosmic evolution resembles your mud cooking, and has led us to nowhere!" Bob finally blurted out, looking at the astronomer. "We are all in deep shit because of your scientific impotence!"

Suddenly, Bob abruptly stood up, as though stung by a bee. He grabbed the pan of tea, and spilled its entire contents on the bonfire. The dying ashes immediately sent out a hissing reminiscent of an agitated viper. The dense smoke began to ascend from what was left of the former bonfire. Then, Bob, who flew into a rage, turned away with scorn and walked briskly towards his tent without ever looking back at us. At first, shocked by his prank, we remained sitting in muteness and staring at the smouldering ashes, as though nothing unusual had just happened.

That night we all slept like children: deeply and peacefully, despite the fact that by our middle years the old-age insomnia had already infected our lives. Only men condemned to death are known to sink that innocently into sleep the last night before their execution.

We woke up late. The star was just approaching its zenith. We tried fishing, but soon found ourselves uninterested. With more dead salmon carcasses washed to the shores, the stream's bank resembled a fresh battlefield still scattered with lost lives.

"I have to leave earlier today. Got to meet my gals at the bar," Phil admitted and began wrapping his gear.

"I simply forgot, that I have to weed my little garden and then water it," Bob stated abruptly.

"If half of us are going to relish other pleasures of life, then I might as well call it a day," Albert said. "I still have to complete one interesting book on statistics."

"Your arithmetic is nothing but speculation of filthy damn lies," I
rapped out. "When one person inadvertently kicks the bucket, it's a tragedy.
When we are all apt to expire, it's regarded as statistics!"

I showed up at home earlier than my family expected.
"Lilly, look! Your genius daddy has finally decided to drop by on us,"
my wife, Janet, met me with malice. "Look at him. Why are you so sad?
Because you are empty on the hook? The fish outsmart you again? Or,
perhaps, you cannot recover from another rejection from your tent mate.
Was she pretty? Or does the shadow of her denial still hover over your
head?"
"Don't start in front of the kid," I snapped at Janet who was moving
her dirty tongue as swiftly as a snake.
"Why should I hide from our child that her daddy is a bastard. A
lustful son of a bitch with a zest to explore every passing skirt!"
"Guys decided to leave before the sunset, that's it," I mumbled,
angered by the slur.
"In that case, maybe you want to help me lay your daughter to sleep.
She is getting completely out of hand. Can you imagine, our Lilly comes home
from her kindergarten and tells me about the forthcoming end of the world.
What am I supposed to say ?"
I opened the door to Lilly's room.
"Daddy, did you catch me a big fish?" Lilly asked skipping into her
bedroom.
"Yes. Your mother has gone to the kitchen to cook your favourite
fish and eggs for supper. After you wake up from your afternoon nap, the
dish should be ready. Meanwhile, shut your big-as-cherry eyes and try to fall
asleep, fast."
"I don't want to sleep! Our teacher, Mrs. Ramisbottom, said that
soon we will all go to a very long sleep, kids and adults too. I want to play
more with my Dollie before it comes. Daddy, did you have to sleep so much
when you were a kid?"
I was in turmoil. I, the captain of the starship, had just calmly learned
from my own child what we adults are still too apprehensive to openly discuss
amongst ourselves.
"If you close your eyes tight and try to sleep, I'll tell your favourite

story about us," I said after a small pause.

Lilly narrowed her eyes.

"Don't cheat. Or I won't start the story"

Lilly turned to the right, placed her palms under her cheek, and began breathing heavily and noisily through her nose, pretending that she was already in the land of nod.

"A long, long, time ago," I began the narration, "people lived on the beautiful planet called Earth. The planet was surrounded by purling waters, blue sky and white wandering clouds. On the planet's lands grew green plants and scarlet flowers and all kinds of animals lived in its oceans, rivers, soils and air. The people and the beasts enjoyed the delicious fruits of Earth, admired the fragrance of the violets and the purity of the carnations. The men bathed in soothing waters, conceived the lore of nature, and in the eventides watched the friendly, warm Sun sink into the deep, turquoise sea. And at nighttime the yellow moon and the twinkling stars dwelled on the dark-blue firmament. Life was serene and beautiful, and nothing in the world seemed to hint at calamity. One morning the people woke up and discovered that their Sun suddenly looked much bigger and hotter. Its rays became hot and prickly. No positive change in the Sun's appearance occurred in the days to come. Instead, the water from the rivers and the seas began to evaporate, fast. The plants and animals started to die from the heat and exhaustion, and the people became imprisoned in their stone shelters. Then the people really became concerned.

"What is happening?" a neighbour asked his neighbour. "Why does our friend the Sun grow bigger and hotter every day?"

Only astronomers did not ask simple questions or rush around the cities seeking plain answers. These wise men were busy, working day and night: tracking stars, making countless calculations, creating postulates, testing them against observations, and unifying all sorts of theories. Many months later the chief astronomer finally revealed his findings. The Sun, which all the men loved so much, had grown old and began to expire. By swelling and turning hotter than a legion of ovens, the Sun wanted to send the people a warning about its end. The time came for the people to relocate to newer places, where the planets of another, younger sun could provide life and shelter. Delay would mean an eventual death for all mankind. Very soon the expanding Sun would swallow its neighbouring planets, and even Earth with its Moon, before collapsing into a small, cold ball of cinder, called a white dwarf. The alerted people quickly built big, sturdy spaceships. The people brought with them on board, the plants and the animals which they cherished most, and samples of Earth's waters and soils. Soon the spaceships with the earthmen were racing toward other parts of their big galaxy -- towards younger, friendlier suns.

Time passed by, and the people colonized a new planet. When that sun aged, the people moved in search of a newer sun. Since then, mankind has been wandering for millennia from the older suns to the newer ones, from one galaxy to another. The people quickly learned how to live among the aging stars. Nonetheless, the astronomers were always on alert, keeping their eyes on the high skies above them. One day the astronomers saw that the distant suns appeared larger, the distant galaxies seemed to come closer, and the nighttime air waxed dense with stars. The wakeful scientists hurried to their telescopes and engaged in detailed observations, created new hypothesis and verifications, and made calculations . . . rolls of countless calculations. Many months later, the council of the scientists came to a bitter conclusion. *Our Universe has become old. It has stopped expanding.* The stars ceased moving away from each other and, instead, began rushing back to the centre of the Universe, to their inevitable fall into the giant black hole. To sit and wait for mercy from the stars' elements became a desperate gamble. The people built seven big starships which they named after the planets which had orbited their earliest sun: Earth, Venus, Mars, Neptune, Mercury, Saturn, and . . . "

"Jupiter," Lilly said and opened her eyes.

"Thank you," I replied with amazement. "What about your promise to try to fall asleep during my story?"

Lilly closed her eyes humbly, reversed clumsily to a new more comfortable side, and hushed.

"Then, mankind forever left their last planet with its still young sun and sailed into the vast abyss of the cold cosmos, away from the besieging stars and galaxies. Since then, we have been wandering throughout the ether in our starships, desperately trying to beat the inevitable -- our Universe's all mighty gravitational attraction."

I hushed and checked Lilly. My daughter was peacefully snoozing, probably experiencing dreams which all children at her age see: a sandbox with new toys, a stroll with her dolls through the magic forest, or endeavouring to enclose with her miniature, plump hands the orange rendering of a descending real sun. Lilly was born five years ago under the artificial sun which shone on the firmament of our starship. My little daughter could not see a lonely, salty tear inconspicuously sliding down the check of her father's face.

That night I could not sleep and showed up at my shift hours early. First thing I checked was the helmsman on duty.

"How's the night? Sailing over calm waters?" I asked Johnny. He was still green, of the junior class, but already bearded and with tattoos on both hands in the manner of a starbeaten space dog.

"In a calm space, every man is a pilot. But nowadays, flying seems like we are going through virulent rapids during a hailstorm," Johnny replied. "Every time I peer at this abyss, I taste dizziness, and my head goes round. I cannot relax for a moment, so congested the cosmos has become. Take a look for yourself. I have never seen anything analogous to that before."

I glimpsed through the unshielded porthole and blanched, as though being ambushed by a snake. Our starship's projectors were scanning over a rapidly moving array of rocks. The cosmic dust, ice, and boulders were flowing parallel to our starship in eerie silence, occasionally bumping against each other. The stern spectacle reminded me of an awakened river during the springtime ice drift. Behind the demonic influx of debris I observed a countless array of stars, tailed comets, and galaxies. They were fleeing around us, seemingly as a rushing herd of disturbed mustangs.

"Space is getting more dense and thicker with every workshift." Johnny reported. "We should be flying away from this congestion, not trailing behind that cosmic junk like a bunch of stupid rams."

"Remember! We *are* flying away!" I expressed in a loud voice. "And, please, keep your comments to yourself," I retorted and headed to my command station.

At lunch I dropped by the bar, where I ordered a light ale and a sandwich with red caviar. Marinated salmon fish eggs, to be culinarily correct. My recent camping companion, Phil, the navigator, was seated in the company of his sidekicks and chewing the fat about yesterday's fishing trip. The man could not see me from behind. The waiter delivered a baked salmon to his table, probably the one which the navigator had caught himself

the day before. I sipped a cool beer and took a little bite from the sandwich.
One fish egg skipped the crash of my molars and landed on my tongue. I
rolled the salty egg several times against my palate before ingesting it. I
wondered, what were the odds of this yet unprepared fish egg dropping into
the kitchen garbage and landing next to the sperm from Phil's male salmon.
If that rubbish is then released into the water system untreated, then there is
a small prospect that a baby fish can reproduce from a fluky egg-semen
contact . . . . A few minutes later another of my friends, Albert, the
astronomer, holding a bottle of mineral water joined me at the table. I
immediately shared my thoughts with the knowledgeable man.

  "Definitely, there is a small chance of that happening," Albert
nodded. "A rider and time, works wonders and tries all things. I actually
believe, that in all disorder there is a secret order. Thus, with time, chaos and
the transmutation can even breed life into your dropped fish egg. However,
the odds of our destruction before the new life is conceived are much, much
higher. Last night I finished reading that notorious book on statistics. And
immediately, I did some rough calculations. Unfortunately, the results are far
from encouraging. Worse than I thought. Although there is always a hope,
there is always safety in numbers."

  "What can be worse than our continuing helplessness?"

  "It's a predetermined finish, my friend. Everything has its beginning
and end; it's part of the matter of things, isn't it? When a child is born, we sort
of know his average lifetime span; it's programmed in his cells. When the
Big Bang had given birth to our Universe, it also created presuppositions for
its demise. What I read and calculated last night is not new. It's simply a
mathematical machine which allows us to compute more precisely the
occurrence of certain events."

  "Such as?"

  "The collapse of our Universe," Albert declared and pierced me with
his burning eyes. A few speechless moments dragged. The man sounded
to be out of breath, so intense was his excitement. The astronomer hastily
charged a glass of water and emptied it in one shot. Only then was Albert
able to resume revealing his findings. "Following the Big Bang, the matter
in our Universe was distributed non-uniformly. To be precise, in the clusters
which were dispersed throughout the ether in accordance with the Poisson
* distribution. Science can predict the approximate locations of these groups,

---

* Statistical distribution named after the famous mathematician who first proposed it.

and even estimate their sizes and masses. Now, when our Universe stopped expanding and set out to collapse, these gigantic clusters began hurling towards each other with unprecedented speed which defies computation. The closer the clusters get to each other, the faster they run toward their inevitable collision. If our starships are captured by the gravitational field of one of these clusters, which might as well be a giant black hole, then we shall perish before our Universe's end."

"So what!" I exclaimed. "We still cannot escape from the gravitation of our dying Universe. Another Big Bang, and our starships will be blown to pieces! Humanity will vanish forever!"

"All I want to claim, is that another Big Bang will come much later. Meanwhile, we should do our best to avoid encounters with these bundles of falling substance. We must sail in the directions where the probabilities of a crash with the falling material are much less. As we buy time, our lives will be prolonged. Perhaps, new solutions will be found in the upcoming days."

"Tomorrow is the council of the starships' captains," I said. "What would you want me to communicate to them?"

"We've got to alter the blind courses of our starships immediately. Once the falling matter passed through a specific region of cosmos, we can follow its path safely. Presently, the likelihood of another cluster going through the same loci is much less. Retreat, look around, and reorient should become our new navigational strategy. Flying straight away, as we despondently attempt to accomplish nowadays, is illusionary and suicidal. Please, convince tomorrow's council to adopt my new game plan. I've written down all my recent calculations in this report." Albert handed me his blue note-book. 'My arithmetic is simple and clear as daylight. It is mathematically coherent and elegant. It should convince even the dumbest space-rookie. The proposed navigation route lasts until its graduation to singularity."

With a cynical expression on my face, I promised to deliver the astronomer's recommendations. He soon withdrew to his observatory without discovering the main agenda of the next day's council, which was called Adopting a Common Method for Mass Suicide.

The council was held on the largest starship called Jupiter. The split in the captains' opinions came right from the beginning. The captainess from Venus proposed an ending from orgasmic shock. No big surprise. In the commanders' circle that shrewish, independent woman was well known for her lust and a bizarre hobby of collecting heavy-duty vibrators. The muscular captain from Mars put forth a plan for massive war games. He even offered a proper appellation for it: The Game of Life. Mercury suggested a deactivation by the neural tablets, while Neptune insisted on a fast and deep freeze. Jupiter went for a good old solution of the sweet sleeping gas. At the very closure of the exhaustive debates I finally dared to issue a word. Before I even finished sharing Albert's plan, I was publically ridiculed and hissed off the tribune. Angered commanders raised hue and cry.

"How dare I?" was on everybody's foul tongues. "To speak about a brief prolongation of our mental sufferings at a time when people are gathered to select the easiest end for this torment. Your old man is an imposter. The obsolete scientist, who uses his statistics as a drunk man uses lamp posts -- for support rather than illumination. We are sick from his talmudistic remarks:

What is easie-e-er to imagi-i-ine: infinity of our Universe, or its finality?' Dutch! Get off the stage. You, naive, little captain."

Soon I was back on my starship and heading along the passageway. Suddenly, Albert materialized from behind a corner.

"How was the meeting?" he immediately inquired. "I've just learned about its main agenda."

"The commanders didn't even want to listen to your plan. Overall, we walked away from the table without deciding on the unique termination plan for us all. The overall majority of men voted to end it all, because for them living has turned to a wait in purgatory. Everybody is pursuing his or her own termination scheme. Those who do not like it are free to change starships."

"I knew it!" Albert blurted. "I always found that statistics were hard to swallow and impossible to digest. Alas. We grew into a narcissistic civilization of egoists. The overall cause for humanity is believed to be less important than individual cravings. Too bad! I had honestly hoped that you might turn things around."

Suddenly, our starship was shaken up as though we were hit by a strong oceanic wave.

"What's that?" Albert asked with alarm and fear in his eyes.

"Nothing to worry about. Johnny, the junior helmsman is at the wheel today. I've just ordered our starship to change its course and follow your navigation route. I choose a likelihood of our existence, no matter how abysmal, pathetic and brief it might turn out."

Touched by the eye of years, the astronomer beheld me with respect. A smile rose to his visage, and a gleam of hope began playing in his round, although subtly slanted black eyes. Probably the man could not believe his plan was working.

We arrived at the bar entrance. I opened the door to the nearly void hall and invited Albert in. "Let's celebrate life and your knowledge, and become drunk as fishes . . . while we are still around."

Weeks passed by fast, as though they were never here. I was at my command station when the messenger from the telecommunication ward appeared and approached me in a hurry. The man with fright on his face timidly handed me a telegram. My uneasy heart sank immediately. Through a hidden sixth sense I apprehended, even without reading the message, that the notorious end, which we were so fearful even to think about, had finally befallen.   Indeed, the captain from Mars was informing me that communication with the starship Jupiter had been lost this morning. A cluster of the fast-moving dark space matter was spotted in Jupiter's assumed location.

The bad news spread like a fire. At lunch our bar was buzzing like a fish market in the old country. Nearly everybody smoked heavily and gossiped about the same thing. The stupefying cloud of blue cigarette smoke was so dense that the countenances of the bar's patrons could not be well placed, even from a short distance. My eyes were watering and sore. I could not help noticing that people drank more, smoked more, spoke more and with a definite note of fear in their unusually loud voices.

"Dutch, are you alone?" a gentle voice and a soft touch on my cheek awoke me from my trance.

I turned backward and recognized Sabrina, the captainess from Venus.

" I am surprised to find you in here." I welcomed Sabrina by raising a goblet still full of red wine.

"I've just transferred to your starship this morning. After pondering your navigational plan, I relinquished my command post and decided to put my life into your capable hands."

Sabrina approached me and impudently removed the goblet from my hand. Then the temptress moved even closer. I could feel her hot breath blowing against my cheek. The potent, teasing aroma of her perfume had diffused throughout the toxic tobacco clouds and crept inside my head.

"Don't you want to check out how I've settled in? It's only a few blocks away from here. You never missed checking my abode when paying a visit to Venus."

Her petite hand grabbed my silk tie and imperatively hauled it toward herself, as though she was a young shepherdess who was dragging a stubborn lamb to the slaughter.

"I can't do it today," I uttered in bewilderment. "I am in uniform."

"Come." Sabrina whispered in supplication. "I will help you to take it off. We are all naked inside our clothes."

With a hand around my waist and nestled close to me, Sabrina guided me to her private quarters ignorant of people's seemingly indifferent glances. A few minutes later, rushed by the gust of desire, our two craving souls finally had a chance to amalgamate into one. The frantic flux of kisses and embraces rekindled our hungry hearts which, in turn, started to strike more resonantly and expeditiously, endeavouring to outrace the ebbing of time on a wave of fleeting passions.

In my wild ecstasy I was close to weightlessness. I mused in a drowsy delirium of joy: *Why had I always waited for such sweet and brief moments so long? How much time had been squandered for nothing? Why do I have to realize it only in this day and age, when the sun finally bears down on the horizon?*

Late in the evening, feeling a hundred years younger, although still a bit tired and sweaty, I headed home. Before I entered the house, my intuition sensed something wrong. The doors were wide open, the curtains taken out, and the household items were displaced throughout the backyard and on the stairs. An even greater mess was inside the dwelling. I called, but no one answered. Unless I knew what had happened, I would imagine that people attempted to flee this place in a hurry, taking only the most important, precious things and with scorn dropping the rest on the floor. Although deep in my guts I also knew that a woman must always leave a mark; it's in her blood. In the kitchen I finally found the harrowing answer. The letter from my once beloved consort was attached to the refrigerator's door by a magnetic clip shaped like a horn.

Thank goodness. Janet wrote. *There are still good people around who tell the truth. Besides, I suspected it all along. Let you die with your whore! I cannot live like that any longer. I am taking Lilly and flying away to Neptune, to my mom. We want to spend our last days in prayers.*

P.S. I took only our personal items and the sewing machine. Don't even dare to follow us.

I hope you'll burn in hell! Your ex-spouse Janet.

Following my family breakdown, I moved to Sabrina's home. My life began a new chapter. Like a cataract the shroud fell from my eyes in one night: the bridges were burnt, and the doors to my past were closed forever. From then on I began living as I had never lived before. I was honest with my emotions, frank with my girlfriend, unevasive with my colleagues, and tried to enjoy everything that life could offer. The grass for me seemed to be greener, the skies bluer, the air sweeter, and the water more palatable than ever before. I even put a stop to cursing about mosquito bites or when accidentally dropping stationary on the floor. After learning about the council's resolution and my choice of the starship's destiny, I observed how other men around me altered their behaviour. The people became more straightforward, less haughty, some even tried to appear as nimble as youngsters. What was earlier hidden inside, now soared to the surface. Curses become more common. It seemed as if the people, with a sweep of a magic wand, suddenly ceased hiding whom they despised or fancied, whom or what they were afraid of all their lives. Nowadays, even if the Lord sneezed, the humblest of the humble would know what to say. The little everyday lies which accompany men's lives, big and small, like dim and ugly stains on fresh snow, became relics of the past. The nice men became even better, the bad ones grew much worse. Although, overall, living became much simpler and clearer.

The semi-empty bars abruptly became crowded with noisy beer lovers. The legions of hungry buyers imbued the shopping malls, which lately had stood nearly empty. The eloquent preachers called forth to spend all you have, since nothing personal can be taken into the big journey of no return.

All forms of the ecclesiastic congregations, like dugup archeological ruins, rose from the obsolescent, cellar's stench, and soggy semi-darkness and filled the churches with new worshippers. While mostly women were the dominant parishioners in the saintly institutions of faith, men preferred other sinful pleasures. 'Be fruitful and multiply' became the motto of our happy, passing days. The bad news -- first about the loss of Jupiter, then Saturn and the most recent one, the disappearance of Venus -- stopped being taken as calamities. Tired from the never ending fears and strains, the people matured fast. The men conquered their fears and became wiser, more united with each other -- ready for new, deadly strikes of the cosmos.

On a gloomy, windy day a huge cloud covered the skies, and big, shaggy snowflakes hovered towards the bleak ground. The freshly fallen snow seemed to me like the unwelcomed, although I did not realize right away of what. Albert showed up at my command station unexpectedly. The grime of deep sorrow was imprinted on his wrinkled face. His thick African lips were trembling under the still dark, but drooping mustache. The man was looking at his feet as though endeavouring to avoid a direct eye to eye contact. I barely glimpsed at him as I flinched, as though I suddenly learned something horrible. My sixth sense perceived a disaster in a flash.

"Don't give vent to it, my harbinger of death," I forced myself to utter. "It's the Neptune, isn't it."

"Yes," Albert uttered. "Dutch, I am sorry."

"I just spoke with Lilly yesterday. She said nothing about the sleep."

"It had happened so suddenly and unexpectedly, I doubt anybody had time to reach the deep freeze sarcophaguses."

"What!" I screamed as though hit by a javelin in the heart.

A loud echo reflected from the walls and the blinking consoles. The nearby working crew hushed and turned towards me.

"Their starship had accidently crossed the path of a meteor shower," Albert began talking fast. "The communication had halted abruptly. We could only intercept agonizing unhuman shrills before a church-like hush. Then followed the whoosh of the barren Universe. It was quick but painful. The hit starship immediately lost control and became depressurized. In a flash the blood had boiled in the their veins and burst all the living tissues."

I could not listen to Albert's explanations any longer. For me the world had already turned upside down and wrapped in upon itself. I was fleeing in haste, from the buildings, from the streets, from the people's open-eyed stares. On the nearby desolate late autumn lakeshore I undid my shirt, removed my shoes and ran barefoot towards the lead-coloured lake, oblivious of the biting snow and the cold pebbles. I didn't feel a thing. A deadly spike was thrust in my heart. I earned it. For thirty seconds of lust I bartered the life of my dear child. And for whom? For the treacherous bitch who a few days ago kicked me out of her home and took up living with an officer who was lower in rank -- the famous starship's navigator, Phil. A fellow who in the recent good old days was my fishing friend. A better man than I! ... Now, it's all over. I will blame myself for the rest of my duration. Hopefully it will be short.

Only pain and time, the priestess, can wrest a man from his bitter memories. Grief is itself a medicine. It took several months for my recuperation from the pneumonia and the subsequent depression, before Albert could address me as the starship's commander.

"Dutch! You have to make the final decision. How and when do we end it all!"

"Didn't you ever hear that it's not over until it's over?" I stalled.

"With time ebbing at an ever increasing pace, all of our survivor's routes have been traversed, all possibilities have been depleted. We are desperately entangled in an immense cloud of the cosmic matter and dragged inside the funnel of a colossal black hole. It has recently become the centre of our collapsing Universe. There is no escape from the black holes, you know it. Although, there is some room to manoeuvre between the falling substance."

"I don't want to live. Why did you save me from drowning? Allow the cosmos to take me as I am!" I snarled at Albert. "We came from the stars and we should return to them. Ashes to ashes ... "

"Don't be foolish. There are other men, women and children who do not share your fatalism. Besides, our starship is the last out of seven where life still lingers. While you were
scorching in the feverish deliriums of your illness, we had riots on the remaining starships. People demanded a quick and easy end. Nobody had the guts to wait for the repetition of Neptune's doom."

"Did Neptune plan the deep freeze?" I asked after taking some time to ponder.

"Yes. All others had earlier used a sweet sleeping gas."

"Let it be the freeze," I uttered as an augur. "Deeper than the guts of the ether, and deadlier than the infernos of hell."

"Wise choice." Albert said and patted my back.

The starship's headquarters was picked to be the final resting place for my crew. The beasts were refrigerated first. Then all other men and minors had laid themselves to sleep. There were many lofty speeches, heart-rendering cries, outbreaks of despair, and many examples of valour. The frost has shadowed it all.

The array of hollow, grim sarcophaguses was situated in front of me. The lids on all the caskets were wide open. Newly fabricated deep freeze coffins, still smelling of fresh factory paint, patiently waited for their new dwellers. A graveyard's breeze seemed to be blowing from the coffins' hollows. Phil, my traitor in love, was the first being guided towards his casket. Two officers assisted the whining comrade. His tremulous legs seemed to be filled with cotton. He could barely walk. His forehead wet from sweat; Phil's face was red like the pulp of a ripe watermelon. The man's arms were shaking. Phil, with care, lay down on the casket's mattress.

Albert consoled his crying pal. "Buck up. You won't feel a thing. I tested it on myself three times. It felt like consigning yourself to oblivion, without major thoughts, feelings, or
sensations. All the times I was able to come back to life as though nothing had happened. Be proud. When the time sets to age again, the new planets are formed, your sarcophagus like the plant's kernel shall fall in the furrow and stem new life. Few members of mankind have ever lived for such privilege. You are the chosen one. Relax and sleep well my friend. Your term has not been wasted. Perhaps, we'll meet once more in another life."

The lid on Phil's casket had been let down, and soon the blinks from the red diodes on the sarcophagus's display marked progressions of the freeze. The anxious chief helmsman, Bob, hurriedly left the tense, hushed crowd. He drew himself close to Phil's sarcophagus and impatiently turned the deep freeze knob to the end of the cold scale. The control lights on the casket's display immediately began running wild, issuing crying peeps.

"That gutless wonder has spoiled my mood." Bob cried spinning around. "Let him feel the freeze while he still can. To cheer up before taking a permanent vacation is as life-giving as a cleansing enema." Bob began to cackle like an idiot. "I never felt Phil was conceited, anyway. Although, now, I feel a deep sorrow for the man on the make. Suddenly, I crave to cover myself with dung for a day or two, if I had time. But who will mourn for m-e-e-e! Not a bug remains to shed a few tears for all of us."

It just came to my attention that Bob had a bottle of hard liquor clenched in his right hand. He was already drunk. The man lifted the half-empty bottle, overturned it and emptied it in one hasty shot. He then unseemly let the gas from his thorax out. Then Bob approached his final resting place in a rocking gait, and nearly fell into the hollow. The casket's lid had been let down, and we never saw that man again.

"Truth sits on the lips of a departing man," Albert uttered regarding Bob's coffin. The astronomer brushed at his watch and added, "Meanwhile, the world was, indeed, diminished by his passing. Our term is running out." Albert turned towards me and extended his arm for a farewell handshake. "All good things come to an end, and so is our pilgrimage of life. We warmed our hands near the flames of life, and right now we are ready to depart. It was nice knowing you, Dutch."

The man headed towards his casket. His humble gait was slow and timid, more dunning a land turtle than a man.

"One more question?" I asked after a long pause.

"What?" Albert posed having one leg already inside the coffin.

I set to pull towards the astronomer.

"What did you actually mean when you told Phil that a new life can spring up again?"

"I had told you once that choosing the deep freeze was a wise choice, hadn't I. After playing with numbers, I started to believe that our life was the result of a cosmic accident, which was determined by chance, not law. Indeed, this life such as it is has a narrow chance of being reborn from cosmic dust, into a Phoenix-like rise from the ashes of despondency. The circumstance of that happening is tinier than locating a needle in a billion stacks. Far smaller than a dozen untamed monkeys banging on a keyboard to compose a symphony. Much, much smaller than your salmon egg dropped in a sewer. To be truly honest, even much less than were our probabilities of surviving up to this day." Albert regarded me with his vivid eyes and exhaled. A sudden, tense pause followed before he continued. "I know, it boggles the mind, but the chance is still there, as you can witness for yourself. Based on the pure suppositions and the preliminary calculations, I believe that a new Big Bang should happen long before our torn pieces can disintegrate and fall into singularity. Without doubt, our last starship will be destroyed by the waves of this mega-explosion. But a few of our cells might outlast the cataclysm and remain frozen, lingering in the icy cosmos for eons. Sometime, somewhere in the new Universe the cells will finally drop into the propitious liquid of a newly formed planet and give rise to bacteria, primitive organisms, animals, and eventually another mankind." Albert exhaled deeply and stretched out on his mattress in relaxation. " 'No root, no fruit' as people say. However, the probability of life's revival can be greatly increased if someone is willing to attempt navigating our starship till the very end. A grievous mission. The last helmsman should be a real hero, unsusceptible to pain, and fearless of death. For this valorous son, time, like a grain of verity, will be precious. With every backward tick of a clock, time quickens, and the cosmos gets denser and thicker, making his space navigation extremely hazardous. The finale can befall in the twinkling of an eye, without granting an occasion to react and break the salvaging ampoule. The last helmsman, caught in the middle of his noble task, might even witness how his flesh dies before his reason falters. His head separated from the body continues to see and analyze for thirty seconds. It's a known fact. B-r-r-r!" Albert was shaken up as though suddenly pinched by a frost. "Who knows how long a mind can persist on that ghastly chill, among the starship's scattered pieces."

I groaned and nodded. I was so balled up that my eyes remained wide open, glued towards the man's coffin. I seemed to be hypnotized by his farewell words.

"Hello! Wake up!" the astronomer waved his arm in front of my glassy gaze. "That's what I meant when endorsing a deep freeze, captain. Anyway, enough with prophecy. It can be contagious. Go to sleep my commander and don't believe an old man's statistics. Unlikely life plays those dice."

I stood as enchanted, and fixedly scrutinized the lid lowering on Albert's sarcophagus. Somehow the vivid gleams of diodes on his casket's display struck me as performing a farewell march.

As a captain I should be the last to abandon the sinking vessel. Contemplating Albert's prophecy I am resigned to wait until everybody is asleep. Finally, I am truly alone in the world. Like the hunting animal pursuing a scent of its prey, I descend to the old, abandoned smithy, begin to beat the bushes, and eventually spot a huge, massive blacksmith's hammer. I carry it on my shoulder back to headquarters. Finally I come to a standstill in front of my sarcophagus. I inhale heavily; my skin is sweating as though in a sauna. Using both of my shaking arms I lift the rusty hammer high above my head. It's as ponderous as a church-bell, and as big as a chime's pendulum. I narrow my eyes and painstakingly aim as though I am a sniper. A few creeping moments pass by, and I am ready. Never to risk is to miss life. Besides, I have nothing to lose except my blues. Slash! With all my might I strike my damned, vacant casket which appears as sound as a pyramid. Blow! The smashed pieces are finally darting around me. Clap! My ears are deafened from the din. Slash! Several sharp splinters thrust into my flesh. Blow! I feel that I am bleeding but I choose to disregard it. Slash! Blow! Slash! Blow! Beyond my patience's overflow. I stay solid and keep on hitting and striking my heavy pendulum against the brittle coffin until nothing but the deformed pieces of glass and metal remain from it . . . Dripping with cooling sweat and exhausted I finally drop the heavy, loathsome tool of destruction on the floor. Hum! And the last echo dies. Suddenly it becomes so quiet that my deafened ears begin to ache, and my inflamed mind starts to hallucinate. Gradually I hear how a hiss of delightful hush fills the room. It is bliss! It seems that I am in heaven, but I know that I am still here.

"Hurray! Viva de bravery! Despair gave courage to a coward! Ultimately I am freed from the doubts of 'to be or not to be'. My fear is gone, and my bosom is relieved from a might of stones. I've finally liberated myself to pursue my chosen destiny."

I switch off total illumination on the starship. Who needs it? Instead, I lift the shields on all the portholes. A pythonic string of blazing lights is stretched out in front of me. It is beautiful, but perilous as a busy night highway. Millions of suns, stars and celestial bodies assembling one endless chain, behold me from the cool and murky emptiness. They are humble children who are lined up to reenter their mother's womb. Like salmonids, the wandering stars come back to the place of their birth. I can't see the great black hole, the mother of all stars, but I know it is there. Big and dim, ready to consume its off-spring and to grind them into dust. We are all equal: stone and flesh, gas and liquid, light and darkness. All are the selfsame candidates

for the final judgement. Indeed, the time of reckoning is near. I feel it in my
shivering guts. Everybody will get what they deserve. I know, for sure,
where I will go. My life was a tale on the lips of a blockhead. I did not commit
any major crimes, but the sins of the heart. Disregarding the word of my
mother, I had married a nice looking woman. But the marching years of life
and a grievous childbirth had transformed my wife into a hideous, obtuse
bitch, a true damn wretch. The growing, darkened hair on her body, arms and
legs became a birth control device. We hardly made love any more. My
spouse's filthy tongue, constant ignorance of my opinions, and duck's brains
compelled me to seek female acquaintances on the side. And I had a number
of them, and I cherished them all, without exception. I used all the freedom
I had, and the virtue that my position had allowed. A bluff gust grew into a
desire. A covet turned into an aspiration and an urge became a thirst, a thirst
for me is nothing but the satisfaction. All my women looked like negatives:
blonde hair, tanned features and white teeth. My girls were so sweet, my
'manhood' never learned about the prophylactic. Not because the holy
church said that wearing them was a sin. I simply loathed having
impenetrable rubber separate me from the objects of my admiration. Their
names are like whispers on the wind that keep on passing through my head:
time and again . . . First there was Mary, my secretary. For me it was
inexpressively delicious to keep an eye on her posing half-naked on her bed,
wearing a pale silky night gown and doing a manicure. Then there was
Janifer, the waitress with breasts so high, so offering. It seemed as if she'd
been created for tender passions. My hands relished kneading her bloomers,
as though they were fresh balls of pastry dough. Then, the night bar's
stripper, Lynda. She fancied camping with me. Lynda moved around
gloriously, and with a flowing motion, her shoes scarcely touched bare
ground. The latest one, Sabrina, the captainess and the redheaded, freckled
bitch . . . Just to mention a few of my girlfriends who had helped to sooth my
pang of the hostile home ruled by the fishwife. Still, I am smutty and crooked
like my bowels. In some people dwells God, in others the devil. Inside my
bulk lives nothing but the intestinal worms. I became a philanderer, the
unharnessed toy of my testosterone's whims. I sucked in vices and ended
up execrated by everybody, loved by none. I had practically killed my own
child, my little flower. Lilly's life was like a cherry blossom: short and
beautiful. And I had destroyed it, as though I mindlessly slapped at a mosquito

which sucked the blood out of my cheek. I am carrion. I do not deserve to live, but I will stay on to witness the apocalypse come heaven or hell!"

It is hard to manoeuvre day and night without repose, but I recognize that I must. Hope keeps me alive through my final days, philosophical reflections make me breath. A-h-h-h! A clear and burning hollowness finally settles inside my bosom. I have already given air to my previous condition, but yet to commence immersion into my coming state of mind. I feel that I am at my wits' end, but I still manage to stay on. Gradually I sink into morose moods or escape into thought, where my dissipated reflections carry me away, God only knows where . . . The sculptor finds his statue in a lump of marble; I am seeking mine in the salvation. I faithfully believe that each human being must possess a thing in his life he is ready to sacrifice his term for. If not politics, then something very personal, but it must be there; otherwise he is not a human being, but an animal. For years, centuries, and epochs on end, everything strived for warmth from frosts and blizzards. Why do I head towards the collapsing oblivion? If not flying in the face of logic, I am reckoned to flee from this devouring black hole. I do not demand glory or grandeur. I am my own undertaker, but I shall not let myself down. Like a moth I fly towards the flame on my own accord. Soon my final flight will cross an event horizon and meet its finish. The blast, not singularity will become my reward for this audacious act; the vague chance of life's resurrection lies in my hands.

Suddenly, I sense a gust of great relief through my mind. I finally feel placid, cool and serene.

"At long last, my purpose is finally understood. I should have known better what the salmon knows best."

With a deep joy I begin to inhale the air, as though I am a sailor who goes back to the sea after a prolonged stay home. "It is better to meet your end this way, behind the wheel, than in a soft and soggy bed from the colds, anginas, prostates or itching haemorrhoids. And then to become decaying food for the disgusting grave worms."

How light it feels now. I breathe deep and easily, like after a heavy thunderstorm. Now, I
truly feel that drowsiness overwhelms me. I am tired out and almost cut in half by hunger. I switch the autopilot on, give up the wheel and head towards the pool. Let the soothing water clear my drowsy mind and refresh my

loosened sensations. In solitude I swim and play as a child, raising fountains of spray and vaulting out in my birthday suit in dolphin imitations. Finally, I draw a deep breath and take a dive. The deeper I plunge into the abyss, the more I realize the importance of my mission and of my remaining life.

Who is a man? A handful of earth which is doomed for disappearance, or more than this quintessence of dust, from whence man sprung? Financial worries distinguished man from animals. Even though the principal business of man's life was to enjoy it, the mass of men led lives of quiet desperation. Deep inside, man was the most savage, egocentric beast who remained on friendly terms with the victims he intended to eat until he devoured them. Though still, man was nobler than a bee. There was a dignity in everything man did. Man was the only beast that laughed and wept; for he was the only animal that was struck with the difference between what things are, and what they ought to be. The homo sapiens could make decisions, often the painful ones, which appeared as going against man's instinct for survival, or preservation of his species. Although man was alone among creatures who had more than an inexhaustible voice. Man also had a soul, a spirit capable of endurance and compassion -- even when man was not good for anything, but holding the world together. Man was the originator of himself by virtue of his thoughts which he chose and promoted. Man's reflections -- big and small, low and noble -- which travelled through eternity became his monument's monument. All man's resulting acts and deeds -- stained in gore from fighting, bloated from corruptions, glorified by short-lived successes and enriched by lasting failures, but ultimately, treacherously pierced by rusty nails -- became immortal. Still, in every case, even the most hopeless one, man was not an end but a beginning.

Inspired by the epiphany of my lofty thoughts, I forcefully thrust with both of my legs, widely stroke my arms and drop deeper and further. Half way through my descent to the sandy bottom a strange, weird rumble reaches me. This unknown roar is blaring and continuous, comparable to the bellowing of a thousand waterfalls. I bend my head up and notice a stirred surface gleaming with erratic lights. As moving shafts of light pierce the water, I feel wrapped in blue light and displaced in time. I perceive something wrong and immediately begin to rise to the surface in a panic. Before I reach the air, a force mightier than the oceanic tide splashes me with the waters away from the pool. Deranged as a cornered beast, I manage to grab a sip

of much-craved-for air. I also see a widening break in the ceiling of my
starship. The crying inferno is storming all over the partitions. The debris of
machines is twisting in the air as though snatched by a passing hurricane. For
the cosmos, we are all women: it can trifle with us, or it can violate us. The
swishing whistle deafens my ears and petrifies me. I realize that the starship,
left without a helmsman, was hit by a meteor shower and transformed into
a burning hearse.

"This is the end. I know it. Even here I blundered!" In my wife's
words, I was a failure all my life and it looked here like she was right. I am
doomed to falter till my very last breath.

Meanwhile the split broadens and I am sucked like a straw outside
the starship, together with the waters and the debris. Instead of flapping like
a fish on a deck, I take a dive as though believing naively that the liquid abyss
can safeguard me from the inevitable. My plunge resembles a scared frog
desperately seeking refuge in the fuscous Stroke! Stroke! Suddenly I
experience my environment cools fast and then solidifies. Stroke! In a few
seconds I can't manoeuvrer. A bitter frost bites me but I can't scream. It
feels like the hot sting of a bee, like a scoop of melted metal poured on my
flesh. In a flash of agonizing recognition I am burned, frozen and paralysed
with my arms wide spread. I am reminded of a crucified redeemer of
humanity in a transient state of post-crucifixion, in a prelude for resurrection.
My stupid brain and thin flesh are clenched by the marching crystals of ice
which sound to be in a hurry to squeeze the piss and blood out of my body.
My crying bones are crunching in distress, my long tongue is paralysed by
frost and fear in one instance, but the inflamed mind still lives. To palpitate
from a sting of pain, 'to see a world in a grain of sand, and a heaven in a wild
flower, to hold infinity in the palm of my hand', to apprehend eternity by my
bowels -- is yet another cause worth living for. I still can use my head and
thus, I can resist. I know I am hopeless but I am not prostrated yet: I float
on and fiddle with death. Every moment is mine, every thought is precious,
each pang is a vital signal . . . Good! ... Good! ... Overthrown at last, my
agitated spirit finds its escape from the mocked body and launches, hovering
along a narrow, dim tunnel between agony and bliss. My expiring bulk is left
behind. The stars and planets behold me with horror. With my every
advancement the luminosity from them grows dimmer and weaker; the realm
of darkness slowly devours me. I begin to distinguish disembodied voices of

friends swarming around their gay bonfires. The hot flames of hell start to lick the soles of my feet. Ebbing time begins to look like eternity, analogous to the trees' shadows which are lengthened by the passing of the day. I am not afraid to bite the dust. For me it would mean a state to which I finally come home. I only regret having accomplished so little in my life .... Suddenly, a dazzling flash, brighter than the lights from all the remaining suns in the Universe hits me. My tight fetters are melted in one instance and the icy vice is released at last. I am frightened and, like a grape snail, briskly re-enter what remains of my body-abode. There I am warmed up fast from the ghastly frost which had possessed my soul. My zombie ears begin to ache and the eyes begin to see, the pulse begins to throb, the brain to work again, the soul to feel the flesh and the flesh to feel the pain. I see Time's winged chariot hurrying near; and yonder all around me fly breaths of awaken eternity. The Universe around me is transformed into one raging bang. It's silent as a vacuum and motley as a peacock. No one is left to tell, but I know, I feel keenly by each of my particles that the mega-explosion, another Big Bang, has finally come.

"I made it! Despite all doubts and remote chances, fate has, at last, turned towards me by its right side. The fountain of Time has erupted again. I hear and see its life-giving pulse. There is a light at the end of the tunnel, after all. The darkness materializes from those blazing rays? Never! The recursive enigma of Time has prevailed once more."

These were my final thoughts before I saw a pale horse with a horseman on it; and its name was the Grim Reaper. She swung her terrible scythe and my blood and vital fluids boiled up in one instance. And then the leviathan forces of the incoming cataclysm shattered my poor flesh to pieces. The cosmos took me and dissipated my dust, transformed into ice, throughout the ether, towards immortality, where life and time are one.

Perhaps, that's how it was? Or, may be how it will be? Nothing comes of nothing; everything must have its seed. Our lives, their growths, hopes, fears, loves are all the results of the accidents which made us the way we are. Although no one knows for sure how we came to be, or even where we are going. We are all at the mercy of Fate. When autumn night is quiet, and silent distances harken to God, the Universe rewards us with a star. Watch the starlit nighttide sky faithfully. When you finally spy how the falling star burns through a night firmament, do not divert your eyes. Take a pinch of your precious time to contemplate the event, where probable gives way to improbable, where a sobbing cry of our scattered past resounds in the future. Alas. In the high skies the stars are destined to be born only once. They radiate lights and can move in a flash, as our thoughts do, but the stars cannot acquire wings, like the fowls. Also, the falling stars burn down rapidly before arriving to Earth's distant shores. The stars' songs melt as though they are golden candles, often without permitting us to bend an ear to their lilting verses.

Listen attentively to the hush of the falling stars and do not believe in the evil prophesies. Let your subconscious overshadow your reason. A touch of luck and resonance of a faraway cry should reward your forbearing heedfulness ... Do you hear my voice entombed in the stillness? Do you perceive how in the black womb of poppy is hidden life's sedition?

> Do not believe in life or in death!
> Life, is a fleeting instance between
> Our past and our future,
> Where hours and minutes mean nothing.
> Only the caviar of the cosmos,
> The wandering star, can alter the world,
> And nothing else.
> The ripple it sends out can spring
> a fever of life once more.
> And death is when there are no more stars!

Maybe this sonnet is a dropped messenger of my days gone by, when I disappeared from the scale of time, remaining alive, nevertheless. How, when I left this world, I continued to exist and watched the ashes from my life's hot fire turn grey in one instance, then cold. Maybe my star was that very right seed which has lingered in our silent Universe for eons before finally reaching the Earth's furrow.

AGMV
MARQUIS
Québec, Canada
1998